A PLACE TO START

WANDER CREEK BOOK ONE

AMY RUTH ALLEN

D1738928

CHAPTER 1

*A*bby Barrett let herself into her fourth-floor studio apartment located in a modest neighborhood in Minneapolis. Compared to her former home—a thirteen-bedroom lakefront mansion with a movie screening room, indoor and outdoor pools and a tennis court—the apartment was claustrophobically small, to say the least. It was actually closer in size to her former walk-in closet, which consisted of two rooms for clothes and accessories and another with a vanity and hair and make-up station.

Each time she turned the key in the apartment lock, pushed open the door, and was about to step into the dingy living room, she found herself wishing that it had all been a terrible dream, and that she would instead step into the huge front foyer of her former house, as if returning through a fourth-dimensional time portal. She would look down and see the black-and-white marble floor under her feet, then gaze up at the crystal chandelier hanging from the thirty-foot ceiling. But of course, that never happened. Instead of coming home from a fabulous vacation or day at the spa, most days Abby returned from her minimum-wage job at the Paperie, a fashionable paper store that in her former life she frequented as a customer. She loved the owner, Carmen, and was truly grateful for the job, but there was really no room for advancement. She was stuck.

It had been a year since the FBI seized Abby's home and belongings, and three months since her husband Jake was sentenced to fifty years in federal prison for defrauding his clients out of hundreds of millions of dollars. All of her fashionable, fair-weather friends had dropped off, one by one. Most of them were appalled at Jake's "light" sentence. After all, Bernie Madoff, who pulled off a similar Ponzi scheme, got one-hundred-fifty years.

Abby flicked on the light as she closed the apartment door behind her, and tried to pretend that the navy pull-out couch, which served as both a sofa and a bed, and the banged-up Formica dinette set, both purchased from a thrift shop, were really a huge sectional luxury white leather sofa set, and a dining room furniture suite that could seat twenty guests. No such luck. She took the few steps on thread-bare carpet to the couch, and instantly collapsed. She certainly wasn't used to being on her feet all day.

The only belongings the FBI allowed Abby to keep were all of her clothes, her childhood keepsakes, and her laptop, which they had kindly, as the agent-in-charge put it, "cleaned" for her. They replaced her old cell phone with a new one, for which she was actually grateful because it meant no one knew how to get ahold of her, including Jake. Of course, it would only be a matter of time until one of her old "friends" came into the Paperie on her shift. But she wouldn't worry about that now. *No sense in borrowing trouble.*

Abby's "closet" now consisted of a beat-up dresser and a metal rolling clothes rack. Her beautiful Chanel suits, Prada dresses, Louis Vuitton purses, Jimmy Cho shoes, and countless other designer labels, were mostly folded in tissue paper and lovingly packed away in suitcases and cardboard boxes. A few favorites hung on the rolling clothes rack. When she got home in the evenings, instead of changing into something more comfortable, she would take off her casual pants and top and randomly pull out something from her treasure trove of clothes. It made her feel strong and powerful to wear the clothes she loved. But she couldn't wear these clothes to work. Or anywhere, for that matter.

This particular evening, she pulled out a fuchsia evening gown that had cost thousands of dollars. *That's enough to buy a small used car,* she reflected, although she herself had never actually bought a small car. She stepped into the dress and zipped it up the side. The silk fabric was soft against her skin. She rummaged around in another box and found a pair of strappy gold sling-backs. In the tiny bathroom, she pulled back her shoulder-length, honey blonde hair into a high pony-tail, and expertly fashioned it into an elaborate up-do, fastening it with a gold hair clip. Next, she pulled out her box of designer make-up and applied eye liner and shadow, rouge, and a pink lipstick that perfectly matched her dress. For everyday use, she had been reduced to make-up she could afford from the drugstore, so she saved her designer stash for the special occasions she created for herself. Like this one.

"Not bad, if I do say so myself," she said to her reflection. She admired her high cheekbones, emerald-green eyes, and swan-like neck. At thirty-eight, her jawline had begun to sag a little, and crow's feet had appeared at the edges of her eyes. She leaned over the sink and examined the bags under her eyes. Sleepless nights agonizing over the hundreds of people Jake cheated out of their life savings had left dark circles under her eyes. On a positive note, her complexion had never been better. Instead of fancy coffees and expensive wines, she drank water from the tap. No sodas. No juices. No energy drinks. Sometimes, she splurged and bought a fresh lemon to squeeze over ice cubes before pouring in the water, and for one beautiful second, the zest of the fruit was so decadent that she moaned aloud. She had learned that now she needed to find joy in simple pleasures. But who knew that one lemon cost more than a dollar? She could buy two breakfast yogurts for that amount. She bought only generic brands, and they tasted as bland as she felt most days. She was terrified to spend any more money than necessary. She had gone from spending freely without a thought to what things cost, to saving thirty cents by buying a store brand yogurt instead of the kind with the real fruit on the bottom, and a little side pocket with nuts and raisins. *Those things cost a fortune!* Everything was expensive it seemed.

In her apartment's galley kitchen—really only a fridge, microwave, sink, and stove, with a counter the size of a postage stamp—she put on a large apron over her gown and made a grilled cheese sandwich to accompany a bowl of delicious tomato soup. Outside her window, she could practically feel the icy Minneapolis winter making plans to descend upon the city. But it was mid-September, and although the sun set earlier and rose later each day, the fall leaves were still vibrant, and the crisp air gave Abby an unexpected spring to her step. She contemplated buying a stand-alone gas fireplace to cheer up her dim apartment. If she could find one on sale, she would splurge. And it would be worth it to have tuna from a can for dinner and to skip breakfast for a month to have the beautiful red and orange flames embrace her apartment and help her through a long Minneapolis winter. She thought of her bedroom back home and the heated floors in her in-suite bathroom, and sighed. How pampered and fortunate she had been. And she had taken it all for granted.

After eating her dinner at the dinette table, Abby settled on the couch, still in her designer dress and shoes. She picked up her library book and opened it to her bookmark. For just a few hours every day, she could almost forget her circumstances as she lost herself in a different time and place. These days she gravitated to books about secret billionaires falling in love with ordinary women and cowboys who seem like hired hands but turn out to be the ranch owner and sweep the heroine out of a life of drudgery and into a life of luxury. She knew that she had to accept reality and leave her old life behind. But she didn't want to. Before she got past the first page, her phone rang. Glancing at it, she shook her head. This number had been calling for weeks now, and the caller was leaving messages about some timeshare property or something in a place called Wander Creek in northern Minnesota. She only half listened to the messages because they were all practically the same. The ringing stopped, and Abby returned to her book. Then it started again. And again. And again. This time there were no messages.

Probably some reporter trying to trick me into talking about Jake, she told herself. She had been on the news again earlier in the week when Jake's lawyers filed another appeal, and the whole story splashed over the local networks again, along with her photo. She was just grateful that without her expensive haircut and highlights and designer make-up she no longer resembled her former glamorous self. The news anchors always asked the same question and speculated on the answer: How could a woman with a master's degree in philosophy and another in English literature be so clueless that for an entire decade she totally missed the fact that her husband was lining his pockets— their pockets—with hundreds of millions of dollars stolen from innocent people? For almost a year, Abby had asked herself the same question.

After ten minutes, the caller finally gave up. And then the knocking started.

"Ms. Barrett," a man's voice said from outside her apartment door. "I need to speak with you, urgently. I've been calling and leaving messages, but you haven't returned my calls. I'm sorry for just appearing on your doorstep unannounced, but you've left me no choice."

Abby crept toward the door, walking on her toes so the

stiletto heels wouldn't make any noise, and peered through the peephole. A small, prim-looking man in a three-piece grey suit stood on the other side, holding a briefcase. He sported a fairly decent attempt at a comb-over and wore small wire-rimmed glasses, and Abby guessed he was about seventy. He looked more like a lawyer than a reporter. Or maybe he was an FBI agent coming to interrogate her again. Abby knew, all-too well, that looks could be deceiving.

"Go away," she barked through the door. "I'm not interested in your time share. And if you're a reporter, well, then just go away and don't come back."

"What time share?" the man asked.

Through the peep hole, Abby saw his face scrunch up in confusion.

"The one in your messages," she said. "The one in Wander Creek, Minnesota." Abby leaned against the wall. Why had she engaged with this man? She had waited out many a reporter simply by outlasting their persistence at her door. All of them eventually gave up. Every time one of them came knocking, she flashed back to that early morning more than a year ago when she had woken up to the sound of her front door crashing open. She had jumped out of bed and hurriedly pulled on a peach silk bathrobe that matched her expensive nightie. She was just cinching the belt around her waist when the first agent entered, demanding to know where Jake was. Men and women in FBI windbreakers, guns drawn, swarmed in behind, crowding into her bedroom.

"Ms. Barrett, it's not a time share. It's a bequest of property. To you." The man's muffled voice behind her apartment door jerked her back to reality.

Abby heard something on the floor and picked up a business card the gentleman had just slipped under her door. She read to herself, *Monroe, Able and Associates, Attorneys at Law*. So he *was* a lawyer. Moreover, Abby recognized the name of the law firm.

Each year, Monroe, Able and Associates purchased several tables at a fundraiser she co-chaired for a local children's hospital. Correction. *Used* to co-chair. The firm's donations and pro bono work were legendary on the charity circuit. She also knew the name Jerome Monroe. She peered through the peephole again. Sure enough, it was *the* Jerome Monroe who had been featured recently on the cover of *Minnesota Business* magazine, which she had seen at the library.

"What kind of property?" she asked through the door.

Jerome Monroe shifted the briefcase to his other hand. She saw him visibly sag at her question. She almost felt sorry for him. It was a cold night, and the stingy landlord would not turn on the heat in the hallways until the first snow, and the lawyer wasn't wearing an overcoat or gloves.

"Ms. Barrett, please let me in. I promise it will be worth your while." He paused, then continued. "I think we've met before at the charity auctions for the children's hospital. I'm not going to hurt you, I promise."

Hurt me? That hadn't even occurred to her. She worked out every day at her home gym and swam laps four times a week. Correction. *Had* worked out. But she was still reasonably fit. Her Spartan diet certainly hadn't added any weight to her five-foot-seven-inch frame. And walking up and down the stairs twice a day, and to and from the bus stop, kept her in reasonably good shape. He was in his seventies. She could take him. Unless he had a gun. Or what if an accomplice lurked out of sight?

Stop it right now Abby! You are being insane, not to mention ridiculous.

She turned the three locks on the door, opened it and stepped aside, motioning for him to enter.

Jerome Monroe walked into the apartment and blinked at her in surprise, and Abby realized he was probably not expecting to find her in an evening gown, and the juxtaposition of the elegance of the colorful dress against the shabbiness of the apartment almost made her laugh.

Jerome Monroe held out his hand and she accepted it. "It's nice to see you again," he said. "Can we sit down and talk?"

She nodded and glided to the dinette set where she invited him to take a seat. "Can I get you a glass of tap water?" she asked, always the gracious hostess. "Or maybe you'd prefer a glass of tap water."

As she hoped, Jerome Monroe laughed. She had broken the ice, and with that accomplished, she sat down opposite him and waited for him to explain himself.

CHAPTER 2

"*L*et me get this straight," Abby said after thirty minutes of listening to the lawyer and glancing at various legal documents that had emerged from his briefcase during the conversation. "An anonymous person has given me a building in a town up north and wants me to open a business and live there?"

"That's mostly correct," Jerome said, moving a pen so it was precisely perpendicular to the edge of the table. "But as I mentioned, there are caveats. You have to run the business for at least a year, live in the apartment on the second story, and employ at least one local person."

"And after a year?" Abby prompted, not really understanding why she was even entertaining this ludicrous proposition.

"After a year the building is yours to do with as you see fit. You can stay and keep the business going or sell the building and leave. It will be your choice."

"And this mysterious, anonymous person..." Abby asked.

"Your benefactor," Jerome corrected.

"Died and left me this property, why?"

"Not died," Jerome corrected again.

Abby looked around the apartment as if to see if the benefactor was lurking behind the couch. "They're still alive?"

Jerome Monroe nodded.

"Look, Mr. Monroe, I don't mean to be rude, but look at this from my perspective. This really is an outrageous proposition. I can't just go off to this town I've never heard of on a whim without knowing who is giving me this property, and why."

Mr. Monroe shook his head and said in a lawyerly tone, "I'm not at liberty to disclose any of the information you want to know. I know this is difficult, but you have to take this on faith."

Faith. That was a joke. Take his word for it? After what she'd been through, how would she ever learn to trust another person again? And more importantly, how could she trust herself and her own judgement? For ten years she had been oblivious that Jake was robbing their friends and his clients blind. How could she not have known?

Abby returned her gaze to the lawyer who still sat patiently in the same position.

"I would have to be crazy to go along with this," she said.

"Considering your recent circumstances," Mr. Monroe said, gently and with kindness, "you might look at this as a silver lining. A chance to start over out of the public eye."

Abby blushed. No doubt Mr. Monroe knew all about her downfall. The whole city of Minneapolis knew. In her old neighborhood and among the country club set, she could hardly throw a stone and not hit someone Jake had swindled. Mr. Monroe definitely knew of her reduced circumstances. One look around the apartment told him that.

Mr. Monroe slid a tablet from his briefcase, tapped a few times, then handed it to her. Wordlessly, she swiped through the photos he had brought up on the screen. She stared at a charming, historic downtown area with maybe a dozen stores on a main street that ran parallel to Wander Creek, one block over. The shops were situated in handsome brick and stucco buildings of various sizes and colors. The majority of the windows had colorful awnings. To Abby's eyes, the creek looked more like a river, and a small wooden bridge led traffic to the other side where dense forest and trees were covered in a light dusting of snow. She shivered. Winter had already arrived in Wander Creek. It would soon arrive in Minneapolis and she would no longer want to take her long walks through the many city parks and museum gardens. With the wind whipping and temperatures below zero, Minneapolis was a tough place to live when you were used to the finer things but had no money.

Mr. Monroe narrated as she swiped. "As you can see, Wander Creek has a small but vibrant commercial district, but it is still very much a small town that just happens to attract tourists. That's the Inn there on the west side of town and all the way east is the outfitters that rents canoes, tubes, snowmobiles and the like."

"It really is beautiful," Abby conceded, feeling a slight flutter in her stomach. And was that a smile trying to emerge?

"Keep going," Mr. Monroe said as she tried to hand the tablet back to him. "There are photos of the building."

And then Abby was staring at what was, almost, her building. A building she owned. Almost. The thought of it thrilled her, even though the circumstances were outrageous. The façade was a deep red brick, and it had a glass door with a brass mail slot. A large bay window was prominent on the first floor, and three windows were on the second floor. Awnings, in robin's egg blue, topped the door and all the windows. It was beautiful and obviously well cared for.

There were several photos of the interior, showing white walls, a sales counter plus a number of product display cases and racks against the walls, ready for inventory.

"What was in the building before? she asked, handing the tablet back.

"It used to be the office of the weekly newspaper, but it went out of business. The editor lived upstairs. Over the years it's been a used bookstore and a pizza parlor, among other things. Someone also tried running an art gallery there, but that lasted only a few months from what I understand. Sad really. When the building was constructed in the 1880s, it was the town's first mercantile store."

"It is lovely," Abby conceded again, almost longingly. It was a far cry from her mansion, but compared to where she currently lived, it was a castle. "But I don't know anything about the town. I've never been to Wander Creek, much less heard of it."

Jerome Monroe took out another folder from his briefcase and slid it across the table. "I've compiled a dossier about the town, everything from demographics to the town's history and current business district. And there's some information there about the local Chamber of Commerce. You'll probably want to join after you settle in."

He'd thought of everything. And Abby couldn't help but notice, he was under the impression that she was going to accept the offer.

Abby took the folder and put it in front of her. She'd read it later. Maybe. "Even if I were to do this," Abby reasoned, "I don't have the money to invest in starting a business from the ground up." She spread her arms wide. "Everything I have in this world is contained within these walls. Everything else in my life— the cars, houses, bank accounts—all of it was in my husband's name. And the FBI took everything."

Mr. Monroe picked up a long white envelope that had been sitting on the table between them and handed it to her. "This should help. And before you ask, it's free and clear. No strings attached. As long as you stay in Wander Creek according to the terms of the gift you don't have to pay the money back after the year is up. And as far as the government goes, this is income independent of your husband. They can't touch it. You aren't liable for your husband's debts. Now all you have to do is figure out what kind of business you want to open."

Abby colored slightly. She would never admit it to him, but as she scrolled through the photos of the building, she had let her mind fantasize about opening her own paper boutique where she would sell stationery, cards, gift wrap, and other paper goods. Even though there were days when she resented having to work at the Paperie, she had to admit that being there among the beautiful things, both as a customer and an employee, brought her joy.

Abby lifted the flap and drew out a check. She blinked twice and counted the zeros. And counted them again. Then she looked at Mr. Monroe who, for the first time, had a tiny smile on his round, pale face.

If she didn't spend it all on the business and was frugal—she was used to that by now—there could be enough left over to return to Minneapolis and live in a nicer apartment in a better neighborhood. She could go back to school and maybe learn a trade and get a better job. Maybe get a business degree. Something more useful than philosophy or English literature. With this money, she could have a fireplace this winter. She could buy fancy yogurts. But for now, she would have to do all of it, and more, in Wander Creek.

"I'll have to think about it," she said. "I have no idea how to run a small business. Prior to my current position as a sales-clerk I hadn't worked in a decade."

"I'm sure an educated woman like yourself could learn the ropes fairly quickly," he responded immediately, as if he had predicted her protests in advance, which she supposed he had. He was a lawyer after all, and a good one. Mr. Monroe nodded at the check, which she still held. "And that will certainly help with the learning curve."

After Mr. Monroe left, Abby sat at the table for a long time, remembering the robin's egg blue awning above the building's front door, and the beautiful bay window overlooking Main

Street. It looked as if the glass was original to the historic build-ing, and it was undeniably charming. Mr. Monroe had told her that year-round, people came to Wander Creek, drawn by the ATV trails, hunting, river activities, and ice fishing and snowmo-biling. The lovely small inn overlooking the water attracted a clientele of hunting and fishing widows. *Who knew there was such a thing?*

Abby flipped open the dossier and reviewed the information. Wander Creek's population was just under five thousand. Tiny compared to Minneapolis. That would take some getting used to. Abby laughed aloud. After what she'd been through, she figured she could get through just about anything. The closest decent grocery store was twenty miles away in Two Harbors. Duluth, the closest proper city, was an hour away. She studied the topo-graphical map Mr. Monroe had provided. Wander Creek was nestled in a valley and surrounded on three sides by thick forest, and on the fourth side by Wander Creek. A waterfront path and park ran along the creek. The main street, with flourishing shops and restaurants, was one block inland from the water, and the residential neighborhoods stretched behind. Mr. Monroe had said that it was the tourism that made the town thrive, and that without it, it would not survive for long. Tourism in Wander Creek meant jobs, sales taxes that paid for infrastructure and beautification, and a community pride that made people work mostly in collaboration, not competition. Each person in Wander Creek had a role to play, Mr. Monroe had explained, and what they each did impacted their friends and neighbors in an economic way.

It felt like she had stepped into one of those quaint Hallmark movies she used to watch with her mother growing up, and right about then, that didn't seem like a bad thing at all.

Abby looked around her apartment. As far as she could tell, she had two choices. Live in this dumpy studio apartment, work at the Paperie, unable to save any money, and hope things would change. Or accept the money, move to Wander Creek and open a business. Choice one was not optimal. And if choice two didn't work out, after a year, she could sell the property and return to Minneapolis to reclaim some semblance of her old life.

But for now, what did she have to lose? She had already lost everything. Literally.

CHAPTER 3

he next day, Abby arrived at the Paperie more than an hour before the store opened, knowing that Carmen would already be there. Carmen, a sixty-something, five-foot-two bundle of energy, was the only person from Abby's old life who stuck by her during the entire sordid ordeal.

After storing her coat and purse, Abby grabbed a cup of coffee and the two women sat in the break room where Abby recounted the whole fantastic tale of the previous evening. Carmen listened with rapt attention and didn't speak until the end of the story.

"You're going to do it, right?" she said. It was more of a command than a question.

"I'm thinking about it," Abby admitted. "But it's a big decision. And sort of crazy."

"So is staying here," Carmen said.

"What do you mean?" Abby asked.

"Staying here is a decision you're making, too. Even though you don't have to do anything, it's still a decision. And it's crazy, too. You can't stay here the rest of your life making fifteen dollars an hour. You know I'd pay you more if I could."

Abby put her hand over Carmen's. "You've been my Fairy Godmother," she said.

"So it's time for you to go find your glass slipper. Forget Prince Charming. You go on out there and find your slipper up in Wander Creek, and then get a matching one, too, and show it off!"

Abby laughed. "You have a very colorful way about you."

"I'll take that as a complement," Carmen said, giving a slight bow.

"You should, I meant it as one," Abby replied. She looked at her watch. They still had thirty minutes before the store opened.

"There's something I've been wanting to ask you for a while now," Abby said.

"Shoot," Carmen responded. "I'll answer if I can."

"Why did you hire me? I had no work experience, was an emotional train wreck and was basically a social pariah."

"Yeah, but you looked good," Carmen remembered, and grinned. "The day I hired you, you were wearing that dark maroon Chanel suit and suede ankle boots that matched perfectly. I remember, because the next day I went to the discount shoe store and bought a knock-off pair just like them."

"So you hired me because of the way I dressed?" Abby asked, surprised. That did not sound like the Carmen she knew.

"Of course, not," Carmen said. "I'm getting there. I was just remembering what I saw when you came in, asking about the sign in the window. Do you remember about two years ago, you came into the shop to order invitations for one of your friend's wedding showers?"

Abby took a sip of her coffee and nodded. "Sure. Mimi Albright was marrying one of Jake's work colleagues. I threw the shower at the country club." She started doing the math in her head again. She couldn't help it. The cost of the appetizers and open bar would have paid her current rent for six months. The amount of money she tipped the wait staff could pay her renter's insurance for a year.

"After we had gone through the invitations and got your order together, we stood up at the same time and bumped each other," Carmen said. "All the paper samples and envelopes on my desk fluttered to the floor, along with pens, the stapler and some other things I can't remember. But what I do remember, is that you didn't hesitate for one minute. You crouched down and scooped things up, the whole time saying how sorry you were for being so clumsy. At one point, you were on your knees, reaching for something under the desk."

"So you hired me because I'm clumsy?" Abby laughed.

"Of course not. Now just hold on while I get to the point," Carmen admonished. "I hired you for three reasons. One. You knew my name and used it every time you came into the store. Two. You didn't hesitate to clean up the mess. I know it seems like a small thing, but do you know how many other people like you would have done that?"

Abby didn't need to answer, and Carmen wasn't expecting one.

"Zero," Carmen continued. "My customers, the ones that are rich and fabulous, like you, treated me like a servant. They don't know my name even though I have helped them with all of their party invitations and Christmas cards for a long time. I mean a loooong time. Your friend Marcia, the one who wears only white. She used to come into the store with her mother when she was a teenager. I picked out the invitations for her sweet sixteen party and high school and college graduation parties, and her wedding. She has known me for a decade. Never once has she said my name or asked how I'm doing. My customers have no idea that I actually own the store. They think I'm just an underling, and they treat me accordingly."

Abby hung her head, embarrassed. "That's awful," she whispered. "I can't believe I was friends with those people."

Carmen reached across the table and squeezed her hand. "You may have been friends with them. But you weren't like them. You were always nice. Always. There was one day about five years ago, not long after my mother died. I must have looked how I felt. Sad, exhausted, lonely. You could tell. You asked me if I was alright and we talked about our mothers, how they both had died too young."

"I remember that," Abby said, feeling better and sitting up a little straighter. "My mother had died a year earlier. We were both going through the same thing. It helped me, too, to talk about it with you."

"The point is that you were trying to make me feel better. You saw me as a person, and you made a human connection with me. I never forgot that."

"Okay stop, you're making me cry. But what was the third reason?" Abby asked.

"What? Oh. Right. The third reason is this. But first, a story. When I was eight, my mother sent me and two of my friends down to the corner store to buy milk and eggs to make us breakfast. We had a sleepover the night before. Those two girls were my best friends, and we had stayed up all night laughing and giggling, and we did pinky swears that we would always be friends. So we got to the store and I picked up the milk and eggs, paid for them, and left. Except as the three of us went out the door, the cashier yelled for us to stop. The next thing I know, one of my friends threw two candy bars at my feet and they both ran away. No matter how much I swore up and down that I hadn't stolen the candy, the man would not believe me. Even when my mother came to the store and explained the situation, he still didn't believe me. My mother paid for the candy, then handed it back to the man, who promptly banned me from the store. I sometimes drive back to my old neighborhood and go in and buy the same kind of chocolate bars. The man is still there. He must be a hundred by now. He has no idea who I am. Anyway. Despite all the evidence, my mother believed me when I told her I hadn't stolen the chocolate. She was the only one. Even my dad didn't believe me. So it was the same with you. Despite all the evidence around you, and despite all the people who thought you were guilty, I knew you weren't involved in your husband's scam. And when I heard on the news that your membership to the country club had been revoked and you had been banned for life, I thought about that candy store. When my full-time salesclerk quit, I was going to call you and see if you were interested, but you beat me to it. You can imagine my surprise when you came into the store."

"I never knew any of that," Abby said. "That's quite a story. I owe you so much. You helped get me on my feet again. I don't know what I would have done if you hadn't given me a job." She used the back of her hand to wipe away the tears. "You extended me your friendship when everyone else was withdrawing it."

"Your mascara is running," Carmen observed. "I told you, you need to stop wearing that cheap stuff." They both laughed, and Carmen continued. "You would have found another job somewhere else. You're a survivor. And by the way, friendship goes two ways, you know. And you gave me yours."

"Little good that does for you," Abby said wryly. "I don't have anything to give you."

"That's where you're wrong," Carmen said. "Every day when you come into the store, you hold your head high and face the day with dignity. It takes a lot of courage for you to take a job waiting on people. I really admire that. You set a good example of grace under pressure."

Abby smiled. "I don't feel that graceful, but it's good to know that I project that. I always tried to, but I held on to the resentment for longer than I should have. I know that now."

Abby was grateful that the shop was busy that day. It was still September, but people were already thinking about Christmas and came in by the droves to order their personalized holiday greeting cards.

At the end of the day, Abby rang up a customer's purchase of five hundred dollars' worth of greeting cards, rolls of high-gloss gift wrap, stationery and other sundry paper items. Abby herself used to spend that amount of money and more in the shop, before the tornado hit her life and split it in two. In fact, she could drop that amount of money in ten minutes, then have an expensive lunch with her fashionable friends, and then drop another five hundred dollars at a shoe store, then at the gourmet food store she and Jake liked to frequent. There was a time when money was plentiful. It kept rolling in, day after day. But that day eventually—and rather abruptly— came to an end. And now Abby worked in her favorite stationery store, instead of patronizing it.

"Here you go," Abby said as she handed the bulging bags across the counter to the stylish customer, who wore her Burberry raincoat and scarf like a pro. "Enjoy." Abby thought to herself that nowadays five hundred dollars would pay for groceries, her electricity, and her gas and cell phone bills for a month.

When the customer left, Abby took advantage of the lull in shoppers to take a break. She took off her smock and draped it over the stool behind the cash register.

"Going to take my fifteen minutes," she said to Carmen.

"Okay, honey," Carmen called from where she was stacking boxes of Crane notecards. "Take thirty if you need to. I doubt we'll get much more traffic in the next hour, and I know you haven't eaten yet today. Plus, you look exhausted."

"Thanks, I'll owe you forever," Abby quipped. "Someday, when my fabulous fortune is restored, I will take you to New York City for an all-expenses-paid girls' weekend. We'll go to the Elizabeth Arden spa and have seaweed wraps and mud baths while hunky

Swedish guys serve us Mojitos in crystal glasses rimmed with real gold."

"Can we get hot stone massages and facials, too?" Carmen asked, playing along. "And I want a manicure with real diamonds imbedded in the polish. Something to make my nails really sparkle."

"Of course," Abby said. "We'll do all that and more. I'll hire us both a personal stylist, and we'll get private shopping sprees at all the best stores. It'll be fun. Just like the old days."

"I won't hold my breath," Carmen said, bringing them both down to earth again. She turned to look at Abby. "And neither should you. It's time to forget about the past and concentrate on what's ahead. You need to get out of Minneapolis, and the opportunity in Wander Creek is perfect. God knows I'll miss you, and not just as an employee—you're the best I've ever had—but as a friend, too. You need to be where no one knows who you are, and where you can start over."

Abby stood next to Carmen who was now fussing with a holiday display, and lovingly fingering the boxes of Christmas cards adorned with delicate designs of holly boughs tied with red and white holiday ribbon. Abby had sent out similar cards the previous year to her Christmas list of almost four hundred people. She mentally did the math. Four hundred people. Ten cards to a box. Thirty dollars a box. That was twelve hundred dollars that she had spent on Christmas cards. That amount would now cover two month's rent.

"Minneapolis is my home," Abby said wistfully. "I can't imagine living any place else."

Abby had grown up in a working class neighborhood, attended the University of Minnesota where she had earned a bachelor's degree, followed by two master's degrees. She had worked for a large and trendy event management firm for a year, which is how she met real estate mogul and financier Jake

Stinette. But she hadn't held a job since. That seemed like a life-time ago.

In the break room, Abby sat down with her bland yogurt. She knew she had to get rid of her anger and bitterness. And she knew Carmen was right that she needed to start over where no one knew her. But why should she have to leave? It was Jake, not her, who stole millions of dollars. She hadn't known a thing until FBI agents came knocking at their door and seized computers and files from Jake's office. It had taken them almost a month to find and seize Jake himself. He had been tipped off somehow, and he had emptied their bank accounts, and fled to Costa Rica with a twenty-something assistant named Dee. She had no idea where Dee was now. And frankly, she didn't care. For weeks during the trial, Jake had made collect calls to her from prison every day. And every day, she refused the charges, or just didn't answer. She wasn't holding a grudge, exactly. But come on. FBI raid? Collect calls from prison? Extradition? Abby felt as if she deserved the right to some self-pity, just for a little while longer.

At closing time, Abby and Carmen cashed out the register and straightened the store. This was the part of the day that Abby looked forward to the most. She loved looking at all the beautiful things and slipping them back into their rightful places. The large, loose sheets of thick and vibrant gift wrap hung from a floor-to-ceiling rack with dowels. She arranged a stack of blank journals into a fan-shape stack. As she walked past a table dedicated to every imaginable type of pen, she paused to return the rogue drifters to their rightful places based on color or nib size. There were so many variations of pens, it made her head swim.

Abby sighed. She might not be able to bring order to her own life, but she could impose it on the store, and for now, that would have to be enough.

Carmen had changed the soundtrack after closing, tuning to a station playing only Christmas music.

"Isn't it a little early for Christmas carols?" Abby asked.

"Well, I figure that since you're not going to be around for Christmas this year, we'd start celebrating a little early."

"But I haven't decided yet," Abby protested.

"Yes, you have," Carmen said. "You just don't know it yet."

As Abby and Carmen walked toward the bus stop and parking deck, Carmen slipped her arm through Abby's. Around them the fashionable boutiques were closing, and shoppers headed to the bistros and bars for happy hour and dinner. Abby loved to be surrounded by the bustle of the city before she headed home to the stale quiet of her apartment.

"I've never said this before, because I know it's harsh," Carmen said as they turned the corner at the bus stop where they would part. "But you need to hear it. You're lucky you aren't in prison, too. And you need to grab hold of this opportunity and run with it. You've been given a second chance and you need to take it."

"I didn't do anything wrong," Abby said flatly, "but God knows I still feel guilty about the lives Jake ruined."

"I know you didn't do anything wrong, and you know it," Carmen said patiently. "But the rest of the world, not so much. And there's nothing you can do about what Jake did. Even if you gave every cent you ever earn to the victims, you couldn't even make a dent in the amount of money Jake stole. You need to stop worrying about what you can't control and start worrying about what you can. Beginning with yourself. You've got to stop living in the past and get on with your life. Most of all, you have to forgive yourself for not realizing what Jake was doing."

CHAPTER 4

*D*uring the two weeks that Abby prepared to make the move to Wander Creek, she took the bus downtown to Jerome Monroe's office, signed the paperwork and deposited her benefactor's check into her account. In the evenings, for hours after the shop closed, she and Carmen poured over accounting software and inventory tracking systems, insurance policies and business licenses. Carmen generously gave Abby a crash course in starting and running a small business. They talked about marketing and using social media to advertise specials and sales to draw in customers. Carmen explained the ins and outs of holding an event on site and how to maximize holidays and special occasions by making creative and breath-taking window displays. She talked balefully about not relying too much on local business in a tourist town, but not to overlook the needs of the residents, either. They poured over websites and catalogs and Abby got intense lessons in pricing strategies, diver-sifying and cycling inventory, and calculating profit margins.

Each night, Abby returned to her small apartment, her head swimming with ideas and possibilities. And instead of dressing up in her pretty clothes, Abby settled immediately at the kitchen table, often skipping dinner, and reviewed her notes and made sketches and observations. Based on Carmen's input, she drafted a list of what she would need to get started and made a corresponding budget. She would need a new laptop with software for accounting, inventory and graphic design. Carmen had shown her how to use a specialized printer to make her own signage and marketing materials. Abby pinned so many pins on Pinterest she thought she might break the platform! Her head swam with ideas. Space-saving ideas, like attaching a rack with wooden dowels to the sides of the display blocks to hang the loose wrapping paper sheets on, rather than take up wall space. Decorating ideas about how to present her wares, like selling ribbon by the yard, and ideas about the variety of gorgeous but useful items she would carry, like pretty cocktail napkins and coasters, cloth-covered boxes, and basic office and organizing supplies. Wander Creek was a small community and Abby instinctively knew she needed to make herself and her store valuable to its residents.

She thought about the different rooms in a house. Not her mansion, but the house she grew up in. A simple bungalow with a small kitchen, two bedrooms, two bathrooms, a small den where her parents watched television, and a living room and dining room. They had given her a very happy childhood. She didn't know they were "working class" until junior high school and she had asked her mother to take her to the mall to buy a two-hundred-dollar pair of jeans she wanted to wear the next day. Her mother had gone white and sat down on a kitchen chair. Abby had watched as she worried her hands in her lap. They were red and chapped from the industrial strength chemicals she used to clean offices throughout the city.

"I'm sorry, sweetie," her mother had said with tears in her eyes. "We just can't afford those kinds of things. But we can go to the Goodwill on Saturday. There's a good one in Eden Lake. We might even find a pair of the jeans you want there."

It was the first time Abby had seen her mother cry. She

wished now that she had comforted her mother. Instead, she stomped upstairs to her bedroom and slammed the door. The next morning when she came down for breakfast, her mother put a plate of blueberry pancakes in front of her and took a little jug of syrup out of the microwave and set it on the table.

When Abby sat down and picked up her fork, she saw a ten dollar bill tucked under her plate. She knew even that amount was a stretch for her parents.

"I thought it would be nice to have a treat this morning," her mother said, as if the previous evening hadn't happened. She didn't mention the jeans or the ten dollars, and Abby never asked for anything extravagant again.

Abby stood up to stretch her legs and made a circuit around her small apartment, rubbing her neck and rolling her shoulders. It had been a long time since she had thought of those expensive designer blue jeans and the distraught look on her mother's face when she was forced by circumstance to deny her daughter the one thing she wanted more than anything in the world. Looking back, she realized that the feelings of lack and denying herself never left her. Throughout school and later in college and graduate school she had been content just getting by, with no extravagances. She loved her studies and her friends, and that was enough. But then she met Jake and every glittering thing he dangled in front of her drove her closer to him and further into a material lifestyle and mindset.

The image of the first home she had shared with Jake popped into her mind. It was nothing like their lavish mansion, but it was large and brand new. Much too big for the two of them. In her mind's eye she saw the little built-in office nook off of the kitchen, and the stacks of cookbooks she had bought soon after they were married. And there was the large pantry, which she had organized in a precise manner, labeling the shelves with a label maker. She kept an inventory list on a clipboard.

As she thought of all these things, she scribbled furiously. She could expand her inventory to include kitchen items and have a corresponding display table. She remembered the beautiful museum shops she had visited during her many travels across the country and internationally. But she was getting ahead of herself. Time to put on the brakes. She had to draw the line somewhere. At least at the beginning.

With each new thing she learned, Abby's heart grew a little larger. She almost felt like the Grinch in the Dr. Seuss tale, whose heart was smaller than all the Whos in Whoville. It seemed that since her life had been turned upside down by Jake's sins, Abby had let her heart shrink to the point where there was no room for anything except resentment. But as she poured over the plans for her new endeavor, she felt the stirrings of the old Abby, the one who had been excited in college and grad school to learn new things and meet new people who could enrich her life and broaden her horizons.

She wished she had asked Jerome Monroe to email her the photos he had shown her but decided she would be there soon enough. Besides, she could rely on her memory until then to sketch out where things would go. She went to bed excited and exhausted every night and woke up before the alarm, ready to tackle the day.

Somewhere along the line she realized that the nightmare of the previous year had turned into dreams. The kind of dreams of her childhood on Christmas Eve, the anticipation of Santa's visit and the gifts to come so intense she could barely stand the excitement. For the first time in a long time, she felt hope. She was finally doing what Carmen had been telling her to do. She couldn't help but wonder what would have happened to her if she hadn't received the gift of this incredible second chance. She liked to think that she would have worked it out, that she would have fought her way out of her situation and made a fulfilling life for herself. But part of her wasn't so sure. Until a year ago, her life had been a never-ending parade of parties, socialites, shopping and frivolities. And somewhere along the way, she had lost herself. When she met and married Jake, she put away her master's degrees and dreams of owning her own special events company. She had been so in love and so dazzled by the lifestyle Jake offered her, it hadn't been a hard choice. Going to work every day versus shopping and jet-setting? No brainer. But Abby now realized that her life with Jake had changed her. With Jake, her identity was tied to possessions, like their beautiful lakefront mansion and her huge walk-in closet filled to the brim with all the latest designer clothes and shoes and handbags; and what she did, like traveling the world, going to the best spas, shopping in the poshest stores, and being the glamorous trophy on the arm of her rich and amazing husband. She had forgotten who she really was. She had lost her true self.

Abby knew in her heart that she was only going to stay in Wander Creek for the required year. She pondered whether it made sense to pour herself into starting a business only to turn around and sell it, but she decided that a prosperous and well-run business would attract more buyers. Everything she needed to do, she would do well. And she'd keep her eye firmly on her future. Wander Creek would be a place for her to start anew. A stepping-stone. But her life would really start again when she returned to Minneapolis. And maybe, after a year, things would have cooled off some and she might be accepted back into her old social circle. Stranger things had happened. It wasn't too much to ask that her friends might forgive her, was it?

You're coming to visit me, right?" Abby asked Carmen on their last evening together.

"Of course, I am," Carmen answered her. "I'm your business consultant, remember? I'll come in a few months and assess your progress."

"A few months?" Abby asked, surprised at the panic she felt when she thought of leaving the security of Carmen and the Paperie.

The older woman patted her hand. "Don't worry. If you need me sooner, just call. I'll come. But basically, you're on your own now. And I know you can handle it."

She and Carmen sat at a nearby up-scale Tapas bar nibbling on small plates and sipping wine. It was Carmen's goodbye treat. Although she was now fortified with plenty of funds, and she felt right at home in the expensive restaurant, Abby knew it would take her a while until she got used to spending it.

The two speculated as to the identity of the benefactor. Carmen pointed out the obvious, that the timing of the gift was perfect and couldn't have come at a better time and suggested that the benefactor must know her personally, rather than being a random person who happened to hear about her situation.

"That makes sense to some degree," Abby agreed, popping a toast point topped with olive bruschetta into her mouth. "But why did they wait an entire year? I could have used this boost a year ago, even six months ago."

"Fair point," Carmen conceded. "Maybe it is a philanthropist who followed the trial and waited to see the outcome before they put their plan into action. Or maybe it all comes back to the most obvious—it's someone you know who's trying to help you but doesn't want you to know for whatever reason."

"But does it make sense that it could be one of my old friends? Jake scammed practically everyone I knew. All my friends. I mean, all *our* friends. I guess it's possible that someone took pity on me, but the terms of the arrangement in Wander Creek are pretty specific to be coming from a someone in Minneapolis."

Carmen nodded in agreement. "Maybe they thought if they concocted this outrageous scheme, they could distract you from their identity," she suggested.

"Maybe," Abby said, very grateful that apparently there was at least one person—well, two, counting Carmen—who still cared about her. And there was one last person she needed to see before she left Minneapolis. Maybe she could find the answer in him.

~

THE NEXT MORNING, Abby broke down and bought a small used silver SUV. Despite the expense, she was thrilled to have her own transportation again, instead of relying on the bus and the Minneapolis light rail system. A vehicle gave her a freedom she hadn't felt for a long time. As she drove off the lot, she tuned to her favorite radio station, and was delighted to hear her favorite song playing. *This must be a sign.* She pushed the button to open the sunroof, and when it had fully opened and the bright northern sun was blaring down from a spectacularly blue sky, she felt better than she had in ages.

There was no bus or train system in Wander Creek. No doubt about it, she would need this car, and would need the four wheel drive. She was going to the north country, after all. As she had written the check at the used car lot, her mind automatically started calculating. The cost of the car would pay rent and insurance for a year.

Enough is enough. No more calculating, she admonished herself. Those days needed to be over.

By late that afternoon, she sat fidgeting nervously at a table in the visitors' room at the Sandstone Federal Prison a little over an hour's drive from Minneapolis. She knew she was on Jake's visitor list. His lawyer had told her that during the trial, so she figured she would be able to see him.

When the door opened and Jake shuffled in, Abby hardly recognized her former husband. Once her dynamic and healthy husband, the man before her displayed no characteristics of his former self. His hair, no longer stylishly cut or highlighted, was grey around the temples, and had been shorn into a buzz cut. His pallor was pale, lacking the usual vibrancy of his year-round tan. But then he flashed her his roguish half smile, displaying very expensive white veneers. Although she would never forgive him for what he had done to her, and to so many of their friends and acquaintances, she was relieved, for his sake, that he was still in there, in a way safe, somewhere. Safe from himself, too. He was going to be in prison for a long, long time.

Jake slid over a plastic molded chair and sat down. Around them, other visitors chatted while others cried. Children screamed and laughed, but to Abby it was all muffled background noise that she could hardly discern.

Jake reached across the table for her hands, which she jerked away and folded onto her lap.

"I'm sorry," he said. "I am really, really sorry. I never wanted to hurt you."

Abby didn't say anything. Her mouth was dry. She hadn't prepared for this.

"I tried to protect you," he continued, "by putting all of the assets in my name so nothing could be tied to you. So you couldn't be blamed for anything."

"Well instead of protecting me you left me with nothing," Abby pointed out.

Jake hung his head. "I know. I didn't think it through. I guess I didn't want to believe that I would actually get caught, so I didn't make a real contingency plan."

"And running away to Costa Rica?" Abby asked, "with your secretary? What a cliché. I thought you loved me. I thought we were happy." She willed the tears away, but one rolled down her cheek despite her efforts. She had promised herself over and over that she had cried her last tears for Jake Stinette. But apparently, there was one left.

"I know, I know," Jake said, giving her that roguish, boy-next-door grin. "I wasn't thinking. I don't know what that was about."

"You didn't think about a lot of things, especially me," Abby snapped. "But it doesn't matter anymore."

"You look awesome," he said. "Beautiful as ever. I knew you would land on your feet."

Abby intensified her gaze, hoping that somewhere in his face or his eyes, she could discern the truth about whether or not he was her benefactor, or had knowledge of who it was. Jake had always had an intensity about him, and a certain set of his jaw or tilt of his chin conveyed his mood. But all that was gone. Now, he just hung his head in shame.

At least he has the decency to be ashamed, she thought.

Could Jake have pulled off the elaborate scheme from prison? Only if he had resources somewhere that he had somehow managed to hide from the FBI's forensic accountants. After a year apart from Jake, Abby found she could no longer sense his mood or anticipate his next move. What had she expected? Jake had deceived her in the past. Their whole life together had been based on lies. Why did she think that all of a sudden she would be able to tell whether or not he was lying to her in the present?

THE CALCULATOR constantly running in Abby's brain was annoying, relentlessly pointing out to her exactly what she had lost financially, and by how much her value as a person had been reduced. When the FBI had raided her home and locked up her wayward husband, her income had dropped from eight figures to five. Add one dingy apartment and a forty-hour work week making just above minimum wage, five figures dwindled to zero at the end of the month. Abby was taking six figures with her to Wander Creek where she would acquire one building. But beyond that, she didn't know what awaited her. It almost felt like she was living in a word problem. "If a woman 'A' has six figures and moves three hundred miles from home to unknown city 'B', what is 'X'?"

Abby decided that no matter what awaited her in Wander Creek, she was going to enjoy the ride. She decided she would frame her new situation as a prolonged, working vacation, after which she would emerge rested, refreshed, and ready to return home and re-establish her life in Minneapolis.

CHAPTER 5

On the morning of her departure, Abby rose very early and sat on the couch sipping her coffee. She had packed everything up and had it stacked by the front door. She donated her furniture, such as it was, back to the thrift shop where she had purchased it. It wasn't worth the cost of moving it up to Wander Creek, and she could buy new second-hand furniture at the thrift shop down the street from her new building. One of the employees from the thrift store near her apartment had volunteered to pick up her furniture and help load her SUV.

On the three-hour drive north on I-35, Abby had plenty of time to speculate about the identity of her benefactor. After her tense but unproductive visit with Jake, she had ruled him out. Her short list had just become shorter. She was an only child, and both of her parents were dead. Jake's parents and brother had lost their life savings in Jake's schemes, so she was pretty sure none of them were handing out real estate and cash. Abby had a great aunt in Wyoming, but she was in her eighties and had Alzheimer's. Besides, Abby had never met her and wasn't even sure if Great Aunt Eleanor even knew she existed. Or was

Eleanor a second or third cousin? She never had been able to remember, and for the past decade, it hadn't seemed important.

Abby's mind wandered to the decision she had made. About an hour into the drive, as she left the city behind and was zooming along a long straight stretch of interstate, passing by farm fields and patches of woods and lakes, doubt began to set in.

What am I doing?

Was she about to make another catastrophic mistake? She couldn't be trusted to choose the right man, so what made her think she was in any position to judge the situation presented to her? She remembered sitting in Jerome Monroe's downtown office, signing all of the papers he put in front of her. Had she been so mesmerized by the dazzling proposition that she failed to consider the consequences? Frankly, yes.

She ticked off the list of unknowns in her mind. What if she got there and the building and the town were not as presented to her? What if everyone knew who she was and shunned her? What if, after a decade of luxury and ease and only a little work experience under her belt, she couldn't hack it as a business owner? What if no one wanted to buy pretty stationery and paper items and gifts?

Soon, the hum of the road drowned out her thoughts and Abby began to enjoy the scenery. The further north she drove the more wooded the area became, and the flashes of white birch trees against dense green forest were hypnotic. With her car packed with her belongings, and an uncertain future ahead of her, she almost felt like a college student taking a road trip.

Two hours into her drive she stopped at a rest area to use the ladies' room and stretch her legs. Like so many public spaces in Minnesota, the rest area was a pleasing park-like space with a small brick building, picnic tables under an outdoor tent thingy and even a short walking path for dogs. Abby tilted her face to the sun and closed her eyes. Maybe everything would work out.

When the tip of Lake Superior came into view, Abby was so

taken by its vastness that she missed her exit. No matter. The view of the black and white lighthouse at the end of the pier was meant to be enjoyed, and she could double back. It was a sunny day, but the persistent wind was whipping up whitecaps on the grey water. The lake was just huge, and she gazed in awe at the bulging mounds of coal and grain and iron ore on the gigantic ships docked in the port. It had never occurred to her before that day how the goods that fueled her life moved from one place to another. Everything just appeared before her. Whatever she wanted, it was just there.

At Highway 53 she doubled back then hit Highway 2 that would take her northward into Wander Creek. For some unknown reason this last stretch of the drive reminded her of the vacations she and Jake had taken to California and the Caribbean, and the kayaking and canoeing they had enjoyed. They had once taken a kayaking tour in Alaska, and one summer they had spent a month on a sailboat in Greece learning how to sail. It had been invigorating learning how to control the boat and work with the wind to make it go where she wanted. She loved running from bow to stern, her bare feet slapping against the deck to tie off a line or use the winches to adjust the rigging.

She remembered Mexico. Whenever they went to Mexico, which was often, the first thing she did was change into a bikini, jump into the Gulf of Mexico, and let the glorious pale blue salt water engulf her.

She had always been so active—constantly moving, burning calories, building muscle, soaking in the sun, learning new things, meeting new people. She remembered the pictures Jerome Monroe had shown her of families kayaking and tubing on Wander Creek. *Well*, she thought to herself, *of all the ways a person could choose to heal, kayaking down a picturesque creek as it meandered through the great north woods was not too bad of an option.* It was too late in the season now, but next summer she could rent a kayak, dip the blade of the paddle into the water and guide the boat wherever she wanted it to go. She imagined it would be akin to a spiritual awakening. But in the meantime, she'd find something else to do to be active. She no longer had to sit in her dingy apartment. There was a new world for her to explore, small though it may be.

As she turned onto Minnesota Highway 15, which would take her right up into Wander Creek, she began to understand what drew so many visitors to the region. As she drove, her eyes feasted on a stunning panorama of densely forested rolling hills. The tall trunks of white birch trees competing for attention with the evergreens flashed her their greeting. If she knew her trees better, she would have realized that she was also passing by trembling aspens, a smattering of northern hardwoods, a variety of spruces and pines, hemlocks, tamarack, and perhaps an occasional red or burr oak. She knew from what Mr. Monroe had told her that hidden amongst the lavish forests were beautiful lakes and rivers and streams of all sizes, amazing and cozy family resorts, and cherished privately owned cabins, lovingly maintained by generation after generation of Minnesota families.

If the splendid scene flashing by the windows of her SUV was not enough, it was complimented by a northern Minnesota high latitude sky. A sky that Abby thought could not have possibly been more brilliant or more blue, even if it tried. For the first time since she left Minneapolis, Abby smiled. Not just a twitch of the corner of the lips smile, but a full on, teeth baring, face wrinkling, beaming, happy grin. She hoped the feeling would last.

Abby eased on the brakes when she saw the sign for Wander Creek and guided the SUV over into the right turn only lane, following the direction of the arrow carved into the wooden and rustic "Welcome to Wander Creek" sign. After she made the easterly turn off Highway 15 onto Wolf Path Lane, the road curved around to the north. The town itself just seemed to appear out of nowhere, mostly filling up the raised flat area cut from the trees. It was bordered on its north by Wander Creek, with the remainder surrounded by a smattering of farm fields, gardens, and pastures, gradually giving way to the forested rolling hills. She had entered the town from the south. Wolf Path Lane wound up being a narrow, windy road that trailed mostly northward through neat residential neighborhoods with small-ish, well-kept houses on each side of the road. After a bit, the road straightened and entered the business district, which Abby correctly assumed was downtown. Eventually, Wolf Path Lane teed out at Main Street. Abby maneuvered east on Main Street for a block and arrived at the municipal parking lot, where she parked and sat for a few minutes taking in the view and trying to get her bearings. Adjacent to the parking lot were the county offices. Beyond the county buildings a striking white gazebo sat in the park that ran the whole two blocks of the town's water-front. The creek bottom was perhaps two dozen yards below the town in elevation, accessed by several sets of stairs that led down to creek level. This section of the creek bottom ran pretty much west to east for about half a mile. The creek itself flowed east in a gentle meander within the confines of the creek bottom. Across the bottom, rugged bluffs rose up to more thick woods.

Abby put in the address for her new building, more excited than she ever thought she would be. Her GPS told her to take a right on Main Street out of the parking lot. She retraced the one block of Main Street she had just come down, this time noticing the neat rows of stores on both sides, and after continuing past Wolf Path Lane, got her first glimpse of her building on the left. She almost stopped in the middle of the road looking, but noticing a car behind her, she continued westward until she hit Maple Lane, where she turned around and headed back east. A minute later she was parked curbside in front of her building. *Oh my gosh, this is really mine! And it looks even better in real life than in the pictures Jerome Monroe showed me!*

It was almost lunchtime and the town hummed with small

town activity. The day was fine, the air particularly fresh and crisp, and the sun shone brightly. And she had arrived.

As promised, Jerome Monroe was waiting for her, wearing another stylish three-piece suit, standing in front of the building located at 29 Main Street. Abby didn't notice him until he waved, then she recognized his car parked in front of hers. She quickly hopped out, happy to stretch her legs, and walked toward Mr. Monroe. She had worn comfortable jeans, a navy crewneck sweater and trendy tennis shoes left over from her former life. She wanted to look casual, but elegant. She wanted to make a good impression, fit in, not draw attention to herself, find friends and be alone, all at the same time. *Shheeesh. I'm giving myself mixed messages*, she thought.

"I hope I'm not late," she said, shaking Mr. Monroe's outstretched hand.

"Not at all," he assured her. "I was early. I wanted to make sure things were ready for you. Shall we go in?"

"There's something I've been wanting to ask you," Abby said, as Mr. Monroe unlocked the door and entered, with Abby just behind him. The bell above the door tinkled a greeting, and she stopped in mid-sentence to admire the interior. While it resembled what she had seen in the photographs, someone had done quite a few last-minute upgrades. There was a fresh coat of creamy white paint on the walls, and new light grey Berber carpet covered the floor. And it appeared that the sales counter had been somewhat customized. The sides were made of galvanized steel and the top was a six feet long piece of grey and white granite. It was a stunning effect. The merchandise racks and display cases had been artfully arranged against the walls, with a few placed in the middle of the store. Abby's heart sang with possibilities. *Cards in the racks in the middle of the store. The "men's gifts" section can go over there. This can go on that shelf. That can go on this shelf.* She practically spun around in a circle trying to take in everything at the same time.

"We took the liberty of sprucing up the space," he explained. "You mentioned how much you enjoyed working at the Paperie, so we ordered some specialty merchandise racks and cases that would be suitable for a stationery store." He gestured around the room. "Hope we didn't assume too much."

"It's beautiful," Abby breathed. "Better than I could have hoped for." She turned to Mr. Monroe. "I've been wanting to ask you something," she said again. "The other people in Wander Creek, do they know about this arrangement? With my benefactor, I mean? That could make for some awkward questions."

Mr. Monroe shook his head. "No, you don't need to worry about that. As far as everyone in Wander Creek is concerned, you purchased the building yourself and moved up from Minneapolis."

"That's a relief. Thank you," Abby said.

"Are you worried about people recognizing you?" he asked kindly.

"The thought has crossed my mind," Abby admitted.

Mr. Monroe tried to reassure her. "My client—that is, your benefactor—and I considered this issue. I did some research along those lines. As you might imagine, I have quite a wide network of clients and former clients who are usually eager to assist when I ask. So I asked around. Not a lot, but just enough to get a feel for how well-known you might be up here. It doesn't appear that the Duluth paper carried the story. I have a client who works in broadcast and they offered to nose around the Duluth news studio, and apparently there was one news story when the FBI finally arrested Jake, but your picture wasn't shown. And although you were mentioned by name, people know you now as Abby Barrett . . ." his voice trailed off. "And if you don't mind me saying so, you look very different now than you did when I used to see you at those charity functions. You don't have that glossy veneer about you now. You look more natural. Relaxed."

"You're very thorough," Abby said. "I really do appreciate how you've looked out for me."

"Speaking of," Mr. Monroe said as he withdrew a white envelope from his suit pocket and handed it to Abby. Inside, was a stack of one hundred dollar bills. "I don't understand," she said. "More money?"

Jerome Monroe gestured toward the street where their cars were parked. "We know you've had some personal expenses associated with the move, particularly your new vehicle. It didn't occur to me, to us, that you didn't have a car. Your benefactor was distressed when I told them you were forced to use your seed money on that expense."

It wasn't lost on Abby that Mr. Monroe had not used a gender-specific pronoun. Instead of "he" or "she" he always used the plural "they," "we," and "them."

"Please thank them the next time you speak to them," she said. "Actually, I feel very much like a heel," she continued. "This has been such a whirlwind that I don't think I've adequately expressed my thanks and gratitude. Let me at least write a thank-you note for you to pass on."

Mr. Monroe shook his head. "No need. Your benefactor knows how grateful you are. The only thanks they need is for you to succeed. Make something of this store. Use this opportunity to thrive and rediscover yourself. They know what a difficult time you've had, and all the associated baggage that accompanies your circumstances. Now, shall we finish the tour?"

Abby folded the envelope and put it in her back jean's pocket and followed Mr. Monroe to the back of the store. She lovingly trailed her fingers along the tops of the display blocks, tables and racks.

Mr. Monroe opened a door and they entered into a small office that had been decorated with a beautiful glass-topped desk, a low credenza with file drawers and a beautifully upholstered office chair. Someone had hung cork board on the far wall, and the wall behind the desk was floor to ceiling shelves, with a row of cabinets at the bottom.

"Of course, this is the office," he said, "and there's a small bathroom beyond. You'll probably want to set up a small kitchen area to bring the place up to OSHA and EOE standards for your employee." Mr. Monroe opened the door next to the restroom and they walked up a narrow staircase, emerging into a huge room, fully decorated with dining and living room furniture, a full-size kitchen with an island and bar stools, and beyond that a reading nook with two plump armchairs and ottoman facing a gas fireplace. So, she would have her fire this winter after all.

"The building was mostly empty in the pictures you showed me," Abby said, moving around in a circle. "This just keeps getting better and better. I never expected that the place would come fully furnished."

Mr. Monroe hesitated, as if looking for the right words. "When I visited your apartment, I didn't expect it to be so . . . so . . . . spartan. I knew the FBI would have seized assets as well as personal property, but I expected that you would have been left with some . . . some . . . decent furniture."

Abby smiled. "There's no need to be delicate about it," she said, laughing. "I know that apartment was a dump. All the assets were in Jake's name. But I got to keep all of my designer clothes. I hadn't yet reached the point where I sold them for cash. But believe me, it crossed my mind many times."

"Nevertheless, when I told your benefactor, they decided to furnish the place for you. The bedroom and bathroom are at the back of this living area. The place is fully kitted out with kitchen essentials, towels, and the like. Even condiments." He nodded at her and said, "And the extra money should cover anything we haven't thought of."

After Mr. Monroe left with the promise of checking on her periodically, Abby stood in the still apartment, afraid if she moved or even breathed, the magic spell that had given her all this would be broken. When she heard the bell on the shop door tinkle and Mr. Monroe get in his car and drive away, she did a little happy dance in the living room, pumping her fist and shaking her head like a rock star. She even managed a few quiet hoots and hollers. After all, she didn't know if she had neighbors, but if she did, she certainly didn't want them to hear her giddy celebration through the walls.

With her little dance of delight complete, Abby did what she hadn't felt comfortable doing while Mr. Monroe was in the apartment. She walked every inch of the space inspecting every-thing, down to the pretty glass door handles and the extra bed sheets in the linen closet. It was simply amazing.

The living and dining areas were one large open space with a full-size kitchen off to one side. The floors were a distressed dark grey wood plank and they perfectly matched the grey and white kitchen counter tops and the grey subway tile backsplash. There was even a stainless steel oven fan hood.

The main living area was flanked by two large light grey couches, one of which Abby jumped on, laying on her back and kicking her feet in the air and squealing as quietly as she could manage. A large square matching ottoman had been placed between the couches as a coffee table. Two small navy armchairs completed the suite. To the right of the living area a beautifully distressed farmer's table sat with six straight back chairs enveloped in cream-colored slip covers that fell elegantly to the floor. A long candle holder served as the centerpiece, with white candles in various heights standing ready to be lit. A low credenza stood against one wall next to the front door, and Abby walked to it and placed her phone and car keys on top. There. It was her first official act of moving in. And it felt good. Really good.

Back out on the street, Abby moved her car around to the alley behind the building and began to haul her suitcases and boxes up the stairs into, what? *What do I even call this place?* she wondered in her head. *Home? The store? The apartment? The building? I know*, she finally decided, laughing to herself. *The compound. No, that can't be the name. The upstairs will be* the apartment. *The downstairs will be* the shop.

Abby recalled that the last time she had moved all her stuff, the FBI had been kind enough to have everything delivered and placed directly into her apartment. The last time she had actually moved herself was in college. And she was a lot stronger then.

When she finally had everything inside the apartment, she collapsed on the couch with a glass of water. It was the best damn water she had ever had. And it wasn't even infused with cucumbers and lavender.

Judging from the homey feel of the apartment, the warmth of the colors and the obvious thought that went into choosing them, and the attention to detail when selecting the accessories, Abby began leaning towards the idea that her benefactor was a woman. But that was ridiculous. Even if the person who had decorated the place was a woman, that didn't mean she was the benefactor. Abby's anonymous guardian angel could have easily hired a decorator. He or she certainly seemed to have the means to do so.

That evening, Abby made herself a modest sandwich from the deli items her guardian angel had been kind enough to stock in her fridge. It was the best damn sandwich she'd ever had.

Although she was exhausted, Abby pushed herself to unpack everything. When she awoke the next morning, she wanted to feel as if she was home, and not caught in some limbo between cardboard boxes and suitcases. She would only be in Wander Creek for a year, but she would make sure it was a good year.

After taking a soaking bath with a seemingly inexhaustible supply of hot water in the immaculate white claw footed tub, she put on her flannel pajamas and grabbed her new laptop from her purse. It was time to start planning ahead. Yes, she was committed to being there a year. A year was fine. It was just right, in fact. Just enough time to flush out her game plan. But time could be a funny thing, stretching itself out in agonizingly slow increments, or going by so fast that the present and future seemed to explode together. A year can be a minute, and a minute can be a year. The year that stretched ahead of her could go by very fast, and she wanted to be prepared. If she had learned anything from losing everything, it was to be prepared for anything that might come her way. The calculator running in her head informed her that with the proceeds from the sale of *the compound* and all the beautiful new furnishings and accessories, she could rent an apartment in downtown Minneapolis, maybe one that overlooked the Mississippi River. If she invested her money carefully—noting to herself that she would do it herself— she could live comfortably, though she would still need some sort of income, maybe even a job. Perhaps she could go back to event management. As she woke up her laptop she thought of the boutiques and bars and trendy restaurants and nightspots that dotted the downtown area of the city. She scrolled to her favorite real estate website and started the search for her next home.

As Abby scrolled through pictures of luxury downtown apartments, the thought of Carmen suddenly popped into her head. *I should call her.* Abby grabbed her cell and tapped on Carmen's contact. A couple rings later she heard the familiar voice of her friend say, "Hey! How's it going? I wanted to call, but figured you were really busy."

"Carmen! You really wouldn't believe this place. Apparently, whoever is doing all this checked out the Paperie, because this place is decked out in a similar fashion."

"Wow," Carmen replied. "Wonder who it was? I never noticed anyone casing the place."

Abby spent the next fifteen minutes regaling Carmen with details about all the ways her guardian angel had gone above and beyond. She told Carmen how centered she was, how determined she was to make this endeavor a success. She would create something of value, and then sell it for a profit. A large profit. She told Carmen how she was sure she would be back in Minneapolis, living in a nice place downtown, by the end of one year.

At the end of the call, Carmen said, "I'm so glad you are so, what's the word? Invigorated? Animated? Energized? You sound really good. And your plan. You know, to come back here." Carmen paused, and Abby could hear her breathing. Carmen resumed, "Plans are good. You've got to have plans. But the thing with plans is . . . Oh, never mind. Look, thanks for calling. I miss you and love you. And I promise, I will be up to see you before winter gets too bad. I'm proud of you. Now, go get some sleep." With that, Carmen ended the call.

Abby stared at the phone in her hand, resting on her thigh. *What had Carmen been about to say? Does she not like my plan?*

CHAPTER 6

The first order of business the next morning was coffee, then groceries. Abby descended the stairs to the shop and stood, mesmerized. She was having trouble believing all of this was real. But everything was still there. The display racks and tables. They were really there. Then she saw something that she hadn't noticed before. The tables and racks in the middle of the store all had wheels. She looked around. They could be rolled out of the way leaving a nice large open place for a small event.

She strolled across the street to the Beanery, immediately recognizing from Mr. Monroe's pictures the logo painted on the awning above the front door. Abby thought it strange, and interesting, that the window display was decked out for every major holiday. A decorated Christmas tree with twinkling lights sat in the middle of the display, surrounded on one side by a giant stuffed Easter bunny holding a basket of eggs and on the other side three Styrofoam orange pumpkins on a table next to an ugly and scary witch doll. Under the Christmas tree was an assortment of other holiday paraphernalia, including a stuffed turkey doll flanked by pilgrim dolls. Strands of red paper hearts, green shamrocks, and miniature American flags hung from the ceiling, forming a canopy of sorts.

"Interesting," Abby said aloud. She didn't know it, but she would very quickly come to love the charm of the Wander Creek shops. She would discover that they all felt genuine, and each had a personality of its own, rather unlike the ultra-fashionable and expensive boutiques around the Paperie back home, which all seemed to try to copy and outdo each other. It ended up they all looked the same. Nothing really stood out at home. She began to see that everyone and everything in her previous social circle were cut from the same predictable cloth. Her life had been about fitting in. About doing whatever it took for others to accept her. To like her. To admire her. Her life was about the right dress, the right shoes, the right hair-do, the right jewelry, the right handbag, the right friends, the right husband. *Well, I really screwed that one up.*

Inside the Beanery, a few patrons sat at the tables with newspapers and tablets. Some were chatting amiably. Abby joined the short line in front of the bakery case. The rich aroma of coffee almost made her swoon. No longer would she have to buy store brand instant coffee. Those days were over. Sure, she wasn't going to buy a six dollar cup of coffee every day. After all, there was a coffee maker in her apartment. But today she would have a celebratory cappuccino and mentally toast her first full day in Wander Creek. She would be doing her part to support the local business community. The line moved quickly and soon she found herself standing in front of a young woman at the cash register. Her pink bangs, stark white-blonde hair and fine features made her look elfin, or even fairy like.

"Welcome to the Beanery," the girl said cheerfully. "What can I get you?"

Abby had studied the menu while she was in line and ordered her favorite. "I'll have a grande cappuccino with sugar-free vanilla syrup. And do you mind, can you shake in some Splenda before you froth it up?"

"Great minds think alike," the girl said, punching the tablet suspended on a holder to place the order. Abby realized on closer inspection that she wasn't a girl but a young woman, probably in her mid-twenties. "I hate it when the sweeteners get stuck in the froth. What's the point of putting them in at all? The sweetness doesn't sink down and you get a mouthful of overly sweet milk right off."

"I've never met anyone who shared my philosophy on sweetener and cappuccinos," Abby said.

"You've never been to Wander Creek before. We're full of surprises here."

"I guess word travels fast in a small town," Abby laughed. "I'll have a savory scone, too, please."

"Heated?" the girl asked, and Abby shook her head no. "We heard that someone had bought that building, and we've been watching the renovation for the past few weeks. I'm Sam Nelson, by the way." She used tongs to lift the scone out of the bakery case and put it on the plate. "Here you go. Go ahead and take a table and I'll bring your coffee to you."

Abby obediently threaded through the small dining area and took a seat at a small bistro table by the window overlooking Main Street. It was a quiet morning and the town had yet to wake up. The air felt dewy and fresh. The trees on either side of the street were still bursting with color.

"One cappuccino, hot and frothy, Splenda at the bottom," Sam announced, putting the mug on the table. "How's the scone?"

Abby looked down at the untouched scone. She had been saving it to have with her coffee. She wanted to savor the sweetness of the coffee and the tartness of the scone together. "Just starting now," she said.

"Can I get you anything else?"

"Actually," Abby said, "I'm headed to the grocery store. Can you recommend one in Two Harbors?"

"Sure can. There are two. The fancy one is near downtown. The normal one is on the outskirts. You'll see it in the strip mall on Highway 2, next to the dollar store. It's called Market Foods."

"Normal grocery store, it is," Abby said, then remembered she hadn't paid for her breakfast. "How much do I owe you?"

The girl smiled as if she knew a secret. Abby instantly liked this woman. She reminded her of a younger Carmen, full of energy and sass. "It's on the house," Sam said. "First-time customers get a free coffee and pastry."

ABBY HEADED SOUTH on Highway 15, retracing her path from the previous day. It was a straight shot down to Two Harbors. She cranked the radio and sang along to every song she knew. She even sang along to the songs she didn't know. It didn't matter, because she was feeling good. She was back in charge of her life. Fortified by the rich morning coffee and the plans she had begun to make the night before, Abby felt like she could take over the world.

The trees on either side of the highway were competing for attention. The yellows were definitely winning, but orange, red, russet brown, and burgundy were not far behind. Autumn was always Abby's favorite season, no matter what color the leaves. And this day was no exception. There was a chill in the air, and the pungent smell of woodlands was welcoming, so unlike the indiscernible and sometimes unpleasant city smells of home.

She arrived at the strip mall Sam had described and pulled into a parking spot. It was still early, only eight in the morning, but the parking lot was already half full. Abby grabbed her purse and hurried into the store. It was colder up here than in Minneapolis. Abby sensed that in a few weeks, she would feel that great northwoods cold in her bones. Time to invest in some tights or long underwear. Better get both.

Grabbing a buggy, she wheeled around the store, aimlessly at first. For the past six months, she had not splurged on anything, including food. Of course, she knew she couldn't raid very much of her seed money, but she had budgeted enough to buy everything she needed for the shop, and groceries, and sundry items for six months. She hoped that the store would turn a profit right away, but Carmen had warned her not to count on that. "When I first started the Paperie," Carmen had told her during one of their cram sessions, "it was a year until I turned a profit, and two before I paid myself a real salary."

Abby wheeled into the produce department and inspected the Minnesota-grown apples. There were so many varieties, with so many colors. She grabbed a few Honey Crisps. She had no idea why this variety was so expensive, and at almost five dollars a pound, suffice it to say that she had not eaten a honey crisp since before the FBI raided her home.

She was still daydreaming over the apples when she felt a bump against her thigh and looked up to see a tall man in khakis and a plaid shirt guiding his buggy between her and a display of lemons. "Oh, sorry," he said, his voice sincere. "You were so mesmerized by those apples I didn't want to disturb you so I thought I could just squeeze by." He laughed. "Evidently not."

"Oh, it's fine," Abby said. "I'm standing in the middle of the aisle anyway. Don't you hate it when people do that?"

"I should introduce myself," the man said, "since we are going to be neighbors, well, almost. I'm Ken Turner. I run the river and adventure outfitters on Wander Creek. It's called Northwoods Adventure Sports—Northwoods for short. And you're the new girl. Gosh, that sounded sexist. Ok, the new lady, or new woman, or even better, the new person, in town."

"Nice to meet you," Abby said, smiling and reaching across her cart to shake his hand. "How is it that everyone seems to know who I am? The girl at the coffee shop knew me, and now you."

"Word travels fast in a small town. Plus, I saw you this morning walking to the Beanery while I was out for a run. You just arrive?" he asked, leaning against his buggy.

"Yesterday," she said. "It's really beautiful here. I can see why the town attracts so many tourists."

"Year round," he said. "That's what keeps everyone in business, the creek, and all the lakes, and all the four-season trails."

There was an awkward pause and then Ken moved the conversation along. "I hear the reno of your building went really well. The contractor is a good friend of mine. He told me no expense was spared on materials. Lots of little extras. He said the owner really knew her stuff."

"That's me," Abby said, playing the part. "I'm all about those little extra touches. The devil's in the details and all that."

Ken shifted his cart away from hers. "It was nice meeting you. I've got a hoard of fishermen descending on me tomorrow, so I need to get ready." He considered what to say next, finally asking, "Why don't you come by this week? I'll give you a tour. I stock all kinds of outdoor gear. You never know when you'll need a safety harness or a whistle with a compass. I even sell paddles. You never know when you'll need a paddle. I'll cut you a deal."

"I'll do that," Abby agreed, wondering why she consented so quickly. She watched more closely than usual as Ken rolled away and took his place at the back of the checkout line.

Huh. What a nice guy.

Wow. What a conversation they had had. He was so easy going and natural. She felt like she had just bumped into an old college friend. Someone she used to know and . . . like? Have a crush on? Had he just asked her on a date? Surely not. He was just being friendly and neighborly. He couldn't help it if he was devastatingly handsome. Not like GQ handsome—he was handsome in a rugged, lumberjack kind of way. He stood at least six feet and had deep brown eyes, a full head of sandy blond hair, and he obviously kept himself in good shape. No flab to be seen.

He was just being nice, right?

She would go to see him. One thing she had learned from serving on boards and running charities—it was who you knew that counted. And now, she knew Ken, and until it didn't, that counted. And you never could know too many people. Unless they were reporters or FBI agents. Or Ponzi schemers. And he was right, you never knew when you might need a paddle, literally or figuratively.

AN HOUR AND A HALF LATER, Abby was back in her snug apartment unloading the groceries. She had opted for lots of fresh veggies and fruits, some walleye that was on sale, and a roast chicken that she could make several meals from and even freeze a few pieces. Fresh chicken would be so good on the ten-grain artisan bread she had splurged on, or on a salad with crunchy broccoli and cauliflower. Abby had always eaten clean, at least when she could afford it, and it was something she missed terribly.

She put the groceries away, and then went around opening all the cupboards one after another, like a kid on Christmas opening presents, admiring the contents of each shelf and drawer. Whoever equipped the place had selected simple white dishes, including two sizes of both plates and bowls. There were some casserole dishes and a full set of pots, pans and skillets, including lids. There was even a crockpot which Abby assumed she would use a lot come winter. Jake had tried to talk her into hiring a full-time chef so many times, but that was one of the few times that Abby put her foot down. Abby loved to cook. She loved to cook for Jake. He was so appreciative when she made a meal for him. It made her feel so good. Eventually they compromised. She did the day-to-day cooking, but they hired caterers for dinner and cock-tail parties.

Abby stopped, her hand on a cupboard handle, her body somehow stilled by the memories. Why did it have to hurt so much? After all he had done to her, was it possible that she still loved Jake? She supposed a part of her always would. But that part was getting smaller and smaller, and she wanted it too.

She carried on with her investigations. There were full sets of silverware, mugs, glasses and kitchen utensils. Metal spatulas, rubber spatulas, a potato peeler, whisks, a gorgeous knife set, wooden slotted spoons, kitchen shears, tongs, an expensive meat thermometer. There was a four-slice toaster and an extra nice drip coffee maker sat on the counter. Whoever did this thought of everything, and clearly spent a lot of time and effort making sure it was done right.

ABBY WAS glad that the first encounter with a fellow business owner had gone so well, because the second one was a disaster.

As she sat in the shop opening the boxes that held her new store computer, tablet sale system and printer, Abby heard a knock and looked up to see a rail thin but very tall woman dressed all in black rapping on the bay window and miming that she wanted to be let in.

"I'm not open yet," Abby told the woman, coming to the front of the store and speaking to her through the front window. *Doesn't she see I don't have anything to sell yet?* When Abby saw the fury in the woman's face, she decided there was no way she was going to let her in.

But the woman came over to the front door, and Abby could tell she was extremely agitated.

"I'm Naomi Dale," the skinny woman shouted through the

door. Abby just shrugged her shoulders, having never heard that name before.

The woman continued shouting. "I own the Beanery. I wanted to buy this building," she screamed.

Abby thought of the nice girl, Sam, who had served her that morning. She was sorry she had to work for this horrible woman.

"You bought this building out from under me. And you're going to pay!" the woman screamed. And with that, she turned on her heels and hurried away. Abby watched her cross the street, get into a blue van and screech away from the curb. The whole incident had lasted less than a minute.

That night, Abby sliced up a cooked chicken breast and made herself a big salad. She had splurged on a bag of pre-cleaned mixed greens, with spinach, kale, leaf lettuce, and arugula. She sliced some radishes, tomatoes, and a whole yellow pepper, and arranged the slices on top of the greens. She christened the stovetop by hard boiling an egg, which she then cooled in a pan, and finally peeled and sliced and placed on top of the salad, along with the appetizing cubes of grilled chicken. In a final flourish, she squeezed a wedge of lemon, threw on some goat cheese crumbles, then drizzled a balsamic vinegar on top. It looked as good as the thirty-dollar salads she was used to eating at the country club. But it tasted even better. She ate while relaxing on one of the cozy chairs by the gas fireplace, which she turned on by flicking a switch on the wall. The "whoosh" of the flames was a satisfying sound.

As she ate, she looked around the apartment. Of course, it didn't feel like home yet. That would take a while. But compared to her most recent Minneapolis apartment, this one felt much safer and much more snug. How lucky she was. For all his faults, Jake had been right, she supposed. She had landed on her feet. No thanks to him, of course. But definite thanks to somebody. Abby hoped one day she would know that somebody.

But for now, the exchange with Naomi had left Abby feeling more than a bit unsettled. One of the reasons she had left Minneapolis was to get away from the furious people Jake had swindled and who screamed and glared at her whenever and wherever they saw her. She was grateful that until their house had been sold as part of the liquidation of Jake's assets, the FBI allowed her to live there as she made other arrangements. She still shopped at the same grocery store and went to the country club and gym. Those memberships had been paid in full and she was in her rights to partake. But it quickly became apparent that wherever she went in her upscale lake-front suburb, she would be a verbal punching bag. She still remembered the day the hostess at the country club had asked her to leave. The dining room hushed as soon as Abby walked in and sat down at the table. Then one-by-one, several diners leapt up from their chairs. Some shouted to the hostess to kick Abby out. Others accosted her at her table, shoving their faces so far into hers that she could see their nose hairs and smell what they had been eating. Her friends had turned on her quickly. And she couldn't really blame them.

Abby figured she could handle one furious coffee shop owner who was angry at her for no apparent reason. Just to be on the safe side, however, she texted Jerome Monroe and asked if there was a chance that the sale of the building had not gone through correctly, or that someone else was supposed to buy it. He texted back immediately. *Everything was as it should be. You have nothing to worry about.*

That night, exhausted from the planning and arranging, fighting with unfamiliar technology, and still troubled by her meeting with Naomi, Abby tucked herself into bed early with a steaming cup of mint tea. She still possessed many pairs of silk pajamas, but she had never used them in the dingy apartment in Minneapolis, opting instead to sleep in yoga pants and a t-shirt. Somehow it didn't seem right to expose something so beautiful as her silk pjs to such a non-luxurious environment. But here in her new digs, well, that was a different story. She quickly changed into a navy blue pin stripe ensemble that she was pleased still fit her perfectly. She luxuriated in the familiar feel of silk on her skin. Another small pleasure that brought her joy. She would count these pleasures, no matter how small, one by one, every day, she decided, until she was up to five hundred, or a thousand, or more.

She wished she had something to read, but of course she couldn't bring her Minneapolis library books with her. She would get a card at the Wander Creek library as soon as possible.

Abby had read in a magazine sometime, a long time ago, about a supermodel or actress or some sort of celebrity who gave herself a grade at the end of each day. *How would I grade myself today?* she wondered. She had worked hard on getting everything set up, and had met two nice people, Sam and Ken. Could she call them friends yet? Maybe eventually. She had spent responsibly at the grocery store, but hadn't been miserly, either. She had indulged at the coffee shop, but knew it was a one-time thing. Before she went to bed, Abby set the timer on her coffee maker so she could wake up to the aroma of her own brew percolating in the kitchen. Even though it was technically just the evening of day two in Wander Creek, Abby felt that she was finding a kind of balance in her new life. Surely, she had earned an A today. But then there was Naomi Dale, whose nasty and snarky demeanor was terrifying, if only because it brought back memories of all the people who had been enraged at her back in Minneapolis. *Those people had a point.* Abby had not stood up to Naomi, but that wasn't cause for bringing down her grade, was it? Maybe the "A" was for *not* reacting. After all, there was no point in engaging with someone when they were in a rage. But here was Naomi Dale, threatening her equilibrium. Well, Abby wouldn't let her. She fell asleep proud of her "A."

CHAPTER 7

*E*arly Monday morning was quiet in Wander Creek, but the shops would open around ten and the bustle would begin. After a cup of coffee and yogurt, Abby bundled up and headed out, anxious to explore. The morning was chilly, and she was glad she had grabbed her hat and gloves. She walked up one side of Main Street, past the Pizza Den, and the Pages bookstore, peering in the windows to get a sense of the people who owned them. She made a wide berth around the Beanery, which was the only shop with a light on, and crossed the street, strolling down the block that boasted Beautiful You Salon and Day Spa, Second to None, an upscale thrift shop, and the Bistro restaurant. When she came to the Life and Style boutique, she stopped and gazed into the storefront window. The sun was rising, and with the benefit of its glow she could make out the shapes of lovely accessories for the home—lamps, side tables, plant stands, throw pillows, picture frames, smallish, upholstered chairs, porcelain vases, fine china and even brass tea sets—basically all manner of beautiful and clever items for the home. In the shop window the owner had erected several broomsticks on wooden stands and dressed them like mannequins and surrounded them with home accessories. It certainly was a creative approach. Abby realized quickly that although Wander Creek was in the middle of nowhere, that didn't mean it didn't have its fair share of class and culture.

At Beautiful You she peered in at the beauty stations lined up in a row poised to receive customers. At the front, she recognized some of the designer hair products for sale, many of which she once had on her shelves at home. Reflexively, she put her hand to the hair that fell six inches below her shoulders. These days she used generic hair products from the grocery store. And to be honest, she really couldn't tell that much of a difference. She walked a few more steps and looked into Second to None, taking in the racks of designer clothes and the shelves lined with expensive shoes and handbags. She surmised that the tourist clientele must certainly be affluent if they could afford the high-end items on display, which made her feel better about how well the Paper Box would perform.

She took one last look at all the beautiful designer clothes and realized that for the first time in a long time, she did not feel the familiar intense desire to own and wear beautiful clothes, just so she could dazzle everyone who saw her. She didn't have the urge to buy expensive accoutrements for her apartment, or the nicest furnishings. It occurred to Abby that at that very moment in time, she had absolutely everything she needed. And it felt good. Really good.

She then walked back behind the businesses on the north side of Main Street to the waterfront park and sat on a wooden bench next to a low rock wall. Abby stared in wonder at the absolutely stunning view. In the early morning light, the trees on the bluffs across the creek shone brilliant reds, golds and oranges, and their reflection shimmered on the surface of the creek. She began to more fully understand why the foliage of the area was such a draw. People loved to see Mother Nature's majesty on display, and if they also wanted to spend tourist dollars in the shops of Wander Creek, that was even better.

"Hey there," a breathy voice said behind her, and Abby turned to see Ken jogging down the path toward her, his breath momentarily visible in the frosty air.

"Hi yourself," Abby replied, and was pleased when Ken stopped to talk.

"Mind if I join you?" he asked, gesturing at the bench.

"Please do. I'd love the company," Abby said, smiling. "I think you're the only person I know around here."

Ken caught his breath and wiping his sweating face with his black knit cap, asked, "How is your store coming along? Or is it too early to tell?"

"A little too early," Abby laughed. "I had a bit of inventory waiting for me when I got here but most of it will be delivered this week. I'm busy setting up the social media accounts and trying to figure out my fancy new point-of-sale inventory system. But mainly I've been strategizing about how to create a bit of buzz around the opening."

"Which will be when?" Ken asked, pulling out his phone and handing it to her. "Here, bring up your accounts and follow them from my profiles. Then I'll spread the word. My store has a pretty big following. It might help."

As she tapped on his phone Abby answered, "Thanks. This will help. And I definitely want to open before Black Friday, but hopefully much sooner. I've got a lot to get through and to learn." She handed the phone back to him. "This is my first time owning a business."

He raised his eyebrows. "Really? And you're already using the word 'strategize'?"

Abby laughed.

" Well, the first few years are the toughest," he said.

"So I've heard," Abby said. "Got any advice for me?"

"You know the saying 'the customer is always right?'" he

asked, and Abby nodded. "That's not true. But the customer *is* always the customer. That's it. That's all I got. But I'll come to your opening. Maybe I'll come up with some more brilliant tips." He stood up and did a few leg stretches.

"Thanks," Abby said, "I'll take all the help I can get."

"Anything else you want to know before I take off?" Ken asked.

"Well, since you asked, something's been bugging me. I can't figure out the difference between a river and a creek and a stream. And why Wander Creek is called a creek when it seems to me more like a river."

"Ah," he said. "That's a question for the ages, and the survey-ors," Ken answered. "There is definitely a difference of opinions. You'll see some rivers that are extremely narrow, and some streams and creeks that are half-a-mile-wide, or more. I like to think of Wander Creek as a river. In fact, between the two of us," he said conspiratorially, "I tell people it's actually a river. Seems much more manly for my clients to canoe down a river than a creek. Or fish all day on a river. River just sounds more 'out-doorsy' than creek."

"I can totally see that. Who wants to go home from vacation and tell their friends that they conquered the wilds of a measly creek," Abby said.

"Exactly," Ken agreed. "It's all about marketing. You'll get the hang of it, putting the right spin on everything."

She waved as he resumed his run, sprinting down the path back toward his store. *It's always nice to see a friendly face.*

Abby stood up and headed for the long wooden bridge over the creek. It was narrow, but there was enough room, barely, for two cars to pass. She looked behind her and ahead. No cars on the horizon. It was early still, so she trekked across, hands in her coat pockets and head bent. The wind swirled up from the churning water. There was a class one or two rapid, depending on the water level, that started just before the bridge and stretched downstream about a hundred yards, dumping into a calm pool.

When Abby reached the other side, she stepped onto the asphalt and walked up the road about a quarter mile to the trail-head where so many of the local trails she had read so much about were accessed. There was a pretty extensive trail system in the area, both for Ken's ATVers—when there was no snow—and snowmobilers. There was a second trail system reserved only for cross country skiers in the winter, and hikers and dog walkers, and leaf gawkers for the three months it was not winter. Some years four months. She stepped onto one of the trails and thought she'd just meander a little while and then head back home. She had work to do. But it felt so good to be outside in the fresh air. She stopped mid-trail, looked around, and inhaled deeply. She loved the musty smell of the forest in autumn and relished the sound of leaves crunching underfoot as she stepped. It was practically magical, to be surrounded by such beauty and serenity. She closed her eyes and tilted her head up.

When she returned from her walk and let herself into the shop, she noticed an envelope lying on the floor that someone must have slipped under the door while she was walking. Abby took off her gloves and put them away and sat down, a little out of breath from having walked home rather briskly. The envelope was thick, like maybe whatever was enclosed was made of the kind of paper stock used for posh invitations. The kind of invitations she used to send herself.

Her first name appeared on the front, and Abby thought the attractive handwriting had probably been accomplished with a fountain pen. Abby folded back the flap and pulled out a thick card stock notecard with the name "Mona Sixsmith" embossed in dark green at the top. Very fancy. The note read, "Welcome to Wander Creek. Come to tea at the Wander Inn, today at four." That was it. It was signed with a flourish, "Mona." No phone number or email, no way to decline the invitation. At least, no easy way. She ran her fingers over the fine and expensive stationery.

"Mona Sixsmith," she said aloud. True, Abby had a ton of stuff to do, but it was only eight in the morning. She had eight hours ahead of her to tend to the store before she went to tea at four. But who could resist an invitation to tea from a woman named Mona Sixsmith?

As ABBY TURNED onto Maple Lane from Main Street, the magnificent Wander Inn came into view. Built in the 1920s by a captain of industry who made his fortune in iron ore, the building was solidly constructed from stone and rich brown cedar shake shingles. The many and varied rooflines and windows were smartly trimmed in fresh white paint. It was massive and seemed to go on forever. Abby knew that the back of the Inn looked out over a massive lawn that connected with the creek. Abby decided the view must be magnificent.

Abby walked up the circular drive and through a break in the expertly trimmed hedges that wrapped around the front and side lawns of the Inn. An impressive white-columned portico framed a massive pair of oak doors which were flanked by two large bay windows. Abby knocked, then realized her mistake and opened the door and walked into an elegant lobby with a large walnut registration desk on the far side of the room. A fire roared in a large stone fireplace and the room was decorated with elegant antiques and plush upholstered furniture. A few guests sat chatting and enjoying the fire.

"Ah, you're here," the woman at the registration desk called, and came into the lobby to shake Abby's hand.

Mona Sixsmith was an imposing woman with ash blonde hair styled in a page boy that Abby imagined never moved. Mona must have been almost six-feet tall and was impeccably dressed in a navy blue wrap dress, sheer stockings, navy blue pumps and a lot of sapphires. Sapphires around her neck. On her wrist. On her ears. Abby almost blurted out, "Are those real?" but was able to check herself and instead gave a perfunctory but polite, "Hello, nice to meet you," greeting. To which Mona responded by saying, "Let's take a look at you, our newest resident."

Abby fully expected Mona to ask her to twirl in a circle so she could inspect her from every angle. All of a sudden, she wished she had worn something other than her jeans and blouse. She thought of her clothes stored in her closets. She owned several stunning blue dresses by famous designers that would have competed comfortably with Mona's outfit. And jewelry. Well, she used to have a collection of diamonds, and rubies, and even a couple sapphires, that would have matched Mona's jewelry in its brilliance.

Mona led Abby into a small parlor, sumptuously decorated like the lobby, and invited her to sit, and then closed the door. A beautiful arrangement of refreshments sat on the table in front of two comfortable armchairs. A silver tea service, delicate white porcelain cups, saucers and plates were surrounded by small silver trays of small crustless sandwiches, scones with clotted cream and jam, and macaroons in every color of a pastel rainbow.

Mona poured tea and passed a cup to Abby. "I want to officially welcome you to Wander Creek," Mona said, "and offer you any help and support as you settle in. We're both women of commerce in a man's world. Us ladies must stick together."

Abby took the tea and took a tiny sip of the steaming liquid. "That's very generous of you," she said. "I'm really looking forward to settling and getting to know the town."

Mona raised her cup. "Another time we'll have something a little more festive, but right now we can toast your new endeavor with tea. Cheers."

Abby clinked her cup with Mona's. "Wander Inn," Abby said. "I like that name. Clever and catchy."

"I know," Mona mused. "I just couldn't resist." She laughed a tinkly laugh, making Abby picture in her mind champagne glasses clinking together in a toast. "Can you imagine? The Wander Inn? How ridiculous. But then it grew on me, kind of like a simple tennis bracelet a special beau might give you, only you don't play tennis and it doesn't go with anything you own. But after you put it on, and every time you look at it on your wrist, the bracelet brings you joy."

"I hadn't thought about it that way," Abby said, not sure she followed the analogy.

Mona must have sensed her confusion because she explained, "Sometimes the most obvious thing is also the most unexpected. An intriguing combination."

"Do I detect a slight accent?" Abby asked, helping herself to a watercress sandwich. "Almost British?"

Mona smiled. "Please, have a macaroon, too. Yes, almost British is the best way to describe it. I attended Smith College, you know, in Massachusetts, and did my junior year abroad in London. That's where I met my husband, Lord Elton Sixsmith and after thirty years of marriage some of his accent rubbed off on me. He was mesmerizing, handsome and rich. Very rich. And he was taken with me instantly. Instead of returning to college and finishing my degree, I married him six weeks after we met, and began my new life in England as Lady Sixsmith. I was only twenty-one. Of course, I was ostracized and ridiculed behind my back. Everyone thought I was just an American gold-digger. Then Elton got on a tear that he needed to live in New York City for a while because he wanted to study American artists. Luckily for me, we wound up staying in New York. So I was home, essentially. But it turned out Elton was mean as a snake. He soon tired of me. In the United States I was just one of many beautiful American women. I was no longer a novelty. And he absolutely refused to discuss divorce. So I just lived my life parallel to his. I stayed out of his way, and he stayed out of mine. I raised my son, collected, took classes, decorated, socialized, things like that. I had good friends and lots of interests. In some ways, it was a rich and full life. In others, utterly loveless.

"Any way, after thirty years of a miserable marriage Elton finally did something nice for a change—he died and left me everything, including the family home in Kent, which I promptly sold to a Russian billionaire, to the great horror of Elton's Family. It gave me immense pleasure, let me tell you. They were always so horrid to me. So I bought this place, renovated it into an inn and moved everything I could from my Park Avenue penthouse to furnish it. That was ten years ago. And that, as they say, was that. I've wanted to own a grand inn like this one ever since I was a child. My parents owned a bed-and-breakfast in Vermont, and I grew up cleaning rooms, serving muffins and coffee at six-thirty in the morning, and tea and scones at four-thirty in the after-noon. I was a kid, but they worked me like a beast of burden. And I loved every minute of it."

Abby gazed at Mona, enamored with her story, hoping she could consider her a new friend. She could see why Elton, and anyone for that matter, would be mesmerized by Mona. She was amazing. "But how on earth did you end up here, of all places?" Abby asked.

"How did *you* end up here?" Mona responded, turning the question back to her. "It might only be four hours from Minneapolis, but Wander Creek's a world away. They call the city the Minneapple in some circles, you know."

Abby took a sip of her tea to stall as she considered her answer. Mona was sharp. She wouldn't fall for a wishy-washy explanation about wanting to get away and start over. No one just ended up in Wander Creek. It might be a reasonably popular tourist destination, but it was still in the middle of nowhere.

Abby returned the teacup to its saucer and grabbed a pale

pink macaroon, carefully balancing it on the side of the saucer next to the spoon. She looked Mona squarely in the eye. "Husband trouble," she said. "Divorced."

Mona nodded, her facial expression indicating that she understood completely. "Bad marriage?"

"Actually, no," Abby said, thinking back over the ten years she and Jake had spent together. They had been very happy together. They shared interests, but also had their independent pursuits. They laughed and danced and enjoyed each other's company. They had traveled extensively, and Abby had been to almost every continent. Maybe that was why the end was so crushing. Not because of what Jake had done, but that he ran away and left her behind.

"I thought we were very happy, but apparently we weren't happy enough," Abby said.

"We're quite a pair then, aren't we?" Mona said. "I knew I was in an unhappy marriage, but I stayed anyway, for convenience. You had a happy marriage, but it didn't last. And now you're here with us in Wander Creek. Troubled."

"I wouldn't say troubled, exactly," Abby countered. "Maybe in the process of healing, but not troubled. I'm getting on with it. A broken heart takes time to stich back together. But mine's on the mend."

"A broken heart, eh?" Mona asked, raising one perfectly plucked eyebrow, smiling kindly but slyly. Abby tried to remember the last time she'd had her eyebrows waxed and shaped. She tried not to look at them in the mirror when she put on her make-up in the morning. There was only so much you could do with a pair of tweezers.

"Is that so hard to believe?" Abby asked.

"No, but only if it's true," Mona said.

Abby did not respond. She took a bite of the delicate, airy macaroon and adroitly changed the subject. Later, when she was home in her cozy apartment above her soon-to-be store, she would take apart this conversation with Mona. But now she said, "You never answered my question about how you ended up here."

"You're right," Mona said. "I didn't. Now, would you like another cup of tea? I'll give you a tour and you can bring it with you if you promise not to spill it."

It didn't seem farfetched to Abby to at least consider that Mona had some secret knowledge about her. Could Mona be Abby's benefactor? Perhaps Mona had followed the trial for some reason and wanted to do a good deed. She was rich as Croesus. That was obvious. Just the jewelry she was wearing was worth more than Abby's building. Probably than all the buildings on Main Street combined.

Mona led Abby around the first floor of the Inn. They visited the dining room, and a couple of guest rooms, two different parlors—every room beautifully and tastefully adorned with sophisticated antique furniture, rugs and accessories. Lamp light illuminated the rooms with a pleasing glow. The Inn reminded Abby of something out of an historic home magazine or *Architectural Digest*.

As the paired wrapped up the tour Abby brought up the subject of Naomi. "I met Naomi Dale," she said, opening the conversation for Mona to wade into as deep or shallow as she chose. Abby sensed that Mona wouldn't pull any punches, one way or the other, when it came to her feelings about anything or anyone.

They had returned to the sitting room where they had tea. "Poor you," Mona said. "Let me guess. She accosted you about buying your building."

"How did you know?" Abby asked.

"She's been saying she wants that building—your building—for years now. Ever since I moved here. She apparently wants to open a diner, but, alas, she never has the cash or the gumption at the same time. She's bad news, and if I were you, I'd steer clear of her. Sometimes, she even scares *me*," Mona tinkled with laughter. "And believe me, I don't scare easily."

That night, Abby fell asleep wondering if the identity of her anonymous benefactor would ever be revealed. Jerome Monroe certainly wasn't going to tell her. If Abby wanted to know who it was, she'd have to figure it out herself. Suddenly, she wasn't sure she wanted to learn the identity. Would knowing change everything? Maybe the fairy tale, the spell, would be broken and nothing would be the same again.

CHAPTER 8

The day after her curious visit with Mona at the Wander Inn, Abby was in the shop working on getting the store up and running. She looked up to the sound of knocking on the glass of the front door. It was Sam from the Beanery, and always happy to see a friendly face, Abby let her in, grateful for the visit.

Sam held up a bag. "I brought sustenance. Savory scones and cookies. Not the lunch of champions but it's better than nothing."

Abby looked at her watch. Was it lunchtime already? It felt like only ten minutes ago that she had come downstairs to arrange some of the inventory and start pricing. The hours had flown by.

Sam was still wearing her shapeless brown bakery uniform of polyester pants and a polo shirt that was at least one size too big. Abby flashed back to the polyester Burger King uniform she wore in high school where she worked for a couple years. Abby squinted, taking in the red, green and mustard yellow trim. A Beanery logo patch had been sewn on the top right side of the shirt. Sam was such a lithe, lovely creature and these clothes did not suit her in the least.

"Sam, you're a lifesaver," Abby said. "How did you know I was famished? Sometimes I get so engrossed in what I'm doing that I forget to eat."

Sam looked around the store. "Looks like you're off to a good start." She motioned to the sales counter. "I am loving that galvanized steel. So creative."

Abby blushed, knowing that the complement that was directed to her rightfully belonged to whoever designed the sales counter. But that would be too hard to explain, so she just said, "It is, isn't it," and led Sam into the small office at the back of the store.

The two women settled at Abby's large office desk, and Sam produced two napkins and divided the food. "I'll tell you something, the one thing I can say about Naomi is that she sure can bake."

"Mmmmm," Abby agreed around the scone as its flavor burst in her mouth with fresh herbs and a delightfully sharp bite of salt. Abby avoided mentioning Naomi's outburst from yesterday.

Sam continued. "Are you going to be hiring someone to help you in the store?" she asked shyly.

"Eventually I plan to, yes," Abby said. "Just out of curiosity, are you still in school?"

Sam nodded. "I'm taking business classes at the University of Minnesota in Duluth. I have to pay for classes as I go, so I can't really enroll full time. I take a lot of classes online, too, which saves me from having to make that long drive every day."

Abby thought about Carmen, and how she had given her a job when she most needed it. Carmen had hired Abby by instinct. Should Abby do the same? She liked Sam, who seemed very capable and resourceful. Plus, she had experience running a cash register. Abby glanced out the open office door, knowing that the POS system, computer, and unfamiliar software were all out there waiting, taunting her. She was certain that at her age, Sam could make quick work of it all. Young people were just so much better at technology. And it would save Abby the trouble of having to advertise and interview. Plus, if she had an extra set of hands around now, maybe she could get the shop up and running sooner rather than later. There didn't seem to be a downside to hiring Sam.

"Are you looking to make a move from the Beanery?" Abby asked, already knowing the answer. Naomi had been so mean and nasty to her, Abby couldn't imagine having to work for her.

"I am," Sam said, looking Abby directly in the eyes. "And I'd like to work here, for you."

"That's very direct," Abby said.

"That's how I roll," Sam responded.

"Alright then, let's do this," Abby proposed. "Let's get you started for a month on a trial basis. How much notice do you have to give Naomi?"

"I'll give her a few days. I know she has people she can bring in, even if only temporarily until she finds someone to replace me. I was supposed to be temporary, too, for that matter. But I won't be leaving her in the lurch if that's what you're worried about."

Abby was pleased with Sam's conscientiousness. "Then how about you start Wednesday morning. Let's say eight to five with an hour break for lunch. Once the store is open we'll work out a schedule. I plan to be open a few evenings a week, plus the schedule will be seasonal I imagine. I'm just making it up as I go along, so we can figure it out together."

When Sam left Abby tried not to think about Naomi's angry fist pummeling her shop door. How would Naomi react when she found out that Sam was leaving the Beanery to work for her?

ONE AFTERNOON ABBY drove into Duluth and bought fabric and hemming tape at a local fabric store. She wasn't about to try to sew anything. The drive was pleasant and she took Highway 15 back down to Two Harbors retracing the way she had come just a week earlier. As she drove, she found herself thinking about her benefactor. Again. She was no closer to determining who it was than the day Jerome Monroe had visited. If she did ever find out who it was, what would she say?

That evening, she spread the fabric out on the trestle farm table in her apartment and cut, pinned and taped the fabric, making beautiful tablecloths. She had selected several patterns of upholstery fabric, all with the same robin's egg blue, which she had started to think of as *her* blue. At the craft store she purchased several large picture frames and she framed pieces of the leftover fabric, hanging the finished product on the walls. This was her favorite part, layering and accessorizing. It was hard to restrain herself. There were so many beautiful things out there, and it had been a long time since she felt comfortable spending money. But she'd have to be careful and not careen off in the other direction and start spending too much.

As the store came together, she snapped pictures and uploaded them to her social media accounts so would-be customers could follow the progress. And thanks to Ken and Mona, she was already gaining a nice following.

Every morning she donned a warm fleece track suit, coat, gloves and a hat and made a circuit walking along Main Street, up Hickory Street and into the neat residential neighborhoods. People greeted her by name, like they were old friends.

At the Lutheran Church she turned back into town, taking Hickory Street down the hill and onto Maple Lane, which took her to the Inn. Mona had said she was free to walk the grounds if she wanted to, and Abby found herself looking forward to doing just that. The back lawn of the Inn extended out across the creek bottom to the water. The trees were mostly conifers, and someone had landscaped the yard beautifully with bright yellow, orange and purple mums. White Adirondack chairs were arranged around a fire pit. At both the back and front entrances to the Inn, large cornstalks bookended the doors, with piles of pumpkins and gourds of all colors arranged beautifully. After gazing at the water, a dazzling deep blue in the early morning light, Abby continued along the waterfront walk until she reached the bridge, where she turned around. She remembered her time in the tiny Minneapolis apartment. The only real pleasure she got during that period was her time at the Paperie, with Carmen. She realized she had been existing in a sort of zombie state. There, but not there. Alive, but not vibrant. But those days were over. She could begin to hold her head high now. She could allow herself to be happy and to anticipate gradually returning to the kind of life she thought she'd lost forever.

Somewhere along the way, Abby decided on the name of her new venture: the Paper Box. During the weeks leading up to the grand opening she was visited by the owners and managers of many of the local businesses, all of whom wished her success, and offered their assistance wherever they could. They knocked on the door at all hours of the day, and Abby always greeted them pleasantly and accepted whatever gifts they were carrying—a dozen cookies, a casserole, a six-pack of sodas and a couple bags of chips. She was grateful for it all. She was particularly pleased to meet Dennis Grey, the owner of the Pages bookstore next to the Paper Box.

He was a small, pinched sort of man whose name matched his pallor. But he was friendly and when he smiled his entire demeanor changed.

"I come bearing gifts," he announced, as Abby ushered him inside the store. He handed her a book wrapped in a newspaper.

"That's so nice of you," Abby gushed. "You didn't have to do that."

"Go on, open it," Dennis said, keeping his eyes on her as she undid the string and pulled back the paper.

She read aloud, "The Diary of a Country Woman." She

admired the cover, which was a beautiful scene of rolling hills, blue sky, and a family picnicking in the foreground.

"It's beautiful," she said. "Thank you."

"Well, I couldn't decide what to give you, so I just picked something pretty. I've owned Pages for almost twenty years now," he said, "and before you ask how a small town bookstore has stayed in business all these years, you should know I have a great online store, too, plus selling the odd rare book on eBay helps." He looked around the Paper Box. "I'm thinking you'll do fine," he predicted. "Especially when the fishing and hunting widows arrive. They're more ribbons and pearls than dusty old books. You're in for a treat."

"Mona said the same thing," Abby responded. "I'm anxious to see what all the fuss is about."

"It's a lot of lively women with money to spend and husbands who don't care how much," he explained. "Come January I always stock the latest romance bestsellers and mysteries with female detectives. I usually come up with a clever window display. Plus, I'll make sure I have whatever memoirs are out of the hottest ladies in the news. They tend to like those, too. But to be honest, people on vacation just like to shop. Good for us!"

Abby also was befriended by the UPS man who came more times than she could count, rolling in stacks of boxes on his hand-truck, which he kindly stacked for her in the storeroom. Abby figured that after she got established she could spend more time fine-tuning her stock, but to begin with, it was just easier to use the same vendors as Carmen did. Each box was like a Christmas present.

She had selected a variety of work and home planners, undated calendar templates and mini binder organization systems. She stocked designer calculators, scissors and staplers, rulers and letter openers. Just because something was functional didn't mean it couldn't be beautiful.

Like Carmen, she decided to have a small wine gift corner and set up a table with a variety of wine glasses, stoppers, openers, cocktail napkins with wine-inspired sayings, and an assortment of other gifts meant for wine lovers.

In the kitchen gifts area she utilized lovely wooden stands to display her selection of gourmet and specialty cookbooks, notepads for grocery shopping lists and meal planning, cloth-covered recipe boxes with tabbed index cards inside, recipe binders with plastic sleeves and "From the Kitchen of _____" labels.

Following Jerome Monroe's advice, she had ordered office and school supplies which she hoped that the locals would appreciate. Everyone needed scotch tape, mechanical pencils and file folders, didn't they?

Abby had seen the local mail carrier making his rounds around the Wander Creek business district several times, but so far had not had the pleasure of making his acquaintance. So, Abby was more than a little pleased when he politely tapped on the glass on the front door. She turned the deadbolt and pulled the door open, stood aside, and motioned for him to enter.

"Hi," Abby said pleasantly. "I'm Abby Barrett."

"I know," said the mail carrier, and when he noticed Abby's expression of surprise, he added, "I mean, I figured." With that he handed Abby a single piece of mail. It was an advertisement from the craft store in Duluth where she'd bought the picture frames earlier. Her eyes scanned the front of the mail piece, and she was delighted to see it was addressed to *Abby Barrett or Current Resident.*

"Wow!" Abby exclaimed. "This is actually the first piece of mail I've received in Wander Creek."

The mail carrier smiled at her brightly. "Well, congratulations, I guess. Sorry it's just an ad and not a check or something good. My name's Pete, by the way. Pete White. Obviously, I'm the mailman around here."

Abby held out her hand and said, "It's very nice to meet you, Pete White." Pete took her outstretched hand and gently shook it.

"The pleasure is all mine."

Pete just stood there staring at Abby, and when it occurred to him that an awkward silence was about to commence, he said, "Well, welcome to the neighborhood. I hope you'll be very happy here."

"I already am," Abby declared. And realizing that she was, indeed, very happy for the first time in a long time, she gave herself a little hug.

CHAPTER 9

*A*bby had just turned the dead bolt on the front door of the Paper Box. It had been a long, stressful day, and she leaned her forehead against the glass. Something caught her eye, and Abby glanced up. On the other side of the door, a very attractive, smiling woman in jeans and a camel's hair coat peered at her through the glass. The mystery woman held up two wine glasses in one hand and a bottle of wine in the other and smiled. Abby wasn't about to turn down wine. She opened the door.

"Hi," the perky woman said breathlessly, "I'm Jessica Lake from the Life and Style boutique." She gestured to the right with a nod of her head. "Caddy corner across the street next to Gems, the jewelry store. I thought you might need a friendly face after what happened with Naomi the other evening."

"Wow, how'd you know about that? Does word really travel that fast around here?" Abby asked, worried.

Jessica laughed. "Not at all. I was across the street and saw her pounding on your window and screaming at you. I'm sorry I couldn't stop but I had to pick my son up from daycare. They charge fifteen dollars for every five minutes you're late picking up."

"Ouch," Abby said. "That seems a little harsh."

The look on Jessica's face expressed her complete agreement, but she stayed focused on the topic at hand. "I'm glad you didn't let her in."

"That was just instinct. She's not dangerous, is she?" Abby asked, alarmed. "And please come in instead of standing out there in the cold."

"No, she's not dangerous. She's just mean," Jessica said, as she stepped through the door into the warmth of the Paper Box showroom. "Otherwise, I would have intervened, fifteen dollars or not."

Abby led Jessica toward the back of the store and Jessica oohed and awed. "Wow, this place is really coming together," she said. "It looks like you're almost ready to open."

Jessica surveyed the store. "Everybody's been wondering what kind of place this is going to be. I know you've been keeping the poor UPS man hopping. Let me throw out a wild guess— stationery store? I love all the pretty fabric. I may have to start my Christmas shopping early. Oooh, what's this for?" She pointed to rack containing about a dozen wooden dowels attached to the side of one of the display tables.

Jessica, whom Abby decided must be in her early thirties, was like a kid in a candy shop, taking everything in with obvious fascination and enthusiasm. She practically hopped from one display to another.

"I'll hang sheets of gift wrapping paper on those," Abby pointed. "But it will be one of the last things I do so the paper doesn't get damaged. I haven't even ordered it yet. Come on, I'll show you the upstairs."

Abby led her guest up the narrow stairway to the apartment, looking over her shoulder and saying, "It's so nice of you to do this."

"Wow," Jessica said, looking around as she placed the bottle of wine and glasses on the kitchen island. "This is amazing. I remember what it looked like before. You really went all out."

Abby handed Jessica a bottle opener from a drawer, and Jessica proceeded to open the bottle and pour them each a modest glass.

"Don't mean to be blunt, but this place was downright dumpy before," Jessica said, handing a glass to Abby, who gestured for them to settle on the spacious couch. "I didn't want to be rude and ask outright to come up here, but everyone is dying to see what the place looks like after the renovation. George, the editor for the now-defunct weekly paper—in case you didn't know—used to live here. He didn't do any updating the whole twenty years or so he lived here. And I'm sure nothing had been done for twenty years before that, at least. It was pretty bad."

The two talked like a couple of old college buddies. Abby sensed Jessica's energy and genuine warmth. *I can relate to this woman.* Jessica was a breath of fresh air. Abby raised her glass. "Let's toast to new endeavors and new friends."

They clinked glasses. "And of course, welcome to Wander Creek," Jessica added.

Abby settled back into the couch, perfectly content. She had had a productive day in the shop, gotten her first piece of mail, and was now was entertaining her first guest in her apartment.

"So, what made you decide to open a stationery shop?" Jessica asked.

Why indeed? Abby wondered. Sure, having enjoyed her time with Carmen at the Paperie so much must have informed her decision. But it was more than that, too.

"I don't really know why, exactly. But, when I was a kid growing up in Minneapolis my mother had a friend who was a clerk in an old-fashioned stationery store. It was almost like a newsstand. That was back when people wrote letters and read actual newspapers and magazines. Back when paper, actual paper, mattered. Anyway, I loved it when we went to visit the store. While Mom and her friend chatted, I would roam. The shop was small, but I was perfectly content to look at the same pens and notebooks and postcards over and over again. We couldn't afford to buy anything, so every time we went there, I would imagine what one thing I would buy if we had the money."

Abby hadn't thought of that store in decades, and she was instantly embarrassed at having shared such an intimate memory with someone she had just met. And even though Jessica didn't look the least bit uncomfortable at the turn the conversation had taken, Abby changed the subject anyway.

"How long have you lived in Wander Creek?" she asked.

"Oh, I'm a lifer," Jessica said. "The furthest I've ever been from home was when I went to Lake Superior College in Duluth. I graduated with a degree in Media Studies. Like an idiot, I got married right out of college, and like a genius I had my son. Somewhere along the way—it all runs together—I got divorced. Anyway, it all seems very boring now. What you need to know is that I opened my store three years ago."

"How's business?" Abby asked. "I'm dying to know how all the businesses are doing."

"The town's proximity to Lake Superior makes summer the busiest season, followed by autumn. You'll stay pretty busy June through October and those will probably be your biggest months revenue wise. At least that's how it is with me. Winter will keep you going with the ice fishing, but January is typically slow. And spring, well, that's my slowest season. Last year I closed up for a week in mid-April and took myself on a Caribbean singles cruise."

"And did you meet anyone?" Abby asked, impressed with this bold, sparkly woman.

"Naw, but really I just went to have fun. I really only booked a singles cruise so there wouldn't be any screaming kids around. I have enough of that at home." She reached for the bottle of wine and refilled Abby's glass. "This place is very impressive," she said.

"I love the neutral color palette. It's really airy and light. I like that a lot. Very big-city-esque."

"Do you live above your shop?" Abby asked, wondering just how many people did live on Main Street.

"I use that for storage," Jessica said. "We've got a cute cottage down on Pepper Lane—it's in that first neighborhood you come to when you come from the south. It's close enough that I could walk or bike to work. But of course I never do. So who all have you met since you've been here?" Jessica looked at her watch. "Since you've been in Wander Creek, what, all of ten minutes?"

Abby laughed. "Almost a week now," she said. "Let me think. Hmmm, besides that unfortunate run-in with Naomi Dale, Mona Sixsmith invited me to high tea at her inn the other day."

Jessica raised an eyebrow. "That's impressive," she said. "Some people around town still don't know what to make of old Mona, even after all these years. But she's good for business. She brings in an affluent clientele and they spend money in our stores. And because she's mega rich, she donates money everywhere, from beautification projects to various civic activities. She's very altruistic."

"Do you know why she chose Wander Creek?" Abby asked.

Jessica shook her head. "Nobody knows and she won't say, no matter how many times people ask her. But I think it's just part of the mystique she creates around herself. I bet she just went online, googled historic buildings to buy and liked the looks of the one here. Who else have you met?"

"Samantha at the Beanery who is a real sweetheart," Abby said, not mentioning that she had just hired the girl. "And I ran into Ken Taylor, literally, at the grocery store, and again jogging along the Riverwalk. He was out for an early morning run. Seems like a really nice guy."

"He is," Jessica said. "One of the few really decent men left in this world. And I should know. Somehow I've managed to marry and date only the duds. But Ken's as solid as they come. He built

Northwoods up from nothing. Started with a few kayaks and tubes and now he's got snowmobiles and ATVs for rent, plus fly fishing galore. People pay a lot of money for fly fishing guides. And people come from all over to rent stuff from him."

"So you must like living here. I mean, you're still here," Abby observed, and Jessica nodded her head.

"It's really a close-knit community and anyone, well almost anyone, will help you if you ask. For example, I've got an informal reciprocal arrangement with Caroline Sharp who owns Gems. We both usually have at least two employees, and if she needs help, I'll send one of mine over her store, and she does the same for me. It's all very neighborly. People around here will have your back, once you get to know them. Except for Naomi, of course. She only looks after Naomi. I would never give her my keys, or even dream of asking her for anything. You're probably not used to all this hometown charm coming from Minneapolis?"

Abby laughed, "That's the truth. The last place I worked had surveillance cameras, and an alarm button near the cash register just in case we got robbed. I mean, it was in a nice area and all, but it *is* the city."

"I've always felt safe here," Jessica said. "I doubt you'll have any problems. The biggest problem you'll have is too many casseroles on your doorstep if you get really sick or die." She looked at her watch. "Yikes, I gotta go! My son is with my ex but he doesn't like it when I'm late, either. Though I'd like to see him try to charge me fifteen dollars."

The pair stood as Jessica prepared to go, and Abby said, "I am so glad you came over—you have no idea. Next time I'll get the wine."

"You're on," Jessica said as Abby walked her downstairs. As she reached to open the front door, Jessica turned and smiled impishly. "By the way, Ken's totally available. He's been single for a long time and, believe me, there have been a lot of women in Wander Creek who would have liked to paddle his canoe, if you know what I mean. But so far, he hasn't taken the bait." She laughed at her own joke.

After Jessica left, Abby returned to the apartment and washed the wine glasses and corked the bottle, all of which Jessica had forgotten to take with her when she left. Returning them would give Abby an excuse to go over to the Life and Style. She could return the favor with a batch of cookies or maybe some of the delicious olive tapenade she loved to make from scratch. Abby's mouth watered just thinking about it. And she realized that she hadn't offered Jessica any appetizers. She could have brought out some fruit, or cheese and crackers. And then she also realized that she hadn't asked anything about Jessica's son. How had her manners deteriorated so much? She'd have to be more conscious of that moving forward. She was out in the world now ,where she needed to hold her head up and engage with others, and not be afraid that someone would recognize her and turn on her. She gave herself permission to make friends. *But I also need to remember to be cautious.*

THE NEXT WEEK was a virtual whirlwind of activity, and the Paper Box was starting to look like an actual store. Most of the displays were finished, and most of the shelves were stocked. The wall where the greeting cards were displayed was pretty much full. Abby and Sam were making great progress.

Then, out of nowhere, one afternoon Naomi showed up and stomped into the store while Abby and Sam were stocking shelves.

I really have to remember to lock that door, Abby thought, as she watched Naomi storm further onto the sales floor.

"Why can't you just leave my family alone?" Naomi growled.

"What do you mean?" Abby asked, confused, looking at Sam, as if to seek clarification.

Before Sam could clarify, Naomi barked, "Sam is my cousin."

"I didn't know that you two were related," Abby said. "I mean, you have different last names."

Naomi crossed her arms over her chest and took a step closer to Abby, who instinctively took a step backward. "You don't have to have the same last name to be related," she snapped. "For your information, our mothers are siblings," she finished, as if this fact was the most important thing that mattered in the world.

"C'mon Sam," Naomi said directly to Sam. "Let's go. This has gone far enough. First, she bought my building out from under me, then she tries to steal my boyfriend and now she's trying to put me out of business by stealing my employees."

Abby was flabbergasted but wasn't about to take this abuse. "Excuse me?" she said. "None of those things are true. I had no idea that you wanted to buy this building, I have no idea who your boyfriend is, and I had no idea that Sam was your cousin. How could I?"

"Yeah, go ahead and deny it, but the fact remains that I don't own this building and Sam isn't working for me anymore."

"There's your boyfriend," Abby said mischievously. "Don't forget him."

"What about him?" Naomi asked.

"I stole him, remember? I've only been here a few weeks but we're having a hot and heavy romance and I've already started to plan our wedding and pick out baby names."

Sam snickered from the greeting card section and Abby had to bite the inside of her mouth to keep herself from laughing, too.

"Hardy har har," Naomi snapped. "You just stay away from him. C'mon Sam. Let's go."

Sam reached into a box and took out the remaining greeting cards and carefully placed them on the wall rack. She turned her head and said over her shoulder, "I'm not going anywhere. Abby is paying me more, and I don't have to get up at five in the morning. And she's nicer than you and doesn't yell at me."

Naomi's face turned beet red. She squinted her eyes and hissed, "This isn't over. You're going to be sorry." With that final admonishment, she stomped off and banged the door behind her so hard that Abby thought the glass would break.

"I'm guessing you understand now why I wanted to leave the bakery," Sam said. "Let's just say that my cousin is a little high strung."

"That's an understatement," Abby said. "She's downright abusive. How could you stand to work for her?"

Sam shrugged and smiled over her shoulder. "Let's just say I may have occasionally given my favorite customers a free coffee or pastry from time to time. You know, good customer relations. It made her crazy because she couldn't figure out where all the inventory was going. And I'm so skinny she ruled out me eating it myself."

"Oh my God, you are hysterical," Abby said. "You did that with me, didn't you, the first time I came into the Beanery?"

"Sure did," Sam said. "But if I were you, I wouldn't mention that to anyone. No telling what Naomi would do if she thought you were also stealing her inventory."

"No worries there," Abby said. "I am going to stay as far away from Naomi Dale as possible. Though I guess in a small town, that could prove problematic. How on earth did you deal with her?"

"You'll figure it out," Sam said. "I did."

"Just as long as you don't do that 'favorite customer' thing here," Abby said, and winked.

"No worries," Sam said. "I only mess with people who mess with me."

Abby needed clarification on another point. "Who is Naomi's boyfriend? I'm pretty sure the only guys I've even talked to are Ken, and Pete the mailman."

Sam looked up at her.

"Oh," Abby said. "It's Ken, huh? She's dating Ken, and Ken and

I've been friendly. He's just being a good neighbor. She really doesn't have anything to worry about."

Sam doubled over with laughter.

"What?" Abby asked. "Did I say something funny?"

"It's just that, well . . . Ken is definitely, one hundred percent not her boyfriend. She's had a crush on him since he moved here, and they dated for about five minutes a couple of months ago. But they are definitely not involved." Sam put air quotes with her fingers around "involved."

"Well, someone better tell Naomi that," Abby said, and they both laughed. "And speaking of Naomi. What is the deal with the Beanery display window?"

"You mean all of the holiday decorations crammed together?" Sam asked, smiling. "Naomi figures that if she has all the holidays represented she doesn't have to bother changing the display. She told me once it was 'cost-effective.'" Sam put another pair of air quotes around "cost-effective."

"She certainly is an interesting character," Abby offered. "Interesting in a mean, unpleasant kind of way."

"You don't know the half of it," Sam quipped.

"You can tell me later," Abby said.

Deciding she had learned enough about Naomi Dale for one day, Abby returned to work, filling her mind with fantasies of the store's grand opening.

CHAPTER 10

One morning Abby heard a knock on the front door and she looked up to see Ken standing there smiling at her, with a coffee in each hand.

"Sam, would you mind letting our visitor in please?" Abby asked.

"Our visitor? More like your visitor if you ask me."

"Just let him in, please."

Sam turned the lock and stepped aside, and Ken strolled into the shop.

"Hiya Sam. Coffee?" Ken said, holding one of the coffees up toward Sam. Abby could tell by the cups that Ken had bought the coffees at the Beanery.

"No. I'm good," she said. "But thanks."

Sam headed back to the greeting cards, and when she knew Ken couldn't see her over a display, she made a kissy face at Abby.

"Stop," Abby commanded, mouthing the word silently, and gesturing for Sam to go to the back of the store.

"Uh, I've got some things to do in the back. See ya, Ken," said Sam.

"See ya, Sam," replied Ken.

Ken made a complete three-sixty-degree turn, taking in all the work Sam and Abby had accomplished. "This place looks awesome," he said, handing Abby a coffee. "I didn't know how you liked it, so I put in cream and sugar. Mine's black if you want to trade."

Ken was dressed in a white collared shirt, dark blue jeans, and a bomber jacket. He removed his mirrored lens aviator glasses and tucked them into the interior breast pocket of his jacket. Abby had the thought that he'd gone from lumberjack to Top Gun in just the little time she'd known him. But she guessed that any style would look good on him.

"So you want to switch?" he was saying, holding out his coffee.

"What? Oh, no. No thank you. This is fine." She took a sip of hers as if for confirmation. "This was really nice of you. In fact, everyone has been so nice. It's a lot different than living in a big city."

"There aren't any nice people in the big city?" he asked, grinning. "Don't worry, I know what you mean about everyone being so nice. You'll get used to it. I moved here from Chicago about ten years ago. I got used to it. Eventually."

"What did you do in Chicago?" Abby asked, more curious about this man every time she saw him. She sensed there was definitely more to him than met the eye. He had an easy self-assuredness and confidence that was very appealing.

"I was a trader, you know, on the stock exchange. When I finally realized I had made enough money to get out of the rat race and start my own business, I didn't stay there one more second. It was all cut-throat, everyone out for themselves. I could tell you stories that would blow your mind. But, enough about me. Give me the grand tour."

Abby laughed. "It'll take about three minutes," she said, "and I'm guessing you'd be bored to death."

"Not at all," he said. "You never know when I might need an

engraved invitation or a fancy pen with my name monogrammed on it."

"We do that," Abby replied proudly.

Abby led Ken around the store, trying to avoid eye contact with Sam who had not gone into the back after all and was pretending to be busy at the sales counter just so she could eavesdrop on and gawk at Ken and Abby. Little minx.

"Well, let's see," Abby said. "For the sophisticated professional woman in your life we offer some very high-end desk sets." She motioned, a la Vanna White, at a table, showing him the clear acrylic staplers, stacking trays and file folder collators. "Moving on," she motioned with her arm. "For the culinary enthusiast we've got a variety of items to help organize their kitchens, from shopping lists and meal planners to recipe boxes and binders."

She held up a pretty recipe box covered in a pink toile fabric and Ken took it from her and inspected it with what seemed like genuine interest. His large and work-worn hands looked incongruous as they held the dainty item. He opened the box and flipped through the index card dividers.

"Bread, casseroles, meats, fish, desserts," he read aloud. "Very nice. I'll have to come back to do my Christmas shopping."

"You're the second person whose said that and I'd be delighted to help you select some gifts. I like to think I have a knack for that."

"I bet you do," Ken said, and held her gaze for longer than a man would if he was not interested.

After an awkward pause he said, "I should leave you to it then. I'm sure you have a lot to do."

"Thanks for the coffee," Abby called out as he walked to the door.

"We should do it again," he said, "and the invitation is still open for you to come by Northwoods."

As soon as Ken was out the door Sam was next to Abby in an instant.

"OMG he is so totally into you! I can't believe it. Women in this town have been after him for years. You are going to ruffle an awful lot of feathers when people see you out on your first date. And it will make Naomi crazy." Sam clapped her hands and bounced up and down. "I can't wait."

"Now hold on," Abby cautioned, holding up a hand. "Before you start planning our wedding, he's going to have to ask me out first, and he hasn't done that yet, has he? Besides, he's just being a friendly neighbor, like Jessica, when she brought wine."

Sam scoffed, "Jessica my butt. It's nothing like that. He will totally ask you out and I predict in the next two weeks—max!" Sam assured her. "He is totally shy, and I haven't seen him talk this much to anyone in a long time. He'll wait until you're alone and ask you then. He was going to do it today, I'll bet, only I was here."

Abby thought back to the easy, and by Sam's assessment of Ken's standards, quite lengthy conversation she had had with him the first time they met. Obviously, Sam did not know what she was talking about. The handsome outdoorsman could be interested in her. Imagine that. She thought of them sitting together at an intimate table at the Bistro next door or bundled up and walking along the forest trail where she had walked when she first arrived in Wander Creek. Then she brought herself down to earth. She would be leaving Wander Creek by this time next year. She would be back in Minneapolis living in a gorgeous downtown loft apartment. Then again, there was always the long distance relationship route. Sometimes those did work out. She was acting like she was in junior high and she and her best friend were gushing over boys during a sleepover. *Good grief*. She needed to snap out of it. *Cool and sophisticated.* That's what she was. And would need to remain that way to make a seamless transition back to her life in Minneapolis.

"We'll just have to wait and see," Abby quipped, laughing. "And

I doubt there will be a time when he catches me alone, seeing as you're here all the time eavesdropping."

"I wasn't eavesdropping," Sam insisted. "If I'm going to help you, I need to know the lay of the land."

Abby sighed. She wasn't going to win this conversation with her tenacious assistant. "Alright, back to work for both of us."

"WHAT'S WITH THE WINDOW?" Sam asked a few mornings before the grand opening. They were putting the finishing touches on the store and Abby was finally hanging the glossy wrapping paper sheets on the display rack as Sam watched, so pleased at being a part of all of this. The evening before, after Sam left, Abby had taped pieces of butcher paper over the display window so no one could see in. It was time to get to work on the final touch, but she didn't want any premature gawkers. She would unveil the outdoor sign and the window display the morning of the opening. She was getting so close! There really wasn't much else to do but the window. Ken had graciously offered to have a sign maker he knew make the new sign for the Paper Box. Abby had opted for a simple and reserved "shingle" she planned to display sticking out over the sidewalk above the front door. It was to be a white background, with "Paper Box" printed in a pleasing font in her trademark robin's egg blue.

Sam had taken to Abby's new technology immediately and had shown her how to use the design software. Together they had created a logo consisting of a gift wrapped box between the words Paper and Box. Abby decided that the robin's egg blue would be their signature color, and they printed the logo in robin's egg blue against a white background on signs for the front door, their business cards, and they made social media graphics as well.

"Well, I guess we're as ready as we will ever be," Abby said to

Sam as she admired how the store had come together. "We've just got to figure out how to create a buzz."

"You've already created a buzz," Sam said. "I ran into Gwen Pierce at the Pizza Den last night. She and her husband own the one here and the one in Two Harbors. Anyway, she remarked that she had seen Ken coming out of your shop the other morning."

"And?" Abby said.

"And she was wondering what was going on," Sam explained.

"Why does there have to be anything going on?" Abby asked.

"Because in all the years he's lived here, Ken Turner has never been known to set foot in any of what would be described as women's stores. For example, he's never been seen in Life and Style, The Cooking Shop, Second to None, or the hair salon."

"What about Sweet Pea?" Abby asked. "Doesn't that count as a women's store? I saw him in there one day."

"Naw, he's got a niece and nephew back in Chicago. He buys their birthday and Christmas presents there."

"And how do you know that?" Abby asked, realizing that she *really* had moved to a small town.

"Because Sarah Beth at the Post Office waits on him and he tells her."

"Okay, then," Abby said, winding down the conversation. "Back to the topic at hand."

"Right," Sam said. "The buzz around town about you and Ken."

"Nope," Abby said emphatically. "Try again."

"Okay," Sam grumbled good-naturedly. "The window display."

"Bingo," Abby agreed. "Like I said, I want to create some suspense around the window so that when we unveil it on opening day it will make a huge impact. Let's sit in the office and I'll show you what I have in mind."

Once settled, Abby pulled up Pinterest on her tablet and

flipped through some window displays. Sam scooted a desk chair closer so she could see.

"I want to start with a small desk and a pretty chair, something upholstered, and we'll set the desk up with our best desk set and put it right in the middle of the window. It will be the central focus of the display. We need some height, so I'll get some pretty vases with some nice dried flowers. Plus, we'll position stationery, cards, and an antique inkwell with a fountain pen as if someone is just about to sit down and write a letter to their beau across the pond fighting in the Great War."

Sam looked puzzled.

"The Great War? That was World War I," Abby clarified.

"Oh, yeah," Sam said. "I think I remember that from history class."

Sam made appropriate positive comments, repeatedly nodded her head in agreement, and Abby continued swiping through the images. "I love how these old fruit crates look here," Abby pointed out. "I think I have a couple in the back. We can stack them up and display some pretty trinkets and gadgets on top. On the far wall we'll place a bookshelf, kind of like this." She swiped again. "I'll fill it with journals, office supplies, whatever. I talked to Dennis Grey, and he's gonna let us display some of his rare books. Maybe some more vases, and we can put a couple bouquets of fresh flowers at about eye level."

"I love it," Sam said enthusiastically. "You're setting it up to look like a little study or writing area."

"Right," Abby agreed, "but I don't want it to be stodgy. Look at this picture. I saw a glass chandelier similar to this one in Second to None, so I bought it. It will catch the light beautifully during the day and give a nice glow after dark once I get an electrician in here to install it. For now, I can just suspend it from the ceiling on a chain. Then, for the crowning touch, I want to string fairy lights across about five inches from the top of the window and hang greeting cards from the ceiling. People will be able to look in at night and see the lights and the greeting cards hanging there." She pointed to yet another photo. "It looks like they're falling from the sky."

"You'll need some clear fishing line to hang the cards," Sam said cheekily. "And I bet I know just where you can get some."

Abby was almost tempted to send Sam to Ken's store right away to get the fishing line, but then realized, to her dismay, but even more her delight, that she wanted to see Ken again. *I should go.* She decided she would pick up everything else first and then go to Northwoods. *I'll save the best for last.*

ABBY WAS VERY glad that she had found so much of what she needed for the display at Second to None. She found the owner, Emily Blake, to be very pleasant, and she'd been happy to help Abby brainstorm about her window display. Emily had suggested a brown paper maché dog, about the size of a terrier, standing on its back legs begging for an invisible treat. It would be perfect to put next to the desk, she had said. She had also recommended a five-by-seven floral rug with a pale blue pattern on a cream background. Abby was sure she could make it work, along with a lovely antique bookshelf. But the crème de la crème was that gorgeous chandelier.

"Don't get me wrong," Emily had joked as she helped Abby put the items in the back of her car for the short drive across Main street. "I'm glad for the business, but now I've got to go shopping to refresh my stock. Not that I'm complaining." She closed the back hatch on Abby's SUV. "I've been meaning to come over and say hello," she told Abby, "but just haven't gotten there yet. Not very neighborly of me."

"No worries," Abby had replied, getting into the car. "As long as you make it for the opening next week you're golden."

Abby and Sam set about the task of arranging the furniture of the window display and tastefully accessorizing it. She had sent Sam to Two Harbors to find fairy lights and pretty cream colored vases earlier in the day. Sam returned with the fairy lights and the vases, but also had in tow two framed prints—one a man and the other a woman—sitting at desks writing what appeared to be letters. They couldn't have been more perfect.

"Where on earth did you find those?" Abby gushed. "They will look awesome sitting on easels on either side of the desk."

"I hope you don't mind," Sam said, "but I made sure they were returnable before I bought them. I hope it's okay," she said again, almost apologetically. "I can return them right now if you want."

It was then that Abby remembered how young Sam was. While an outgoing and pleasant young woman, Sam also possessed the lack of certainty that comes with youthfulness and lack of experience. Abby was glad that she had the opportunity to mentor Sam, just as Carmen had mentored her.

"They're better than perfect and you were right to buy them," Abby assured her, taking back her credit card from Sam's outstretched hand. The young woman beamed. "And here are the receipts," she said. "I made sure to get them."

ABBY MADE her way down Main Street to where Northwoods occupied a large, two-story log cabin with a forest green double door and window shutters on all the windows. Abby stopped to admire the view. She decided to have a look around before she went in, and she followed a well-worn path around the side of the building. She saw that the building overlooked the creek, and that there were two sets of wooden steps leading down to access points on the water. Brightly colored inner tubes were stacked behind the building next to a dozen or so ATVs and a rack of kayaks and canoes that had been covered with tarps strapped over them for the coming winter.

"Hey! You came!" she heard Ken's enthusiastic and somewhat surprised voice coming from behind her. Abby turned to see him smiling so widely that it was almost as if she had just told him she had won the lottery. Or even better, he had won the lottery.

"Of course, I came," Abby said. "I came to get that paddle," she said teasingly, "as well as some fishing line to hang a few things in my display window." She followed him back around to the front of the building, admiring the beautiful landscaping.

"Just give me a few minutes to get a few customers taken care of and then I'll give you the grand tour," he said, opening the door and allowing her to step in ahead of him. "Feel free to look around."

Abby was amazed at all the stuff Ken had. It seemed to her he had every kind of fishing lure in the world. There were rods and reels, creels and bait buckets, fillet knifes and neoprene waders, and felt soled wading boots. Who knew there were so many brands and types of fishing line? He had books about fishing, topo maps of the surrounding forest and even the bottoms of the local lakes. He even had a couple gas powered augers that were used to bore holes in the ice for ice fishing. And there was an impressive array of kayaks and canoes in a variety of colors and sizes, all strapped upright against the back wall, standing at attention waiting for some big city adventurer to take them home.

In short order, Ken had passed off the customers to other members of his staff, so he could give Abby his full attention. "Ready for the tour?" he asked, gently touching her elbow.

Abby turned to face him, smiling. "Lead the way, captain," she said. As they walked up and down the aisles, Abby found herself immensely impressed by what Ken had built here. And he was so smart! He seemed to know everything about this business. *I wish I knew as much about my business as he does about his,* she wished to herself.

Before she knew it, Ken was winding up the tour, and they

were standing in front of the fishing line section. "Now, what do you need the fishing line for?" he asked.

"To hang greeting cards from the ceiling. They're gonna hang down in front of the front window. It's part of my magical window display."

"Then you'll just need this two pound test line."

"Two pound test?" she asked, a little puzzled.

"It's how strong the line is. As long as your cards don't weigh over two pounds you're good."

Abby laughed. "Then two pound test it'll be."

Abby followed Ken to the front of the store and watched as he gracefully sauntered around behind the sales counter. "How much do I owe you for the fishing line?" she asked.

"On the house," he grinned. "You can get your fishing gear and bait on your next trip." He gestured to the far wall. "I carry a whole line of pretty pink fishing poles and pink lures. Not all of the wives who accompany their husbands up here hole up at the Wander Inn drinking martinis and gossiping. A fair number of them get out on the ice and many spend the night in their fish houses."

Abby shivered just thinking about being out on the frozen water, as Ken handed her the bag containing two spools of fishing line. "Thanks, but I think I'm more likely to rent a kayak in the summer than go out on the ice, even if the fishing poles are pretty."

"Oh, that reminds me," Ken said, reaching under the counter, and producing a beautifully varnished vintage single blade paddle. He held it out to her, and she took it reflexively. It was only about four feet in length. The wood shone and intricate stripes were painted on the blade.

"This is gorgeous," she said. "It's small. Made for a child?"

Ken shook his head. "You would think, but actually it's a sample. It's quite old. Way back when salesmen didn't have room in their cars driving all around selling equipment. The manufacturers gave them smaller sizes as samples. It's a relic from another time."

"Well, thanks for showing it to me," Abby said. "I love quirky antiques." She tried to hand it back to him.

Ken shook his head. "It's for you," he said. "Remember I told you when we first met that you never know when you might need a paddle? Keep it. It might come in handy, or maybe you can find a place to display it in your shop. You never want to be up the creek without a paddle."

CHAPTER 11

*A*fter having seen how goofy Sam looked in her misshapen brown Beanery uniform, which Sam confirmed was one of a lot of cast-off Burger King uniforms that Naomi bought in bulk at a garage sale, Abby decided that there would be no dress code in her store. Her employees, including herself, would of course always look nice and professional, and would never wear torn jeans. Abby had never seen a pair of torn jeans she liked.

When opening day finally arrived, Abby wore a black wool pants suit with a fuchsia blouse that tied into a bow on the front. She resisted bringing out her fuchsia Jimmy Choo heels and instead selected a pair of sensible black flats. Sam looked almost ethereal in her dressy designer blue jeans, a green gossamer peasant blouse, and thigh high white leather boots with a fake fur fringe at the top. She had died her bangs a light blue. "To match the awnings," she said.

At ten that morning, with Sam wringing her hands with worry, afraid no one would come, Abby stepped onto the platform of the display window and tore the butcher paper from the window, revealing their creation. Then she flipped the "closed" sign hanging on the front door to "open" with a flourish and raised the blind on the front door. She was thrilled to see a small crowd of people milling about out front and she immediately opened the door to let everybody in.

Some of the shopkeepers had stolen away from their own establishments to be there when the store opened. Abby thought she could spot the out-of-towners right away and said a silent "Thank You" to Mona who Abby was sure had admonished her Inn guests to attend. Now it was up to Abby to close the deal and make the sale.

Any doubts about whether opening day would be a boom or bust were quickly dispelled as Sam and Abby observed the enthusiastic shoppers, who came in throughout the day in a steady stream. Sam was so excited Abby basically had to push her into the office to take a lunch break.

Abby was surprised at how much merchandise was going out the door. A group of women from a small town in western Minnesota, having a girls' getaway at the Wander Inn, enjoyed some spirits at Mona's afternoon high tea and before walking the three blocks to the Paper Box. They bought all her Christmas card stock, plus a bunch of blank cards, and pretty much cleaned out the wine accessories section. A group of hunting widows, also staying at Mona's, put a big dent in the kitchen merchandise. And a mother with twins in tow bought a few lined spiral notebooks and crayons from the school and office supply display, and a stack of greeting cards, explaining that she liked to buy a year's worth of birthday cards at one time. Abby was impressed that she could keep up with everyone's birthdays well enough to buy the cards in advance.

About an hour before her scheduled closing time of seven Abby brought out champagne and appetizers for the crowd that had accumulated now that the other stores on Main Street had closed. She was exhausted and exhilarated all at the same time, and she was also very glad she had worn flats instead of heels.

Shortly after the champagne appeared, Ken arrived. He wound his way through the aisles and checked out the greatly diminished inventory with interest, purposefully staying away from the crowd. Every so often someone would strong arm him into conversation, but it wouldn't last long. Abby kept a discrete eye on him as she mingled with the rest of her customers.

An attractive woman in her thirties and wearing a vibrant red pants suit approached Abby. In her hand was a handful of little packs of pretty cocktail napkins she was about to purchase.

"I just love these," she said, holding them up for Abby to see. "I always leave some for my clients along with a bottle of champagne and glasses. It's amazing how far a small gesture like that can take you."

Abby smiled politely and tried to remember if she had met this warm and effervescent woman before. *I don't think so. She's pretty unforgettable.*

"Oh, I'm sorry," the woman said, as if reading Abby's mind. "I keep forgetting that we never actually consulted in person about your apartment—or even on the phone, for that matter—but that nice Mr. Monroe said that anything I did would be fine. Within budget, of course. And it also had to look very professional." She shifted all the napkin packages to her left hand and held out her right. "I'm Nora Talbot, the decorator who worked on your apartment," she said.

"Oh, of course," Abby said, trying not to stumble over her words. She was inwardly pleased that she had been right about how tastefully her apartment had been decorated. "You did an amazing job. I am so happy with it. Everything is perfect."

Nora beamed. "Oh, that is such a relief. Mr. Monroe said you really liked it, but I kind of wanted to make sure I heard it from you, so I figured I'd come to the opening and introduce myself. Definitely let me know if I can help with anything else." She looked around the shop and gestured with her right hand. "You've done a great job with this place. It's delightful."

"Do you live around her?" Abby asked, then wished she hadn't. If she had ostensibly hired Nora, then she naturally would know where she was from and wouldn't have had to ask. But Nora didn't seem to take notice of the question and answered in a bubbly fashion.

"I live in Duluth and run the company from home. I've got two toddlers so working from home is both a blessing and a curse. I have to bribe them with candy and cartoons whenever I have a video client meeting, otherwise one of them will video bomb me." She tinkled a laugh. "But it's all good."

Abby loved Nora's energy, and her happy, carefree manner was downright contagious. Eventually Nora drifted off to mingle with the other shoppers, and Abby made the rounds too, offering assistance and answering questions from town residents and tourists alike. Everyone seemed as interested in her as she realized she was in them. Wander Creek was its own little world—but small as it was, Abby was delighted and excited to a part of its vibrancy.

Mona arrived at about a quarter past six looking absolutely splendid in her Kelly green knit Chanel suit with large pearls everywhere there was space, including on a hairband on her head. Her high-heeled shoes matched perfectly, and when she entered the shop a waft of delectable perfume trailed behind her. Abby recognized it immediately as the brand Felicity, which she knew sold for an exorbitant amount. Abby knew, because it was once her preferred brand as well.

Once Mona arrived it seemed that the party really came alive. Sam changed the radio station from classical to Big Bands music of the fifties. Everyone was talking and laughing, many swaying to the music. It was as if Mona's perfume had mesmerized the entire place.

"This is a triumph," Mona gushed, snagging Abby alone for a moment, and the two exchanged air kisses on each cheek. "People are packed in here like sardines and it looks like they're having the time of their lives. It's been a while since Wander Creek had a new business. Brava, my dear, brava!"

Then she floated around the store oohing and awing. When Mona saw Ken wandering the aisles obviously avoiding the crowd, she went over and latched on to him, literally, putting her arm through his. If Abby wasn't mistaken, Ken was pleased by the attention. *Anyone would be*, she thought. It was impossible for anyone to resist Mona's charms. As she walked throughout the crowd chit-chatting, Abby kept an eye out for Naomi, half hoping she wouldn't come and half-hoping she would so she would see the success of her grand opening. She walked past Ken and Mona a few times and picked up strands of their conversation.

"You simply must come," Mona said, and another time, "It's not at all what you think, darling," and "What a thing to say, you're impossible!"

Mona had been gracious enough to buy several rolls of the glossy wrapping paper and a set of boxed thank-you cards, all of which Abby was certain she did not need.

At seven sharp, Sam grabbed a fishbowl full of business cards and pulled the winner for the raffle, which was a beautiful robin's egg blue leather desk blotter set. Abby had hemmed and hawed about the extravagance of the raffle, but she knew she needed to build a mailing list for the electronic newsletters she and Sam were planning. Things were going so well with Sam that Abby even wondered if, with the right support and a bank loan, Sam could take over the business when Abby made her triumphant return to Minneapolis. Abby would sell the building, but she would make certain in the arrangement that the lease would go to Sam, and that the terms and rent amount were favorable to the Paper Box. *But I shouldn't just assume Sam would even want to take it over. I'm guessing she would.*

"Grace Jacobson!" Sam called out in her bright cheery voice and Abby watched as a pleasant looking middle-aged woman came to the front to accept her prize, thanking Abby along the way.

"I'm the librarian," she said as Abby officially handed her the desk set, "and this will be perfect for my desk at work. Thank you. Now don't forget to come in for your library card. Our funding is related to our patron and traffic count. Every single person helps."

Abby promised she would, and then watched as the crowd thinned out, many coming up to her to say their good-byes. When the showroom had pretty much emptied out, Abby noticed that Ken was standing by the greeting cards, reading what was probably his twentieth card. Abby smiled inwardly. Maybe Sam had been right. She hurried into the small kitchen area where Sam was cleaning up.

Sam didn't look up from her task at the sink. "He's still out there, isn't he?" she asked, laughing.

"You were right," Abby admitted.

"Then what are you doing in here?" Sam scolded, jerking her head toward the sales floor. "Don't keep the poor man waiting. He's been here for like an hour."

Abby ducked into the bathroom, fluffed her hair and applied a fresh coat of fuchsia lipstick. She looked more like her old self than she had in a long time, even with the drugstore make-up and shampoo.

"Thanks so much for coming," Abby said as she joined Ken at the greeting card rack. He was looking at a new baby card, embellished with bears, balloons and glitter. "Are you expecting?" she laughed. She loved that she felt so comfortable with him.

A bit startled, he put the card back into the rack and she could tell he was trying very hard not to bend it. "It was my pleasure," he said, giving her a lingering gaze. Abby decided that if he *was* shy, it was only in groups of people. One-on-one he was quite open and direct. Definitely not shy. At least not with her. She liked that.

"I'd like to take you on a date tomorrow morning, before your store opens," he said. More directness. So refreshing.

"That would be wonderful," she responded, hoping not too quickly. "What did you have in mind?" she asked, hoping that it did not involve breakfast at the Beanery.

"It's a surprise. Dress casually but warmly. I'll pick you up out front at six."

Later, after Ken and Sam had gone home and she was alone in the store, Abby walked the sales floor one last time, straightening the shelves and trying to fill the holes left where something had been sold, and sipping on her first glass of champagne of the evening. Abby was already on a natural high, basking in the success of the shop. In *her* success.

After straightening the shelves, Abby went to the storeroom to gather some additional inventory for the wine display, but paused, shocked, when she opened the door. When she saw the minor catastrophe, her first thought was that maybe an animal had come into the store through the back door and somehow made its way into the storeroom. She knew that raccoons were crafty and could even open doors. She tentatively poked the broken box with her toe, but no raccoons scurried away. It appeared that this damage was manmade. Someone had taken a knife, probably the very box cutter she kept on the shelf above, and slashed into a box of greeting cards, hacking away on every side of the box leaving large gashes. And they had gone even further with their vandalism. Abby picked up a handful of the very expensive cards, the most expensive she stocked, and fingered them. The perpetrator had hacked them all in half and then neatly returned them to their proper places in the box. Abby went through the entire box. Every single beautifully embellished card was ruined.

Abby sat down on the storeroom floor and sagged against the wall, more shocked and confused than angry. She could replace the stock. That would be easy, although costly. But this felt like a message. She felt as though someone were telling her, in no uncertain terms: you are not welcome in Wander Creek! That feeling wouldn't be so easy to shake. Who would do such a thing? Even though the grand opening was open to the public, she had not seen Naomi Dale. Abby was sure the woman had not come because she had been looking for her all evening. Could this be related to her benefactor? Was the vandal someone who knew about and resented the arrangement? Jerome Monroe had promised her that nobody in town knew, but for the past few weeks Abby had seen firsthand how quickly the rumor mill churned around Wander Creek. She surmised she could probably rule out Naomi. But, if it wasn't Naomi, who was it? Somehow, Abby had unwittingly made an enemy. And that thought chilled her, for it felt not unlike being back at home, looking over her shoulder after Jake was arrested. For months she had been constantly on guard for the next angry person to accost her and blame her for Jake's misdeeds. That anger she understood. Jake had ruined people financially. But this. These cards were viciously destroyed under her very nose. On her opening day. And why? Abby hadn't done anything to deserve this. This was vindictive. And personal.

CHAPTER 12

$\mathcal{T}$he next morning when she woke up, the first thing that came to Abby's mind was the box of ruined cards in the stock room. She lifted herself out of bed and padded to the kitchen for a cup of coffee, wondering if she should tell Sam. On one hand, if Sam was in danger, she deserved to know. But on the other hand, she felt very much that the vandalism was personal, and she didn't want to bring Sam down from the high of success. For now, she would not tell Sam. She had hidden the vandalized greeting cards in the back of her SUV. But at some point she would ask Ken about it. Everything she had heard about him was positive, and she felt she could trust him with the secret. If she asked him not to tell anyone, she felt certain he wouldn't.

The second thing she thought about was her date with Ken, and she smiled to herself as she snuggled into her duvet with her coffee cup. It was just after five, and she had an hour before Ken arrived.

In the span of about three minutes her mind had recalled the worst, and the best, of the Paper Box's grand opening. Abby had been thrilled with the turnout and the sales, and hoped the activity wasn't a fluke. Her fellow shop owners had been warm and welcoming, mostly—but she did sense a level of coolness from some of them. Oh well, it took some people time to warm up to strangers. But not Ken. Her stomach flip flopped at the thought of him.

After showering and styling her hair, which she knew to be fruitless as she would be covering it with a hat, she gazed at the options in her closet, finally selecting a pair of black corduroy pants, a black turtleneck and pink pullover sweater. But her base layer consisted of long underwear, tops and bottoms, which she had purchased specifically for her new life in Wander Creek. No time like the present to christen them.

Having sufficiently layered up to the extent that she felt like the Pillsbury Doughboy, Abby stood in the dark on the sidewalk in front of the store, shifting from one foot to the other, and wrapping her arms around herself to fight the early November chill. She could see her breath in the light escaping her storefront windows behind her, softly illuminating her side of the street. She glanced at her watch and saw that she was a few minutes early. Was she anxious to see Ken? No, that couldn't be it. She barely knew him. She liked him, but . . . she didn't need any more complications in her life. The fewer moving parts the better. She was just doing this because she couldn't really say no to him. That would have been rude.

She turned in the direction of a pair of headlights shining from a vehicle that had just turned onto Main Street and was heading her way. *Must be Ken.* A few seconds later, a red Ford Raptor pick-up truck slowed and stopped in front of her. She saw the light come on in the cab, and Ken reaching across to open the passenger door for her.

"What, you're not going to get out and come around and open the door for me?" she asked teasingly.

"I don't become a gentleman until six." Ken glanced at the clock on his dashboard. "I have two minutes left."

Laughing, Abby slid into the passenger seat, and shut the door behind her.

Ken turned in his seat toward Abby and said brightly, "Good morning! I am really glad you said yes."

Abby faced him, and with a brilliant smile that was in no way fake, simply said, "I am too."

In the darkness, Abby hadn't noticed the dark tarp covering a large object in the bed of the truck.

Ken shifted the Raptor into gear and continued down Main Street. When he got to the bridge, he made a left and crossed over Wander Creek. Abby wondered where they were headed, knowing that he had promised to have her back at the store by nine-thirty so she could open by ten.

Her wondering concluded when Ken eased across the bridge over the creek and turned into the parking lot of the trailhead.

Ken parked the truck and got out. Abby just sat there, waiting for further instructions. Ken came around to her side, opened her door and offered his hand, and helped her out of her seat. He then opened the back passenger side door, leaned in, and came out with two helmets.

"You ever ride an ATV?" he asked.

"Well, if you count a golf cart in the Caribbean, sure," Abby answered.

Ken laughed. "Well, they do both have wheels," he replied.

Abby watched as Ken unlashed the ropes that held the tarp in place, finally peeling it back. By now daylight was just beginning to illuminate the morning, and Abby could barely make out a bright red ATV. She was sure that its color matched the color of the truck, and probably also the front to back racing stripes adorning both black helmets. She noticed how precise Ken was. How deliberate. How capable. In just a minute, he had positioned two aluminum ramps from the tailgate to the ground, started the ATV, and backed it down the ramp onto the parking lot. *He must do this a lot,* Abby thought.

Ken helped her into her helmet and assisted her in buckling the chin strap. He flipped the face shield on the helmet up so he could see her. "We'll leave the face shields down while we're mobile, unless we are going real slow. It's hard to talk with them down."

Abby nodded that she understood.

Ken pointed to the ATV, and Abby came nearer. "See this bar?" he asked. "You can hold on to that if you want to." The bar was situated so that Abby would have to extend her hands down and behind her to grab it. "Or the other option is that you can hold on to me. You know, just put your arms around my waist and clasp your hands in front of me."

Abby couldn't decide if this was flirtation, or just sound advice. "I think I'll start with the bar."

"Up to you," said Ken, smiling. "We'll see how long that lasts."

In a matter of minutes, the couple was tooling down a beautiful Minnesota trail, for the most part paralleling Wander Creek. From time to time, the trail would perform a switchback, designed to protect the hollows where streams and lesser creeks —in volume, not value—found their way to their destination.

During the rapid descent down the first big hill on the trail, Abby felt her stomach lurch, and decided quickly that holding on to Ken was the better option.

Abby settled in, her arms around Ken's waist, and she began to take in the scenery they were passing through. The peak of the fall foliage, legendary in this part of the world, had occurred probably a week or two ago. But the tamarack trees were turning now. Abby couldn't decide what color they actually were. They stood out in the dim light of pre-dawn. Yellow? Orange? Gold? She finally settled on gold.

As Ken guided the ATV down the trail, he would occasionally pull into one of the numerous overlooks, all of which offered gorgeous views of Wander Creek, and the bluffs, hollows and forests that cascaded down to its banks. About twenty minutes into the ride, he pulled into a particular overlook, switched off the ATV, and removed his helmet. Abby followed suit and disembarked.

"Wow," she said. "This is gorgeous."

"Of course it is," said Ken. "That's why I brought you here. This is the only place on the north side of the creek where you can get a view actually facing east. Where you can get an unbelievable view of the sunrise."

Ken stood beside Abby and pointed to the east. "We had pretty good timing."

Abby had to agree. The sun was ascending, and a sliver of its glory appeared above a distant ridge. Sun light dappled across the forest, and the reflection of the trees and sky in the smooth as glass water of the creek was spectacular.

Abby stared at the rising sun and then glanced over to see how its light played off Ken's cheek. He was handsome. Very handsome.

Ken then flipped up the seat on the ATV, reached into the storage compartment, and produced a thermos and two disposable coffee cups, complete with lids.

"Coffee?" he asked, smiling at Abby.

"Sure," she said.

Abby watched as Ken reached repeatedly under the seat, each time retrieving a different item. Abby took the lid off her cup and held it up to Ken and watched with delight as he put in just the right amount of sweetener, just the right amount of whipping cream, and even dabbled some vanilla extract into the mixture, stirring it with a stick.

Next, he pulled out a small bag, and offered Abby a blueberry scone. "Sorry. You'll have to eat it cold. But they're really good that way. You'll be surprised."

"Wow. This *is* good cold. Who would've thought?"

The pair stood beside the ATV, sipping coffee, nibbling on scones, wondering what to say next.

Ken moved the conversation forward. "So, how do you like Wander Creek?"

Abby suddenly realized she had never decided whether she liked it or not. "So far so good, but I think I might still be undecided."

"Hmmm," replied Ken.

Abby continued. "It has its good points."

"Of course, you are referring to me," Ken joked.

Abby laughed, then said, "I've had to adjust. But to my surprise, and relief, really, Wander Creek has been pretty great. Nice people. Nice tourists. Nice customers."

"What did you do before you opened the Paper Box?" Ken inquired.

"Well, I had some time between jobs. Lots of time actually. But I did a lot of charity stuff. And I was an event coordinator for about a year when I graduated from the University of Minnesota."

"Any siblings?"

"Nope, no brothers or sisters."

"Parents?"

"No, no parents either. They both died a while back."

Abby realized she was being vague, but she had her reasons.

"So," Abby began, turning the conversation in the direction of Ken, "How do *you* like Wander Creek?"

Ken paused, formulating his answer. "Well, it's the best place I've ever lived."

"Really?" Abby asked, genuinely surprised.

"I mean, I'm a Chicago boy, but this place . . . it's just . . . it's hard to explain. It's like trying to describe the sunrise we just witnessed. How can you possibly say how beautiful it was? You can't. You simply can't describe the sunrise we just saw. And there are lots of indescribable things around here."

Wow, Abby thought to herself. *He's really sensitive, but in a manly kind of way.*

Abby struggled to think up the next thing to say, finally asking, "You think you're here for good?"

Ken took a sip of his coffee, gathered his thoughts, and then replied, "I can't see any reason to leave. I mean, I never say never, but it would take something really spectacular to pull me away from this. I have my business, which I love, and I have plans to grow and expand. My clients are mostly decent people. And I have the great outdoors to wander around in. Who could ask for more?"

Abby just smiled at him warmly. *Wonder if I'll ever be that happy with my situation, whatever that turns out to be,* she thought to herself.

"Ok, enough chit chat," Ken said, slipping on his helmet and handing Abby hers. He placed their coffees in the dual cup holders mounted to the handlebars. "If I'm gonna have you back in time to open the store we better get going."

Less than an hour later, Ken eased the Raptor up against the curb across the street from Abby's store. Abby's instinct was to quickly hop out, to avoid any awkwardness that can accompany the end of a first date, if indeed, this had been an actual date. But to her surprise, she didn't hop out.

She was smiling when Ken turned to her and offered his right hand for a good old fashioned handshake. She took his hand, gave it a shake, and held it.

"Thanks for going with me," Ken said.

"It was my pleasure," Abby replied. "It was nice. Really nice. I had a great time."

Abby let herself in the front door of the shop, locked the door behind her, and bounded up the stairs to her apartment. She landed on the couch, her mind full of thoughts of Ken. She grabbed an embroidered pillow and embraced it. She thought of how easy it was to be around Ken, of how comfortable he was in nature, and in his own skin. With Ken, she could be herself. There was no need to try to impress him. She knew he would see right through it anyway. She had to admit it—she liked him. And more than a little.

CHAPTER 13

a few weeks after the grand opening and Abby's date with Ken, Jessica swung by one Monday evening. She gathered up Abby and Sam and the three of them braved the cold two-block walk up to the police station on Hickory Street. They were bundled up against the chill, with Sam wearing a dark red plaid mad bomber hat complete with fur trimmed earflaps, looking adorable in the crazy head gear. Crazy, but effective. Abby conceded that this type of hat would likely keep her warm but she had never been fashion-backward enough to don one. She might change her mind come January.

"Tell me again about this meeting?" Abby prompted, and Jessica explained, with Sam interjecting.

"The Duluth police department does this every few years. They take their recruits to businesses in a town or city and let them lose in plainclothes to see how much merchandise they can steal from us right under our noses."

"Really?" Abby asked. She'd only worked in retail for about a year, but she'd never heard of anything like this. "Do you mean like a mystery shopper exercise?"

"Sort of," Jessica agreed. "And we get all our merchandise

back, of course. At the end of the exercise, we'll all come back to the community center, meet the recruits and see what they absconded with."

"It's a lot of fun," Sam said. "The last time, even though most of her merchandise is behind the bakery case, one of the recruits snatched a bunch of ingredients, like flour, sugar, butter, stuff like that, from the back. Naomi was pissed. It was awesome!"

Abby had not met the Wander Creek police chief and one of the reasons she had agreed to accompany Jessica was to do that very thing. The image of her slashed inventory still haunted her, and she was no closer to figuring out the who or why. If she could get the chief alone for a casual chat, maybe she would mention it.

The community center was a small building attached to the library and when the trio arrived a few other business owners were already present and helping themselves to coffee and cookies. Sam made a bee line for the refreshments and Jessica had to take a phone call from her son, so Abby was left standing there alone. She surveyed the community room, which was furnished like a meeting room with tables arranged in a square with a square gap in the middle and molded plastic chairs arranged on the perimeter of the tables. A podium stood at the front of the room flanked by the American and Minnesota state flag. She spotted Dennis Grey from the Pages bookshop, Caroline Sharp from Gems, and Becca Simms from the Sweet Pea kids' boutique. She noticed that Naomi Dale wasn't present. As she surveyed the room, she caught Ken's eye and he beckoned for her to come over to where he stood chatting with a man in uniform, who turned out to be Ronald Carter, the Wander Creek police chief.

Abby had not seen Ken since their date. But she wasn't concerned. He had told her that in November he was busy repairing equipment and organizing and booking upcoming tours and trips. People booked months in advance to go fly-fishing, tubing and kayaking in the summer. She supposed that it gave them something to look forward to during the bleak months of winter.

"Abby, I'd like you to meet Chief Carter," he said. They shook hands and chatted amiably. Chief Carter was nice enough, but he was an imposing man, over six foot four she guessed, and solidly built. When Ken excused himself, telling Abby he'd be right back, she took the opportunity to speak privately with the chief.

"I hope this isn't an imposition, but I wonder if I could steal a few minutes after the meeting. I have something I'd like to run by you. It's nothing urgent, but it's something I'd like to discuss in an informal manner."

"You're not asking me out, are you? Because I'm a happily married man with three kids." He said all of this with a straight face, and Abby tried, unsuccessfully, to stifle a laugh.

"I assure you, Chief, I am not going to ask you on a date. Something happened at my store a couple of weeks ago and I'd just like to get your opinion."

He smiled curtly, them strode to the podium, followed by another man in uniform, whom he introduced to the room as Preston Evans, the Chief of Police in Duluth. The two men explained the program, providing not much more information than Jessica and Sam had.

"It's pretty much the same drill as three years ago. Just like we said back then, the best way to prevent shoplifting and theft is to be constantly alert," Chief Evans said. "Hopefully, this exercise will help you learn to always keep your eyes open. At the same time our recruits will learn to think like a criminal, which we have found has benefits in crime prevention efforts, as well as on the enforcement side. Retail participants usually come away with a sense of the weaknesses and security gaps in their establishments. It's a win win. Now the undercover recruits will complete their exercises sometime in the next month. There are fourteen of them in this class, but, of course, they won't all be here at the same time. One recruit could come in and hit one store and leave. Another might hit multiple places."

"And it could be tomorrow, or it could be in three weeks," Chief Carter added. "The point is that being alert for shoplifting and theft should be normal operating procedure. And, if something you really need goes missing, let us know right away and we'll get it back immediately. Once the exercise is complete, we'll process all the merchandise and invite you all back for a look see. You will be amazed at what they manage to take."

At the end of the meeting Abby took a rain check on Jessica's invitation to stop for a dessert at the Bistro, but Sam accepted, and she and Jessica strolled off with the rest of the departing business owners. Chief Carter remained, speaking with several merchants, while Ken helped put away the refreshments and otherwise straighten the room. Abby approached him.

"Can I help straighten up?" she asked, and he turned and gave her his "aw shucks" grin.

"No need," he said, "but thanks. I'm just finishing up. Do you need a ride home?"

Abby tried not to grimace. She was very glad to see Ken, but . . . She had enjoyed their date. Really enjoyed their date, but would it be fair to continue to see him and string him along if she didn't plan to stay in Wander Creek?

"No, thank you," she said, "You are kind to offer, but I think I can manage to walk the two blocks." She didn't know why, but she gave Ken her brightest smile. "I need to speak with the chief about what happened in the store."

"So what can I help you with Ms. Barrett?" the Chief said, approaching Ken and Abby. "Nothing wrong I hope."

"As a matter-of-fact there is," she said, and his eyebrows raised.

Ken, ever the gentleman, sensed this conversation might be none of his business. "I'll leave you two to discuss," he said, preparing to leave them.

"Oh, no," Abby said quickly. "Why don't you stay? You might have some insight, too."

She began her story by telling Chief Carter and Ken about the two previous nasty encounters with Naomi and ended with the vandalism incident at the Paper Box on the day of the grand opening.

"Sounds like kids," the chief said when she was done.

Abby shook her head. "I don't think so. I was there the whole time and I was keeping an eye out for Naomi. If there were any kids there, I'm sure I would have noticed."

"How about your staff? Anyone have a grudge against you?"

Abby sighed. This wasn't going well. "I've only been in business for two weeks and my one employee loves her job and I pay her very well. Believe me, she's very happy. There's no way it was her."

"Maybe kids snuck in the back door and you just didn't see them," the Chief suggested.

Abby noticed Ken's silence up until this point, not sure whether to be pleased or disappointed.

Back to the kids again, Abby thought. "I made sure the back door was locked before the grand opening even started."

"Anyone else have a key to that door?"

This question stumped Abby and she raised her own eyebrows. "Actually, I don't know."

"Didn't you change the locks after you took possession?" the chief asked.

"Ah, ah," Abby stuttered. She didn't know. "I'll have to ask my contractor. I didn't think about that. Thanks chief."

"If you want to come to the office and file a full report the incident will be on the record, which isn't a bad thing."

"Okay, I'll come in sometime this week and file a report," Abby lied. She wasn't about to draw any attention to herself. And on second thought, had she made a mistake talking to the chief in the first place? She sensed he was eyeing her suspiciously as she and Ken wished him a goodnight and left the building. The air was cold but it was a relief to be out in the open. All of a sudden, she had started to feel warm in there. Hot flashes or panic attack? Who knew?

"I ask again, would you like a ride home?" Ken asked pleasantly, pointing at the Raptor in the parking lot.

"Well, if you're just gonna keep asking 'til I give in, sure," Abby said playfully, feeling a need for Ken's company after her unfruitful exchange with the chief.

Ken steered the Raptor down Main Street, pulling curbside just before the Paper Box in front of the Bistro. "I hear this is the best restaurant in town," he stated, matter-of-factly.

"I hear it's the *only* restaurant in town," Abby countered.

A few minutes later, they were seated at a table near the back. After they ordered drinks Abby told Ken that Chief Carter had playfully, she hoped, accused her of asking him on a date. They both laughed, and Abby continued, "You know, that thing he said about changing the locks made sense. I have no idea if the locks were changed before I moved in. There could be who knows how many keys floating around out there."

"You didn't change the locks?" he asked, obviously dismayed to the point of almost scaring her.

"Not after I moved in. I guess I just assumed it would be done by the contractor."

"If you didn't specifically ask I'm guessing they didn't. It's usually left up to the owner to request a lock change," he explained.

"I know," Abby said, pulling her cell phone out of her purse. "I'll just text Mr. Monroe."

"Mr. Monroe?"

"Yes," Abby replied, frantically trying to decide how much she was willing to reveal to Ken. "He handled some of the administrative stuff for me."

Ken didn't pry, and she would not have expected him to.

Abby sent a text off to Jerome Monroe, and was pleased when he replied immediately that yes, the locks had been changed on the front door, back door, and the door at the bottom of the stairs up to her apartment all had different keys. Mr. Monroe had given her two of each, and he kept a backup for all three doors at his office. Unless she had had some made, those were all the keys.

"Nice," Ken said, "then crisis averted."

Relieved, Abby leaned back in her chair, and noticed Sam and Jessica sitting at the bar, obviously staring back at her and Ken. Sam pursed her lips into a smooching motion, hugging herself and kissing the air. Abby suppressed a laugh and returned her gaze to Ken.

They finished their drinks and Ken walked her the few steps to her building. "Do you want me to come in with you?" He paused. "I mean to make sure you're okay. No one hiding under the bed?"

Abby laughed. "No, but thanks. The building does have an alarm system. I only set it when I'm not here."

She pulled her phone out of pocket, thumbed to the app and tapped a large red circle on the screen. A voice came out of the microphone. "Disarmed."

"That's pretty amazing," Ken said. "My alarm is a keypad and I have to run to the other side of the store when I arrive. It doesn't matter which door I come in either. If I don't run fast enough, the alarm goes off. Poor design. And old. It came with the building."

Abby could tell he was rambling, trying to prolong the conversation. She remembered what Sam had said about how shy he supposedly was and took pity on him. "It was fun tonight. Thanks for the drink. And thanks for listening to my saga."

"I wouldn't exactly say a box of eviscerated greeting cards rises to the level of 'saga.'"

Abby laughed, as he continued, stepping a little closer, "I had fun, too. Try not to worry about the greeting cards."

There was an awkward pause, the typical shuffling of feet and averting of the eyes that couples who are just discovering each other experience, but then Ken blurted out, "I would love to take you out again. I mean, not necessarily an ATV ride in the cold before dawn. But I would really like to spend time with you. To get to know you a little."

Abby's head spun from all the contradictory thoughts going through it. *I'm just not ready to date. But he is really nice. It's obvious he likes me, but I don't want to string him along. He'll be in Wander Creek forever. Maybe I will too. No, I won't! He's not my type. So what!? Look what happened the last time you wound up with someone you thought was your type—a husband in federal prison. Well, ex-husband. Ken surely would not want to be married to the ex-wife of a white collar criminal. Married?! Who said anything about marriage?!*

She finally decided she would see Ken again. What could it hurt? In a new place where she was pretty much hiding from scandal and a past life, she could use another friend. Ken was an ally. She felt that in her bones.

"Sure," she said. "I'm game. What do you have up your sleeve?"

Ken raised his eyebrows, and asked almost apologetically, "You ever been hunting?"

Abby laughed out loud, but soon realized Ken was not joking.

"Oh! You're serious. Well, I did humanely live trap a mouse in my kitchen one time and let him loose in the front yard to fend for himself. Does that count?"

Ken shook his head laughing and said, "We'll figure something else out," and before she knew what was happening, he leaned down and lightly brushed his lips on hers. She let him.

ON ONE OF her morning walks out on the Wander Inn's Lawn, Mona called to her from a window. "It's Sunday morning, come in for breakfast. Your shop doesn't open until noon."

Mona had a special way of bossing people around in such a way that they didn't really realize they were being bossed.

Abby's first instinct was to decline. First, she was constantly leery that somehow her true identity would be revealed to the good people of Wander Creek. And second, she decided that since she would be leaving Wander Creek after her year it didn't really make sense to invest the time and energy to get to know too many people. But, recognizing that she was over thinking everything, she waved at Mona and made her way back to the Inn and through the back door. The smell of bacon, eggs, coffee and pastry hit her immediately. She followed her nose and found Mona sitting at the dining room table, plate piled high, reading a newspaper. Abby cringed when she saw Mona reading the *Minneapolis Ledger*.

Nevertheless, she chirped a "Good morning," and sat down across from Mona, reminding herself that she had reverted to her maiden name, grown out her hair and basically looked nothing like the glamorous Abby Trent of days gone by. "Everything smells delicious."

Mona stood up and filled a plate from the sideboard, lifting lids from silver serving dishes and not even asking Abby what she wanted. She delivered the plate and poured Abby both a cup of coffee and a healthy glass orange juice.

Abby gratefully received the coffee and took a long sip of the rich, strong brew. "I don't know what I would do without my morning coffee," she said, half closing her eyes and smiling.

"You're up awfully early," Mona observed, watching Abby as she took a bite of the most perfect Eggs Benedict she had ever tasted. "Don't you ever take a day off from your walks?"

With her mouth full, Abby shook her head then gave the universal sign for 'I'll answer when I finish chewing.'

"I have to take advantage of the nice weather as long as I can. Soon I won't ever want to go outside," Abby explained.

"Oh, but you'll have to," Mona sang. "I take breakfast out to

125

the ice fisherman the first morning their wives are here. It's a tradition. We make eggs, biscuits, bacon, muffins, fresh orange juice and hot coffee, laced with brandy upon request. You don't want to miss it, I promise."

Abby almost choked. "Walk out on the ice?"

"Well of course, darling. How else do you think I get out there? I don't rappel down from a helicopter."

Abby knew lots of people in Minneapolis who ventured out on the city's many frozen lakes. She was not one of them. She and Jake had marveled at the collection of ice-fishing houses that steadily grew as the ice thickened just offshore from their mansion. Of all the ways a person could die, freezing to death in a frigid lake having slipped through a weak spot in the ice was at the top of her list to avoid. But knowing she couldn't say no to Mona she simply agreed. "Okay," she said, thinking to herself, *it's not okay, but if you insist, which I know you will.* The ice fisherman wouldn't arrive until January. Plenty of time to come up with an excuse not to go.

As she sopped up the last of her egg with a crust of toast Mona said, without preamble, "I know who you are."

"That was fast," Abby remarked. For a split second she had thought about denying who she was but thought better of it. She was smart enough not to lie to Mona. "How long have you known?"

"Since the first time I met you. I never forget a face. I was in Minneapolis a few months ago and your husband's appeal was all over the news. They showed your photo. When you first showed up here, I knew right away it was you. And I must say, you have really let yourself go. But I suspect that's something of a disguise. It's a good thing you are a natural beauty, or I would insist on a make-over."

"Do you think other people in town know?" Abby asked, ignoring the remark about her looks. Mona was right, of course, about the disguise part.

Mona shrugged her elegant shoulders and took a sip of her Mimosa. "If they do it's unlikely they'll ever tell you."

"You did," Abby pointed out.

"Yes, well that's because I know what it's like to be an outcast, shunned by your social circle and wanting to start over. Escape to the hills and bury yourself in your work, as it were," Mona said, smiling. "Besides, I think you need a friend. And trust me, I won't say anything. There's nothing like a little mystery to make a woman more attractive."

"I don't feel so attractive," Abby answered. She let out a long ragged breath. "To be honest with you it is a relief that someone knows. And I'm grateful for your discretion."

Just then a tall, gaunt man emerged from the kitchen. He wore a black shirt and white chef's hat and inquired if everything was okay. "If you're done, we'll clear and get tidied up. All of the guests have eaten already."

"Ah, Telly," Mona said, "let me introduce you to our newest resident. Abby, this is my chef, Telluride, known informally as Telly. And before you ask, yes, he is named for the town in Colorado."

Telly raised his hand in greeting but didn't smile. "Just give us a few minutes, Telly, and we'll get out of your way," Mona said. Telly made a slight bow and disappeared back into the kitchen.

"Telluride?" Abby asked, glad to shift the conversation away from herself. "That's certainly an interesting name."

"A name carries a lot of power, doesn't it?" Mona said, raising her perfectly waxed eyebrows. "You of all people know that."

CHAPTER 14

$\mathcal{B}$y mid-November, Mother Nature had seen fit to deliver several moderate snowfalls to the upper Midwest, leaving a covering of close to a foot of snow. Abby was glad her commute to and from work didn't involve going outside.

The town was done up like a wrapped present. The week before Thanksgiving the town's public works department put wreaths, lights, and "Merry Christmas" flags on all the light poles. The workers did an excellent job of clearing the streets, sidewalks and paved trails, so there was the beauty of snow without the treachery that often accompanies it.

Across the creek, snowmobilers flashed along the trail Ken had taken her on. Since that morning ATV ride, drinking coffee together and admiring the sunrise, they had enjoyed only that impromptu date at the Bistro. There had been nothing else. Was he waiting for her to make the next move? After all, he had done the pursuing twice now. *But I didn't reciprocate.* Abby had certainly enjoyed herself and had told Ken as much. Did he sense that she was holding back, not because she didn't enjoy his company, but for some other reason? Like maybe she was uncertain what the future held for her? What did the future hold for her? Was Minneapolis her future? Did she really want it to be?

In the mornings, cross country skiers gathered in groups down by the creek, fiddling with their poles, getting ready to glide along the path. As she watched the skiers drift by, she tried to imagine what Wander Creek would look like with ice fishing huts scattered about. But then she remembered Ken had told her that for the last few years the ice on the creek had never really gotten thick enough for safe ice fishing, so everybody went to one of the nearby lakes. Abby knew that all over the hills, dales and forests of the vast north country, locals and vacationers alike were cross-country and downhill skiing, snow tubing and sledding and snowboarding, snowshoeing and snowmobiling, and in some places, even dogsledding.

In the weeks following the opening, the Paper Box hummed with shoppers and the foot traffic on Main Street was substantial for all the merchants. Sam was proving herself to be a very capable and enthusiastic assistant. Abby made a mental note that she should make her official title Assistant Manager and give her a raise. The store had made a profit from day one, and she knew Sam was a big part of that. Carmen would be proud.

One morning Abby sat working at her computer, when suddenly she looked up as if she had been disturbed by a sound rather than a thought in her head. In her mind's eye, she could see Sam leaning over the sales counter on the store laptop, attending to the Paper Box's social media accounts, which she had pretty much taken over. It had just occurred to Abby that Sam had left a steady job, albeit a bad one, to work for her, totally unaware that after a year Abby would most likely sell the building and move back to Minneapolis. The building itself was worth a substantial sum and selling it would help set Abby up and get her back on her feet in Minneapolis, find another job, and maybe even take a vacation. But Abby felt a pang of guilt that it had taken her this long to realize that she was essentially playing with Sam's future, and the poor young woman was none the wiser. Sam was an eager learner and had absorbed all aspects of the business, just as Abby had done with Carmen. It was a treat to watch Sam come alive and grow confident in her abilities. No longer under the oppressive thumb of her abusive cousin, Sam was free to flourish, suggest new ideas, and find solutions. She had suggested that they stock a few re-purposed gifts made from reclaimed materials. Of course, most of what they stocked was made out of recyclable materials. That was a given these days, but reclaimed was a step up on the eco-friendly ladder. Abby had told her to go for it, but to keep in mind that the Paper Box was mainly a stationery store, and although it did sell gifts, Abby didn't want to see it morph into a gift boutique.

True to her word, Sam had found up-cycled pencil pouches made of recycled gum wrappers, and she made a display with pens, pencils, erasers and small notebooks. She found earrings made of old magazines and refillable gel pens made from recycled plastic water and soda bottles.

As Sam had predicted, all the millennials who came in snapped up all the ecofriendly items, to the point that Abby and Sam dedicated a whole table to re-purposed and ecofriendly items. Since her work on the Paper Box logo, Sam had gotten even better with the design software, and had printed out little placards to put next to each item that explained how it had been repurposed and from what recyclable materials.

Sam was nothing short of a marvel. She had put her personal touch on the store and gladly took care of things—like the design software and social media accounts—that Abby didn't necessarily want to take the time to learn. Sam obviously wanted the store, and by extension Abby, to succeed.

The two never discussed Naomi, though of course Abby caught glimpses of her and Sam together outside the Beanery or walking around town together. They were cousins, after all. One evening, Abby had observed them arguing in front of the pharmacy across the street. If she had opened the shop door she could probably have heard them because Naomi was speaking so loudly. But instead, in an effort to be discreet, Abby had kneeled down by the front door so no one could see her and pushed open the mail slot ever so slightly just in time to hear Naomi say, "You'll be sorry, just you wait," and stomp off. Poor Sam. She was the victim of the same vitriol Naomi had spewed at Abby the first time they met.

The phone buzzed in her pocket and she stood up quickly so she could pull it out and hit her head on the door handle. "Ouch," she said aloud. "Gosh darn it! I guess that's what I get for spying on people."

Rubbing her head, Abby drew out her phone, tapped the green button and said, "Hi Ken, how are you?"

"Ever been to Duluth?" he asked, without preamble.

"Ah, only to run errands. And of course, I drove through it on my way up here," Abby said, still rubbing her head.

"Let's go to Duluth for our next outing, then," he said. "We can go to Canal Park. We can walk across the lift bridge over the canal where the big ships come in. If we're lucky, we can see a cargo ship come in. I know a great place nearby for lunch. There's a great train museum, and a great maritime museum. We can drive up to a bluff that overlooks Lake Superior. It's gorgeous. There's tons to do there."

"Ok. That's sounds like a lot of fun," she said.

After the couple compared schedules and settled on a tentative date, Abby felt herself getting excited about this excursion. Ken's excitement was infectious, and endearing.

For late November, a high temperature in the upper forties was downright balmy. The Raptor gobbled up Highway 61 as it sped southwest along the north shore of Lake Superior. Abby had to look to her left right past Ken if she wanted to admire the grayish green expanse of the lake as it spread out southward toward Wisconsin. *He's going to think I'm staring at him,* she thought. *And just maybe I am.*

Abby couldn't help noticing Ken glance at his watch. "Got somewhere you gotta be?" she asked playfully.

"As a matter of fact, I do."

"Oh, am I keeping you from something? Or, maybe somebody?"

Ken smiled. "As a matter of fact, there's this girl I want to impress, so I wanted to be at a certain place at a certain time to show her something."

"And do I know this girl?" Abby played along.

"I doubt it," Ken said. "She isn't from around here."

Their playful banter continued as they entered Duluth proper. Before long, they passed the northern terminus of Interstate 35, and not long after that, the pair were stepping out of the truck in the parking lot of Canal Park. When they had properly stretched their legs, Ken offered his right hand to Abby, who grabbed it unhesitatingly with her left, and the couple strode hand in hand over toward the Duluth Ship Canal.

The day was unseasonably warm and calm. They walked without speaking along the pier toward the light house at the mouth of the canal. Suddenly, they heard the alarm bell that signified that the Duluth Aerial Lift Bridge was about to rise up from its current height to a height sufficient for a huge great lakes ship to pass underneath.

"That means a ship's coming in," Ken said, stopping so they could both watch as the bridge that minutes ago was serving cars and trucks traveling to and from the narrow spit of land that jutted southward now rise skyward.

"Wow, that's pretty amazing," Abby said, with genuine enthusiasm.

Ken glanced back toward the mouth of the canal and pointed.

"Look," he said. "That's what I wanted you to see." A huge cargo ship was approaching, its massive bow displacing the water as it entered the canal.

"Oh my gosh, that thing is huge!" Abby said.

"Yep. It's over a thousand feet long."

"Wow. What's on it?"

"Probably taconite," Ken answered, and seeing the confused look on Abby's face, continued to explain, "It's a kind of iron ore."

The couple watched the huge vessel pass under the lift bridge, and then the bridge being lowered so cars could once again drive across. They walked over to the nearby maritime museum and browsed the displays. They walked on the lakefront walkway, and Ken took her to his favorite nearby restaurant, where they dined overlooking Lake Superior.

At around six that evening, Ken pulled up across the street from the Paper Box and parked. Before Abby could do anything about it, he jumped out and went around to open her door. She accepted his outstretched hand and he helped her out of the truck. He held her hand as they walked across Main Street to the front door.

Abby spoke first. "Well, that was really fun. I had a great time. Thank you."

"Thank you," Ken said. "I'm really glad you said yes. Again."

"Me too." With that, Abby lifted up on her toes and grabbed Ken by the back of the neck and kissed him firmly.

After the kiss, Ken looked at her kindly, and asked, "Think you would say yes again?"

"Maybe you should ask me and find out."

"Maybe I will," Ken said, turning to head back to the truck.

Just then Abby called, "Ken, one question. How did you know exactly when that ship was going to arrive?"

"Well, I didn't know, exactly. But there are ship trackers online. I checked just before we left Wander Creek, and that ship was pretty close to the harbor. So I just guesstimated. Guess I guessed right."

~

FOR ABBY, Thanksgiving was a quiet affair on her own with a roasted chicken breast, salad, mashed potatoes and gravy. But she did not mind, especially given the fact that Mona had gone to New York City to spend the holiday with her son and Ken had gone to Chicago to be with his family. It wasn't like she had not been invited anywhere because no one liked her. Her friends were just out of town and were not snubbing her. Sam lamented the fact that she could not invite Abby to spend the holiday with her and her parents, but since Naomi would be there, Sam decided not to ask, knowing that if she had asked Abby would not accept. But *not* being committed to a big meal or slaving away in the kitchen for a bunch of people suited Abby as it gave her more time to prepare for what she hoped would be an onslaught of Black Friday shoppers.

She and Sam had already stocked the store with all manner of Christmas themed items. She created a display of stocking stuffers consisting of pretty office supplies and notepads. In the kitchen area she supplemented the display with Christmas cookbooks, snowman cookie cutters, holiday-themed shopping list notepads, paper plates, napkins and fold over name place cards.

With Carmen's help, Abby had found a wholesaler that sold vintage paper tree ornaments and she and Sam erected a small tabletop tree on one of the display tables and hung the beautiful retro ornaments.

After her modest but delicious Thanksgiving dinner, Abby went to work on her display window, having purposefully waited to the last minute to decorate it so she could surprise and delight her shoppers the next day. She put together an artificial Christmas tree and decorated it with traditional decorations, such as twinkling lights, glass balls, tinsel and gold garland. She wrapped a cloth skirt in the store's trademark robin's egg blue around the trunk and placed wrapped packages of all sizes under the boughs. She fantasized about putting a big pile of shiny black coal briquets under the tree with a big sign that said, "For Naomi," but resisted the urge.

At the writing desk, she removed everything left over from the grand opening, and staged it with a large box of crayons, a plate of fake cookies and a mug that said, "For Santa." She cut a long piece from a roll of butcher paper and wrote in child-like letters, "Dear Santa," with squiggly lines representing a list going down the rest of the paper. In the chair, she placed a life-size rag doll, which she had found in a thrift shop in Duluth, and positioned her as if she was sitting down writing a letter. She used a hot glue gun to attach an oversize crayon to the doll's hand. The tail of the butcher paper sprawled across the desk and spilled over the edge of the table until it almost touched the floor. Obviously, this little girl was working on a pretty long list for Santa.

Abby wrapped small and even smaller empty boxes in light blue wrapping paper and tied red bows and ribbon around them. Then she used the translucent fishing line from Ken's store to hang them from the celling at different levels, so that it looked like they were suspended in air. In between she hung white paper snowflakes in all different sizes.

The crowning piece of the front window display was a life-size red mailbox embellished with snowflakes and the words "Letters to Santa," in gold calligraphy. She ordered it online and was surprised that it was so inexpensive, yet well-built and sturdy. She didn't have any problem putting it together, either. *Look at me, Miss Fixit.*

The mailbox fit perfectly in the window and was so cute Abby felt a shiver of delight and contentment. Finally, she brought out the artificial snow spray and applied it around the perimeter of the window. It was perfect. On the display tables around the store she placed poinsettias of all sizes, alternating between red and white, with a large potted one in front of the check-out counter. It would take forever to water them all, but she didn't care. They brought just the right splash of color to her store.

At the last minute, she remembered Ken's paddle. She was pretty sure he wanted her to use it in the display window. She retrieved it from the storage closet, wrapped a wide red ribbon around the handle, and propped it up against one of the table legs.

Outside, she took a few pictures of the window display and texted them to Carmen, then tackled the front and windows. She was so excited about her idea that she was almost giddy. She dug into the box she had carried outside with her and pulled out an evergreen wreath, embellished with a big bow in her trademark robin's egg blue color, and hung it on the front door. She dug into the box again and brought out small posies consisting of green pencils, red and white candy cane ballpoint pens and holly berry stems tied together with white ribbon. She arranged them artfully and evenly on the wreath. Next, she brought out a handful of tiny greeting cards which she had cut to size from Christmas cards she found at the dollar store so that she didn't have to use her expensive stock. She had made many tiny pin holes in the top left corner and threaded the fishing line through to attach the pretty cards so that they blended perfectly with the other decorations.

She looked down at the spool of clear fishing line. How many times had she used it now? She thought back. Quite a few. *I wonder when it will run out?* Maybe that was a metaphor for her relationship with Ken. It was useful and fun while it lasted, but eventually would come to an end. *Wait a minute, am I the spool or the line?*

Finally, she maneuvered a string of tiny white lights around the wreath, tucking the battery pack where no one would see it. She stepped back. Her creation looked amazing. She loved it. As she futzed with the ornaments to get them just so, she realized she was humming a medley of Christmas carols. She put the spool of fishing line in her pocket and headed upstairs to her apartment. Time for a glass of wine.

BLACK FRIDAY SAW a lot of foot traffic, including many guests from the Wander Inn, and Abby and Sam stayed busy all day ringing up customers, answering questions and restocking. Abby was surprised and delighted by the interest in her Santa Claus letter box. In fact, so many children peeked in the window, or boldly came in to ask if they could mail their letters, that Sam and Abby hauled the box out onto the sidewalk. In its place in the window, Abby put a vintage statue of a reindeer with a red nose that lit up. As Christmas approached, Sam spent all of her spare time studying for exams, including down times in the store. Abby remembered the crush of exam study from her own student days, so she often let Sam go home early. She could handle the shop by herself easily for a few hours.

Each morning, Abby loved to peek inside the Santa mailbox to see how many letters had arrived since the store closed. The pile was slowly growing, and she realized that she'd have to do something with the letters. But what? The answer came to her when Pete, the letter carrier, walked through the door and asked, "You getting any letters in the box?" as he handed her the actual mail.

"Actually, I am," Abby said. "And you're just the person I need to talk to about it." She wasn't sure but she thought she saw Pete blush a bit at the attention.

"Whatever I can do to help, I'll do it," he said, accepting the mug of hot cider Abby passed him from the store's refreshment station. He took off one glove and took a sip of the steaming brew. "Thanks for this. Whoever invented hot drinks has my gratitude for life. It really does warm a body up from the inside out."

"I don't know how you can stand the cold all day," Abby said, sipping her own cider. "Doesn't it wear on you?"

"I suppose at the beginning it did, but I've been doing this so long I barely feel it. Plus, if you've got the right gear you won't feel a thing." He paused and said with a sly smile, "You know Ken at Northwoods has just about anything and everything you need to get through the winter up here."

Now it was Abby's turn to color. "So about the letters," she said, deftly changing the subject. "I'm not sure what to do with them. I didn't really think this through. The box was sort of an impulse buy. What do you think?"

"I'll tell you what we do at the Post Office. Sarah Beth, the Postmistress, puts them aside and she and I answer each one of them ourselves. We have it down to an art, actually. We have a form letter that we print on Christmassy looking stationery and use an authentic fountain pen with red ink to write a quick note and add Santa's signature. Sarah Beth writes the name and addresses the envelopes and I put a Christmas stamp on the envelopes. We have a special postmark, too, of Santa and Rudolph."

"Huh, that sounds like a lot of fun, and a ton of work," Abby said. "How many do you do a year?"

"It averages about two-hundred-and-fifty, give or take. But it's worth it. The kids love it. Of course we have to vary the letter and stationery from year to year. Kids pay attention to things like that. And if we don't let them pile up for weeks it isn't as big of a task as it seems."

Abby studied him while he was talking. He was built like a fireplug and wrapped up in his winter clothes he looked more wide than tall, though he stood about five-foot ten. His white hair peeked out from under his knit cap. He seemed to wear the curly locks a little long. His cheeks were red from the cold and his smile emphasized his cheery disposition. Put a white beard and red suit on him and Pete could be Santa himself.

Could be Santa. Should she bring a rent-a-Santa to the store for an afternoon to interact with the customers? No, she didn't want to take on too much during her first Christmas shopping season. She'd consider it for next year, though.

Next year? Where did that come from?

As she was daydreaming about Santa Claus and fighting any and all thoughts of the future, Pete was still talking. "You wouldn't be interested in answering a few letters to Santa, would you?" he asked. "I mean, if you don't have time this year, there's always next year."

"This place keeps me hopping," she answered, not wanting to be rude but not wanting to commit herself to anything either. She changed the subject. "What does the post office do with letters from kids in other areas? I'm sure there are a ton coming out of places like New York City and Philadelphia."

"There's an online program the Postal Service runs called Operation Santa where members of the public can 'adopt' a letter and respond with a card or gift, or both. Kids can also send a letter to the actual North Pole if they use the right address. Parents slip in Santa's reply letter, which they've already written, and a return envelope and the clerks will date stamp them from the North Pole and send them back to the kids."

"That's gotta cover, what, a fraction of kids who send letters?"

"If that," he said. "The estimate is that several million kids write to Santa every year. But here in Wander Creek, every kid gets a reply that I deliver myself. I guess that makes me one of Santa's elves."

They shared a laugh and Abby delighted in getting to know this quiet, kind, and humble man.

"Why don't I collect the letters when I deliver your mail?" he suggested, handing the empty mug back to Abby and putting his glove back on. "Sarah Beth and I meet at the community center for a few hours every Saturday morning at nine and go through the week's letters. If you can, join us. It's a lot of fun and Sarah Beth brings baked goods." He patted his belly.

Like a bowl full of jelly, Abby thought.

"This time of year I gain five pounds at least, keeping up with Sarah Beth, plus all the treats my customers leave in their mailboxes. One year I even got a turkey tetrazzini casserole, fresh from the oven, no covering and still hot as blazes. It was interesting getting that home. But I did it."

Abby tried to get a peek at his left hand but saw he'd already put his glove back on. She couldn't help but notice how often he mentioned Sarah Beth, the postmistress. To her knowledge Pete was a bachelor who lived just off Wolf Path Lane on the outskirts of town. Maybe Pete and Sarah Beth were Wander Creek's "it" couple of the month, and she didn't have the scoop.

Meanwhile, she could tell Pete was anxious to get back to his route as he had moved to the front of the store. Abby stepped through the front door with Pete, reached down and cranked the lever on the bottom of the letter box and a stack of envelopes fell to the sidewalk, like giant snowflakes. She and Pete scooped them all up, and Pete continued down Main Street, a fresh supply of letters to Santa in tow.

What a nice man, Abby thought. As she re-entered the shop, a gust of particularly cold north woods air snuck in behind her. She shivered. She had lived in Minnesota her entire life, but she'd never been through a northern Minnesota winter. There was a difference, she knew. She thought of Ken. Another nice man. Maybe all the good men in the world came to Wander Creek and that's why women all over the country had a hard time finding them and ended up with guys like Jake. What was that old saying? *A good man is hard to find.*

"Amen to that," Abby said to the empty store.

CHAPTER 15

The next Sunday afternoon Mona beckoned Abby to the Wander Inn via a text. Mona's texts always made Abby smile. She wrote them like short semi-formal letters. "Dear Abby. This is Mona. Please come this afternoon at four-thirty for cocktails. Dress is casual. RSVP. See you then. Regards, Mona," followed by the date and time the text was sent.

Promising herself she was going to be better about exercising, Abby never-the-less drove the short distance to the Inn and parked in one of the guest spots. Mona opened the front door and ushered her in. "Quick now, I don't want any snow to blow in." They exchanged air kisses and Mona led her through a door Abby hadn't noticed before because it was disguised as part of the wood paneled wall of the dining room. Interesting.

"I've wondered what else was on this side of the building," Abby told her as Mona led the way down a short narrow hall.

"I have my own three-room suite. It's got a private bath and half-bath," Mona said, as she ushered Abby in.

Abby realized that the two had more in common that she thought. Like Abby, Mona had once lived in lavish luxury on a grand scale.

"What?" Mona asked.

"I was just thinking how alike you and I are," she explained. "We both had large and luxurious lives that have been distilled down to a few rooms and small domains to oversee."

"Well of course," Mona said. "Why do you think we get along so well?"

"I thought it was because I was scared of you," Abby replied, and Mona guffawed.

Like the rest of the Inn, Mona's apartment was tastefully furnished with a mixture of antique furniture, plus contemporary upholstered chairs and a sofa in pastel chintz. Valuable and attractive accessories were scattered throughout, completing a look that exuded class and culture. A Ming dynasty blue and white vase filled with curly willow branches and dried magnolia leaves sat on a gorgeous walnut sideboard. Mona motioned for her to sit in one of the chairs by the fire, where the gas flames welcomed her. Mona poured them each a glass of a deep red Cabernet Sauvignon, then joined Abby at the fire, collapsing into the chair opposite the fire from Abby.

"Ah, it feels good to sit. It's been so busy today I don't know if I'm coming or going." Mona took a fortifying sip of wine.

"How many people work here with you?" Abby asked. "I've only ever seen your housekeeper and Telly."

"Because that's all there is to see," Mona quipped. "Just the three of us little house mice."

"Why don't you hire someone else to help you? Like an assistant manager?" Abby suggested, thinking of how much she depended on Sam. Abby had felt completely comfortable leaving her alone in the store when she and Ken spent the day in Duluth.

"Oh, I intend to," Mona said fervently. "Just as soon as the right person comes along."

"How do you mean?" Abby asked. "Couldn't you advertise the position?"

"I could," Mona mused, "and if it comes to that I will. But I have a good feeling about it. It will be soon. Very soon."

"Is that how you found Telly?" Abby asked. "Or how Telly found you?"

"You're catching on," Mona said, pointing a perfectly mani-cured finger at her. "Yes, Telly and I found each other about three years ago. I was thinking about expanding to offering lunch and dinner. Plus, I had been catering breakfast from the Beanery, and while Naomi's baked goods are excellent, even if her disposition is not, I wanted something with a little more flair for my guests. I was at the farmer's market in Duluth one Saturday, just as the vendors were pulling up stakes. Telly was just about to return his merchandise and table to his little camper pick-up truck when I saw what he was selling."

Mona paused long enough for Abby to take the hint and ask, "So what was he selling?"

"Possibilities," Mona said.

"I don't understand," Abby said.

"You don't have to, dear," Mona responded. "Telly will explain it to you sometime, I'm sure. He likes to tell the story of how we met, and I don't want to deprive him of the pleasure. Now, I didn't invite you here to talk about Telly. My intention is to accli-mate you to the hunting and fishing widows. They are a special breed unto themselves and if they like who you are and what you sell, you'll have friends for life." She pulled out a leather-bound book from under her chair and motioned Abby to move her chair closer. "Let's get started, shall we?"

Mona opened what turned out to be a photo album, and she turned to the first page of pictures. "This was my first group of ice fishing widows, eight years ago." She flipped through the pages and Abby watched the same faces, getting a little older with each turn of the photo album, flash by. "They come every January for a week. Sometimes a few will come for a long weekend in October or November during hunting season. This is last year's photo." Mona turned the book around so Abby could take a closer look.

"They're all wearing matching sweatshirts." Abby squinted and looked closer. "What's that on the front? Do they say 'Ice Widows'?"

"They sure do. One of them bought sweatshirts for the group and they spent a whole day in the back parlor bedazzling them. They each had their own bedazzlers and you have never seen so many sequins, rhinestones and other embellishments. Turn the page."

In the next photo, the sweatshirts had been transformed. "Is that a bedazzled skull and crossbones?" Abby asked, pointing to a tall woman grinning from ear to ear.

"Sure is. That's Elaine Morgan. She's from a tiny town in North Dakota that no one has ever heard of. Her husband owns the Oopsi Daisy frozen yogurt chain."

"No kidding. Huh," Abby mused. "Isn't that a national chain? Does he own all of the restaurants?"

"Every single one, including two in Hong Kong and one in Berlin. They're richer than God. Even richer than me. And Elaine has a wicked sense of humor, hence the death motif."

Abby gestured to the four other bedazzled women. "And these ladies? How do they all fit in the Inn? I thought you only have have eight rooms and you're always booked?"

"Two of the rooms are suites with convertible couches. It suits them to share for a week, sort of like a pajama party. They've been coming here for so long I don't think they would ever consider staying anywhere else. Besides, mine is the nicest small inn in the area. Actually, the only inn. It's either this or the Comfort Inn in Two Harbors." Mona turned another page and pointed to two petite black-haired young women. "Jenny and Jillian are sisters and they live in Chicago with their husbands." Mona moved her finger to the last page, and her finger stopped beside a picture of a hauntingly attractive woman. "Nancy, whose hair is naturally that awful red, by the way—so don't stare when you meet her—is from St. Paul." Mona paused. "Do you recognize her?"

Abby shook her head, relieved that she didn't. She had wondered if she would know any of Mona's rich and fabulous guests from Minneapolis, but apparently, she was to be spared that. At least for now. Mona's rich friends and Abby's rich friends obviously ran in different circles.

"Nancy is the only single one in the bunch. She is a hunting and fishing widow in the real sense of the word. Her husband died four years ago—cancer, if I remember correctly—but she keeps coming anyway and I say good for her."

"So what's the drill?" Abby asked. "What do they do all day? I would think they would run out of things to do after two days. I mean Wander Creek has its charms, but if you're not into the outdoors, what else is there?"

"You would be surprised," Mona said, "and we all have our part to play in this pageant. On their first day here, Tia at Beautiful You doesn't take any other appointments and brings in two manicurists she knows in Two Harbors. The ladies spend the morning getting manicures and pedicures. She does some facials too, and I think she might have expanded into chemical peels. Then I bring lunch over in a hamper and they enjoy some nibbles and cocktails. They all like to nap or relax in the afternoon. We have tea, then cocktails and a formal dinner, usually sans the menfolk. They repeat that for four or five days, doing something different in the morning, shopping here or going to Two Harbors and Duluth, too. They can stretch Main Street out for two or three days if we have planned activities for them. Telly does a cooking class at the Bistro and we often do a wine tasting there. The restaurant has a private room in the back and I fly in a sommelier from San Francisco and they have a ball with him. He is an incredible flirt and the ladies drink too much. They love it."

"Wow, you go all out," Abby observed, suddenly feeling inadequate. "I feel like I need to up my game." She took a big sip of wine, as if the answer rested at the bottom of the glass.

"Exactly," Mona agreed, "and that is why you are going to do a letter writing workshop. I envision you starting with a Power-Point presentation about the history of letter writing, then talk about occasions, etiquette, etc. and wrap up with pretty cards and pens and everyone writes a letter. "

After initially bristling at Mona having the audacity to even think she knew what Abby ought to do, Abby had to admit it was an excellent idea.

Mona was still talking. "Now I'm letting you off the hook for this year, but next winter I'll put it in the brochure. So you have a lot of time to think about it."

"Brochure?" Abby asked, and Mona produced a glossy color tri-fold. Abby read, "A week of pampering, shopping and fun at the Wander Inn. Luxury in beautiful northern Minnesota." She studied the photos, stumped by the notion of 'next year.' First Pete with his Santa letters and Mona with her brochure. *I've got to stop waffling on this. It's killing my long-term planning.* Was Abby even going to be here next year?

"I could probably come up with something small to start with," Abby said, handing the brochure back to Mona. She loved the idea of researching the history of letter writing, and she felt her pulse quicken at the thought of studying and learning.

"I know the ladies would love it. They like to think that they're learning something along with enjoying their wine and luxury. They know how to have fun, but they are all extremely smart, to a one," Mona explained.

"How many times a year do you do all this?" Abby asked. "I mean, pull out all the stops like this?"

"All the stops, like the sommelier?" Mona asked. "That's just for this group. But I probably have a similar group every weekend in January and February who need entertaining, even if it's in some small way. Some of the women come during the school year just to get away from their kids, husbands and stressful lives, to enjoy quiet time and a little too much wine, if you know what I mean. Others come with their husbands who fish on the ice while they work from here remotely. I have excellent WIFI. Men tend to fish in groups, and so their wives often become friends and travel together. But only a few are like the Dazzle Dames, so boisterous and fun. I often go with them on their outings. I've never laughed so much in my life than with those ladies."

Abby laughed. "Dazzle Dames? They gave themselves a name?"

"Of course," Mona said. "They had to have something to bedazzle on the backs of their sweatshirts." Mona turned to the next photo in the album showing the five women with their backs to the camera, looking coquettishly over their shoulders. Sure enough, the words *Dazzle Dames* were spelled out in sequins on the back of each sweatshirt.

CHAPTER 16

*A*s if it was a foregone conclusion, Mona stopped by the shop the week before Christmas to go through the formality of informing Abby that she was expected at the Inn for Christmas dinner. Every year, Mona hosted a huge Christmas buffet and brought in a caterer and servers from Duluth to help Telly with the preparations.

Abby was surprised to learn the Inn was fully booked for Christmas, but Mona had explained that she reserved this week for her regular guests—typically older couples without children —who came for the ambiance, to get back to nature, and to enjoy the splendid decorations and scrumptious food without the hassle of cooking and clean-up. That sounded good to Abby.

The view of the Inn from the western end of Main Street where the driveway began was beautiful. Snow blanketed the vast lawn that stretched across the several acres surrounding the building all the way down to the creek. On many nights a few brave souls would wipe the snow from the Adirondack chairs and start a roaring fire in the fire pit. On those nights, the mood was particularly festive. Snow covered the trees of the surrounding forests almost daily. The trees ranged from looking like they were covered with powdered sugar, to having boughs creaking under the weight of a thick layer of snow.

On Christmas Eve, Ken appeared at the shop right at ten. The door was still locked, but Sam let him in promptly. She called to the back of the store, "Abby, you have a visitor."

She didn't say "Ken's here," Abby thought. She was expecting Ken. Had someone found her? Was the visitor her benefactor? But then Sam called, almost singing the name, "It's Ken," and Abby relaxed. *Wow, I didn't realize I was still that paranoid.*

As Sam headed to the back to give them some privacy, she made a kissy face at Abby who had to bite her tongue to keep from laughing.

Abby knew Ken was just thoughtfully and dutifully stopping by to say good-bye before heading to Chicago to be with his family for Christmas. She was just nervous about whether or not she and Ken would exchange gifts. They weren't a couple. They were just casually dating. What was the protocol? Back when she and Jake were dating, he gave her a present several times a week, either for some particular celebration, or for no occasion at all. Of course, she knew she couldn't, or at least shouldn't, give a guy like Ken presents all the time. But she had to give him something for Christmas. To show she cared. She did care, didn't she? *Don't I?* In the end, she strolled around the store and selected an assortment of different sized notebooks with a classy deer head with an impressive rack embellished on the cover. She threw in one of Sam's recycled pens and a box of chocolates she knew he liked from the candy store in Duluth. It was a modest gift, but heartfelt. She stuffed everything into a festive gift bag with red tissue paper and hid it behind the sales counter.

As he approached, Ken held out his right hand, which she took, and they exchanged a quick but tender kiss.

"Merry Early Christmas," he said, his other hand behind his back. "I wanted to make sure you got your present before I left." From behind his back he produced a box that she couldn't help but notice was expertly wrapped in gorgeous gift wrapping paper and ribbon that she sold in her store. She immediately saw Sam's hand in this.

"Thank you," Abby said, accepting the package. "Should I open it now?" She was already nervously picking at the ribbon, so glad that she had the forethought to get him a gift, too.

"Wait until Christmas Day," he said, taking it from her. "I'll put it under your tree. And by the way, I think the paddle looks great in the display."

As he went to the window to tuck the beautiful present under the display Christmas tree, she ran back and retrieved his present from the back of the store. "Since we're exchanging gifts, I'd better make sure you have mine before you hit the road."

"I'll look forward to opening it tomorrow," he said, smiling brightly. "Well, it's an eight-hour drive to Chicago and my parents are expecting me for Christmas Eve dinner." He leaned forward and kissed her again, this time touching her cheek with his hand. "I'll be back in a few days. Maybe we can plan something for New Year's Eve." And then he was gone.

ABBY ARRIVED at the Inn early on Christmas Day to see if she could help with the preparations and was pleased to see Jessica in the dining room, helping Mona fold napkins into a sleeve shape, making a tiny pocket where they placed sprigs of fresh holly and boxwood.

Abby exchanged air kisses with Mona then embraced Jessica warmly. "I didn't know you were going to be here," she said, happy to realize how pleased she was to see her new friend.

"It's my ex's turn with Burke," Jessica explained. "Breaks my heart to be without him but every other year that means I get to come here." She picked up a champagne glass from the table and took a sip. "Not bad for a consolation prize is it?"

"Okay, you two," Mona chimed in. "We need to finish these napkins and then I need one of you to run up to the linen closet on the second floor and grab the red-padded coat hangers and put them in the hall closet. Chop chop."

The Inn guests began to drift into the largest and most elegant first-floor parlor, where the servers had set out appetizers and champagne.

Pete, the mail carrier, arrived on the heels of Grace Jacobson, the librarian, who had won the leather desk set during the Paper Box's grand opening prize drawing.

Whatever delectable morsels were hiding under the silver chaffing dishes on the two buffets in the Inn's dining room had Abby's mouth watering and stomach grumbling.

When it looked as if not one more person could squeeze into the dining room, Mona gently but effectively tinkled her champagne glass with a knife to get the group's attention. "Merry Christmas," she said, and the room echoed her sentiments. "For those of you who haven't had Christmas at the Wander Inn before, you are in for a treat. Telly, our chef, has prepared an authentic English holiday dinner." She moved to the sideboards removing the tops to the chaffing dishes as she recited their contents. "Roast beef, Yorkshire pudding, braised red cabbage, pureed parsnips, shredded Brussel sprouts with bacon. The list seemed to go on forever. "Dessert will be served in the drawing room. We shall enjoy mincemeat tarts and sticky toffee pudding. Bon appetite!"

As the group moved toward the buffet in anticipation, Abby was amazed that there were sixteen people in the room, and that somehow, Mona had made it possible for all of them to sit at the dining table. There seemed to be no end to the magic and wonder of Mona's aura.

The table was set with silver flatware, crystal glasses and tiny silver salt and pepper shaker sets at each place setting. A huge arrangement of magnolia leaves, holly, mistletoe, and evergreens was artfully arranged in beautiful sprays in the middle of the table. Abby was no stranger to luxury and opulence, but this table setting possessed a quality Abby had rarely seen: Authenticity. Abby imagined Mona lovingly placing every item on the table, infusing it with her own energy and grace. And where in the world did Mona get magnolia leaves this far north? Abby imagined a helicopter landing in the Inn's parking lot to deliver the fresh greens.

Abby was seated next to someone she didn't know, who had already assembled an impressive plate on her first trip through the buffet line and was busy enjoying the spoils of her labor. The woman was short, five three at the most, and was swathed in an assortment of skirts and scarves that gave her the appearance of a gypsy. Her dark auburn hair was swept into an updo held together with another scarf.

Abby placed her own healthy-portioned plate on the table and slipped into the chair reserved for her, clearly indicated by the lovely place card with her name penned in flowing calligraphy. All the place settings had place cards. *Those all came from my store,* she noted to herself. Once seated, Abby turned to the lady, offered her right hand, and said, "I'm Abby." To her surprise, the woman just looked at Abby's proffered hand, which she returned awkwardly to her lap, resisting the urge to smooth back her hair as if that had been her intent all along.

"I'm Elise Winters," the woman said. "Forgive me if I don't shake hands but I'm an artist and if I didn't have these I couldn't make a living." She held out her hands for Abby to inspect.

"Got it," Abby said, even though she didn't really understand. She'd heard of concert pianists and surgeons and people like that not shaking hands, so she supposed the excuse of protecting the indispensable tools of some vocation might as well work for artists, too.

"What kind of artist are you?" Abby asked.

"I work in acrylics. Abstracts mainly, but I'll do anything on commission." She pointed straight ahead to the far wall where a large and attractive oil painting of the Inn hung. "I did that for Mona not long after she opened the Inn. I think it turned out pretty well." With that, the artist took up her fork and resumed plowing through her food as if on a mission. Between mouthfuls, she managed to tell Abby, "I ran an art gallery out of the space you currently occupy."

"What happened?" Abby asked.

"It wasn't the right time for me," Elise said. "It took time away from my painting to come into town and run the gallery. I hired a few assistants to help me, but I could never find the right person."

Abby thought of Sam. She had hit the jackpot with Sam, and she knew it.

"I'd love for you to stop by sometime to see the shop," Abby invited. "I'll keep the Christmas decorations up until the New Year. I'm obviously biased, but I think it looks very festive."

"Yes, I've heard that your shop is doing very well," Elise said over a mouthful of beef pudding, seeming to have lost all interest in talking to Abby, instead focusing her full concentration on what was left of her pudding.

The conversation obviously over, Abby also turned to her plate and dug into her scrumptious meal.

She was surprised, and pleased, when Telly emerged from the kitchen, without his apron and chef's hat and took a seat to Mona's right. Abby realized, with a surge of warmth, that Mona collected people, like someone might collect paintings, or figurines. This was Mona's collection, seated around this table, and Abby was part of it, and was exceedingly glad to be included.

That evening, tucked away on her couch under a velvety throw blanket, she opened Ken's gift. She tore off the paper, then gently pulled the gift from box. It was an eleven by fourteen burnished silver frame displaying a beautiful photograph of the exterior of the Paper Box. Judging by how the light hit the building he must have taken it early one morning as the sun was rising. Assuming it was Ken who took the photo. She hugged the frame to her chest and tears welled up in her eyes. Of all the presents she had ever received throughout her entire life, this was by far the most thoughtful and perfect. She sent Ken a quick text to wish him a Merry Christmas and thank him for the gift. He texted back, "I hoped you would like it. It took me about a week of trying to get just the right shot. I'll come by the shop when I'm back to help you hang it. And thanks for my present. You really do have a gift for anyone and everyone in your store."

Abby was full to bursting, and not just from the embarrassing amounts of food she had eaten earlier at Mona's. She was full of peace and a feeling of contentment washed over her. She was reminded of a line by one of her favorite poets, Robert Browning: 'God's in his heaven. All's right with the world.'

Were things right in her world? After all that she had been through, all that she had overcome, had she found the right place in Wander Creek?

CHAPTER 17

*A*s Mona promised, a caravan of luxury cars and shiny pick-up trucks pulling trailers arrived in Wander Creek late morning on a calm and sunny New Year's Day. They bumped along Main Street like floats in a July Fourth parade, making their way up to the Inn, where the convoy snaked through the entrance and quickly filled up the parking lot. Although the temperature hovered well below freezing, one of the cars had its convertible top down and the female driver, who was seriously but very stylishly bundled up, seemed impervious to the cold.

Abby had promised Mona that she would act as an ambassador of sorts, so when she saw the convoy passing by on Main Street from a window in her apartment, she pulled on her heavy parka over her tasteful black pants suit, stuck her feet in her winter boots, donned a wool scarf, hat, and mittens, and headed up Main Street on foot toward Mona's. When she got there, a mass chaotic unloading was taking place, with a steady stream of luggage being rolled from the vehicles into the main entrance. Mona was on the porch air-kissing guests, and the men were high-fiving each other in anticipation of all the fun they knew they were going to have. Telly, who seemed to be the grand master of this circus, was directing traffic and providing instruction, and seemed to be the only one getting anything accomplished. After the flurry of activity, the women finally all went inside to get out of the cold and the men returned to their trucks, and the convoy, sans the luxury cars, continued down the street and out of sight. Abby knew they were headed for Stewart Lake about thirty minutes away and they wanted to get there in a hurry to get their ice fishing trailers positioned and operational before dark. They were actually going to spend the night on the ice in them. Probably the whole week, with maybe a night or two with their wives at the Inn, or at least taking a dinner or two in the dining room instead of in their fish houses. That's what they were called—fish houses. And they were more tricked out than even the nicest RVs, complete with televisions, kitchens, toilets—even showers. But still, being out on the ice, on purpose, was inconceivable to Abby. But then again, coming to Wander Creek and running her own business had seemed inconceivable just a few months earlier.

Abby hung her outerwear on one of the hooks of the expansive coat rack in the entrance foyer of the Inn, and then prepared to join the guests in the Inn's front parlor where the women, having yet to unpack, were enjoying wine and cocktails, which Mona served from an elaborate drink trolley. The women were gushing and reminiscing, and Abby remembered that Mona told her that the only time most of them saw each other was during this trip. It was truly going to be a girls' reunion week.

Abby hovered in the front parlor doorway until Mona ushered her in. "Girls," she said, "if I could have your attention. I want you to meet Abby Barrett, our newest merchant. She owns the Paper Box on Main Street, which I guarantee you will fall in love with the first time you go in there."

Everyone greeted Abby warmly and introduced themselves. Abby had no problem identifying Nancy of the flame red hair, and the two dark-haired sisters Jennifer and Jillian. Elaine

Morgan of the Oopsie Daisy frozen yogurt chain gave her a warm hug. The fifth woman was Sandy James, an interior decorator from Minneapolis' twin city, St. Paul.

Turning to Mona and then to Abby Elaine said, "You're right, she is gorgeous. But you're coming with us hon, to Beautiful You later this week. You desperately need some highlights and those brows. . ."

"I've got the shop," Abby explained, but Mona interrupted.

"Pish posh," Mona admonished as the other women laughed and smiled, returning to their own conversation. "You know very well that Sam can handle the store for a few hours. And besides, this is Elaine's treat. She likes a good make-over, and you need one."

Mona had not been joking when she said the Inn catered a full breakfast on the ice. "We serve their second breakfast," Mona had explained the previous evening. "Those poor men get up early with only their pitiful granola bars and instant coffee to sustain them. We'll give them a proper hot breakfast and enough sweet and savory baked goods to get them through the next few days. And not just for guests of the Inn, but all the fishermen out on the ice. Think of it as an unofficial Wander Creek holiday. It's the Inn giving back to the community."

As instructed, the next morning Abby presented herself precisely at eight. She had donned her parka, snow pants, boots, scarf, gloves and hat. She had a wool face mask in her pocket. By the time she was done adding layers she was sweating, but at least her walk up Main Street to the Wander Inn was in relative comfort.

The Inn's hospitality van was parked in the circular driveway at the front door and Mona and Telly were packing it with what looked like enough food to feed an army. The day was particu-

larly bitter cold, which Mona assured Abby was cause for celebration among the fishermen, as she greeted her with air kisses.
Through the open door Abby could hear the wives' laughter as
they were tucked warmly inside the Inn, certainly enjoying a hot
breakfast of their own with the dining room fireplace blazing.

Inspecting Abby's outfit, Mona said, "We are going to have to
do something about your winter outerwear. Those things are
atrocious—all stretched out of shape."

Abby looked down at herself. "What things?" she asked.

"All of them. Now, jump into the van, sweetie. Chop chop."

Having successfully and efficiently transferred all the food
crates from the Inn into the van, Telly jumped in behind the
wheel, and Mona climbed into the passenger seat. Abby clam-
bered into the back and sat next to a young woman already
seated who appeared to be sleeping. Either that or she was simply
ignoring Abby. She looked young enough to be an angst-ridden
teenager.

The drive to Stewart Lake was uneventful. From her seat in
the back next to the young girl, Abby could barely hear Telly and
Mona talking, but it sounded like they were discussing what to
do when they got to Stewart Lake. Abby glanced over at the
sleeping girl several times, trying her best not to stare. At one
point the girl squirmed a bit in her seat but did not open her eyes.
Abby noticed she was suffering from a bad bout of acne, and her
mousy brown hair was long and unkempt.

The Wander Inn van glided over the hills and along the
narrow rural road to Stewart Lake as if it had been this way
before, which it had many times. Telly slowed down at the icy
spots, of which there were more than a few. Abby had never been
north of Wander Creek, and she enjoyed watching the thick
north woods forest zoom by outside the window. In what
seemed like no time at all, the van slowed and crept into a snow
covered parking lot. Abby saw the Stewart Lake sign, which was
difficult to read with all the snow and ice clinging to it.

Telly parked the van where the snow-covered lake ice of Stewart Lake met the snow-covered shore. The fisherman, in anticipation of this visit, had pre-positioned a cargo sleigh, the size of a loveseat, the night before for hauling the goods onto the ice. Telly and Mona hopped out and were quickly at the rear opening the doors.

"Help Billie out of the van, will you?" Mona asked. And by way of introduction, Mona gestured to the young woman who had now roused herself. "Abby, this is Billie, with an 'ie' not a 'y.' She arrived last night and is going to be working for me at the Inn."

Abby helped Billie down and the two shook hands and exchanged pleasantries. Abby resisted the urge to inquire as to her serious limp.

The group all did their part as if they were musicians in an orchestra. Mona was obviously the conductor. Telly lifted the heavy stuff, Billie did whatever she was told, and Abby just tried to keep up.

"Is Billie okay lifting things?" Abby asked Telly, because despite her limp and the occasional wince, Billie was transferring crates to the sleigh almost as fast and furious as the others.

Telly looked over his shoulder and saw that Mona was pre-occupied with the task at hand. "Mona won't let her do anything that could hurt her," he said softly, not whispering, but obviously intending this conversation to be strictly between he and Abby. "She's good that way. Looking after people." He turned back to the van and pulled a crate toward him.

"I'm curious," Abby, said, seeing her chance and not knowing when she might get Telly alone again. "How did you come to work at the Wander Inn?"

He smiled slightly. It was the first smile Abby had ever seen on him. "She told you about the farmers market?" he asked. "About the possibilities?"

Abby nodded. "She told me that I should ask you the rest."

"That day when she watched me load my van after the farmers' market, I was selling homemade soap, and scones I used to bake in a commercial kitchen owned by a friend of mine in downtown Duluth. Mona told me the combination of the sweet lavender scent of the soap and the tangy, rich, doughy smell of the scones was like nothing she had ever experienced before. She said it was the most perfect blending of scents, and she hired me right on the spot to be her chef. I learned later that she also smelled the whisky on my breath, which she said wasn't necessarily unpleasant, but definitely something to keep an eye on. But she didn't judge. It took me six months to get sober. All the while I was cooking at the Inn, and fortunately the guests loved my meals, and my baking. Especially my scones. Mona kept talking about possibilities which I took as code for, 'get your rear in gear.'"

"Huh," Abby said. "That sounds like Mona. Do you still make soap, too?"

"Of course," Telly answered, handing her a small crate. "Time to go."

In short order, the van was empty, and the cargo sleigh was chock full of the Wander Inn's special breakfast treats prepared just for this occasion. Telly reached into the van one last time, and brought out two large folding tables, which he placed expertly on top of all the crates.

There was nothing left to do but deliver the goods. Mona and Telly marched out onto the ice like old pros, their steps sure and confident. Mona proudly led the way, looking as much like royalty as any woman ever did, with Telly just behind her, tugging on the rope attached to the front of the cargo sleigh, which yielded to him easily despite its heavy but delicious burden.

Abby held her breath as she watched the pair increase the distance between themselves and the safety of the shore. Mona was decked out in sturdy but fashionable suede boots lined and trimmed in fur, and a calf length fur coat with a fur hat positioned at a jaunty angle. And Abby had no doubt that her suede gloves were fur lined and trimmed. Mona held a basket of baked goods in one hand and her classic Louis Vuitton purse in the other. Ever the elegant lady. The tableau reminded Abby of Queen Elizabeth who was supposedly never seen without her purse. In everything she did, Mona had the aura of royalty walking the rope line greeting her adoring and loyal subjects.

As Telly and Mona got further and further away, Abby suddenly realized that Billie had joined the procession and was not far behind them. She had to admire the young woman's spunk and watched her crunch across the ice like it was the most natural thing in the world, despite whatever was going on with her leg. As Abby watched, she could swear that Billie was wearing one of Telly's large parkas and a particularly bright yellow beret she had seen on Mona a few weeks earlier.

Still hesitating on the shore, Abby gazed out over the ice at the dozens of fish houses sat scattered around the lake. They ranged from crude huts made of wooden planks and tarps to fish houses that looked like nice camping trailers. Some fishermen had no shelter at all and were simply standing or sitting by a whole in the ice, waiting patiently for a nibble.

Abby could resist no longer. She was not going to be outdone by Mona, Telly and Billie. And, she really wanted to see the interior of one of those fancy fish houses. She took a tentative first step onto the ice. So far, so good. No cracking. She moved her second foot and then she was standing on the ice. But not exactly standing, because all of a sudden she was frozen in place. Her heart raced and her mouth went dry. She wanted desperately to leap back onto shore, but she couldn't move. *Is this a panic attack?*

"Hey, you okay?" a familiar voice from behind her asked.

Ken.

"Not really," Abby said, not even able to turn her head to look at him. "I'm sort of stuck."

"Mentally or physically?" Ken asked, and she heard him crunch up beside her.

"Both," she said, "and don't come any closer. Any movement is terrifying me." She heard his footsteps stop abruptly.

"It's okay," he assured her. "You are not going to fall in. I promise you. No one has ever fallen in."

Abby wasn't sure but she felt like he was biting back another thought, such as *here* or *this year*.

"What are you doing here anyway?" she asked.

"These guys are my customers. Most of them have been coming here for years. Plus, I never can resist the site of Mona and Telly crossing the ice to deliver breakfast as if they're just crossing the street to cater a picnic."

"It is comical," Abby agreed.

"So are you just going to stay there until spring?" Ken asked. "You'll fall in for sure if you do that."

"Ha ha," Abby said. She realized that her heart rate had slowed some. Ken's presence was definitely calming her.

"Tell you what, I'll walk down the shore about five feet and walk out on the ice and then move toward you," he offered. "You'll see that there is nothing to be afraid of, and then I can escort you the rest of the way."

"What if I freak out halfway there?" she asked.

"Then I'll throw you over my shoulder and we'll come back to shore," Ken replied.

He was serious, and Abby did not doubt he would do just that. "Okay," she acquiesced. "Just move slowly and don't talk."

"Got it," he said, and Abby heard him walk away.

A few seconds later she could see him in her periphery. He was wearing black snow pants and a red parka, the hood fastened tightly around his neck. As he approached, she expected the panic to set back in, but it didn't. She had never been so glad to see anyone in her life. And then he was in front of her, and he reached for her hands, which she reflexively held out to him.

"Now just take one step," he said gently. "Just one. And if that goes okay, take another one. And then another. Just pretend you and I are walking on the path along the creek," he said. "But you have to open your eyes, first."

Abby laughed and her eyes flew open. "I hadn't realized I'd shut them." She slid her right foot forward and slipped a little.

"Pick your feet up," Ken commanded. "You're walking down the street, remember? You're leaving your shop and heading down to the creek to meet me."

Abby did as she was told, and they made a slow amble following the tracks of the cargo sleigh. She was doing it! She was walking across the ice, and before she knew it she was standing with the group. Telly had already set up the folding tables and was arranging the buffet. Some fishermen had already arrived, while others were walking across the ice toward the feast.

"I see you finally decided to join us," Mona ribbed. "Good for you. I knew you'd make it. Eventually."

Abby couldn't help but notice an assortment of pickup trucks parked out on the ice along with the fish houses, and a thought occurred to her. "Mona, why don't you just drive the van out on the ice?"

"And where would the pageantry be in that, my dear?" Mona replied.

That's pure Mona, thought Abby.

"You okay?" Ken asked, still holding her hand.

She wasn't, not really. Better, but not necessarily okay. "Sure," she said. "I've come this far so I might as well get a closer look at these houses."

"Hey, Marvin," Ken called to a tall, thin man wearing a red and black plaid mad bomber cap, the flaps covering his ears. "Mind if we take a look?" Ken motioned to one of the larger trailers.

"Go ahead," Marvin said. "She's a beaut. Just got her this year."

Abby was grateful that the house was close to them, and she

and Ken walked the ten yards to the door, and Ken ushered her in. They emerged into a cozy, warm room with a galley kitchen on the left, with a small stove top, microwave, fridge and two cupboards.

At the far end of the house, twin bunk beds were attached to one wall and a large table pulled down from the opposite wall, holding a large television set.

Ken flipped a switch. "Track lighting," he said. "And here's the thermostat. Works just like it does in your house. It's propane."

"How on earth do they do all this?" Abby asked, twirling around to take it all in.

"There's a generator out back for the lights," Ken said, "and it will last them about three days between refueling. They'll just head back to town, buy some gas for the generator, take their ladies for dinner, grab a shower and be back out on the ice the next day."

Ken put his hand on her shoulder and pointed to the television monitor where she saw a fuzzy picture of what she could only assume was the water under the ice.

"They have a camera down there?" she asked.

"Yep. And watch this." Ken picked up a remote control that was attached to the wall on a long cord, and flipped through the channels, and Abby could see the other ice houses, as well as Mona gesturing dramatically, in conversation with Marvin. "There's a satellite dish on the roof. They have high speed internet, and as you can see, a surveillance camera system."

Abby pointed to the two hatches in the floor. "So how does it work?"

"It's pretty straight forward," Ken said, lifting one of the hatches, and a rush of cold air blew in. He quickly closed it. "When you get out on the ice you use an auger to make a hole, then you position your fish house over it so you can access it from inside. Then you just fish."

"Huh," Abby said. "So you don't have to be out in the cold shivering all day?"

Ken laughed. "Some of the old-timers do both. They stay on the ice for an hour or two then come inside to thaw out. And some people just like being out on the ice, in the wide open, braving the elements." He picked up another remote control and aimed it at the wall opposite the kitchen and gas flames whooshed up in the small fireplace.

Suddenly, Abby remembered that even though she was standing inside a cozy house, she was still *on* the ice. She sensed her heart rate quicken and felt a little lightheaded.

"Ah, can we go now?" she asked Ken, gripping the kitchen counter to steady herself.

He took her hand and led her back outside. "We're heading back," he told Mona and Telly. "I'll drive Abby back to town."

As with any return trip, the walk back to shore felt blessedly shorter than the walk out, and Abby sighed aloud, letting out a huge breath as she finally stepped onto the snowy bank.

"See," Ken said. "I told you that you wouldn't fall through."

He helped her into his truck, opening the door and almost lifting her inside. He grabbed the seat belt above her and pulled it down until she took it and clipped it closed. She had never felt so relieved and well cared for.

After the drive back to town, Ken pulled into the alley behind her store and helped Abby out of the truck and into the office. Sam heard them coming from the sales floor and wandered back to greet them. She could immediately see that Abby looked pale and a bit out of sorts.

"You okay?" Sam asked, adding, "Rough time on the ice? It's not unusual you know."

"I'm fine," Abby said, "but I think I want to get a hot drink and sit for a few minutes. You know, settle my nerves. Give me half an hour and I'll be down."

"Sounds good," Sam replied. "Ice-phobia rarely lasts longer

than a few hours."

Abby was grateful for the light moment. "Ice-phobia? Is that a thing?"

"It is now," Sam said, grinning. "You're my first case."

Ken led Abby up the narrow stairs to the apartment, and Abby remembered he hadn't seen the place since the renovation.

"This is incredible," he said, walking around the large main room while Abby sank into the couch, spread the velour throw over her and propped her feet on the large ottoman she used as the coffee table.

"It's quite the transformation. I can see why you're so happy here," he said.

That's interesting, Abby thought. Did she give off the impression that she was happy here? She must. The internal battle she waged every day seemed not to show on the outside. She was grateful for that.

Ken walked into the kitchen. "Great island. Love the shelves for cookbooks and the wine rack. Do you have any brandy?" he asked, opening cupboards.

"It's ten-thirty in the morning," Abby resisted, but only half-heartedly. She'd welcome a little something to calm her nerves.

"So what if it's early?" Ken asked, finally finding the bottle. "You need what you need when you need it. No big deal."

Abby loved Ken's homespun logic.

The kettle whistled and Ken rummaged around for mugs and tea bags and finally brought everything into the living room. He had the brandy bottle tucked under his arm and expertly placed everything on the big ottoman. He prepared Abby's hot toddy and handed it to her. "Drink," he commanded. "Then take a few deep breaths, then drink again."

"You're not having any?" she asked, doing as she was told.

"Of course not," Ken said with mock-horror. "It's only ten-thirty in the morning."

Abby laughed. Ken could always make her laugh. Abby

wondered how her life would have been different if she had married a man like him.

"I'm so embarrassed," she said, scooting over so Ken could sit next to her. "Nothing like that has ever happened to me before. I don't know what came over me."

"Don't be embarrassed," he assured her. "These things happen. Besides, you fared better than some people I've seen. You pushed yourself and tested your limits," he said, taking her hand. "That's no easy thing. I'm proud of you."

The words rang pleasantly in Abby's ears. She couldn't remember the last time she'd heard those words directed at her. She'd certainly never heard them from Jake. But then again, had she ever told Jake she was proud of him? She couldn't remember.

"Is it okay, that I'm here?" Ken asked. "I feel like I sort of invited myself."

She squeezed his hand. "It's okay. It's very okay."

THE NEXT DAY, still shuddering every time she remembered her frightful and embarrassing walk on the ice, Abby arrived in the shop before nine to do some paperwork before Sam arrived to open up. Abby didn't have plans to leave the shop that day, so she pulled out her favorite white platform designer sneakers, gently lifting them from the box and tissue paper. She slipped them on her feet with a happy sigh and then trotted downstairs, happy to see the white flashes of her feet on the stair treads. Just like pearls went with any outfit, pristine white sneakers made any casual outfit classy.

Abby gave a little shriek when she saw a man peering in the bay window, but instantly recognized the three-piece suit, burgundy briefcase, and the silver Lexus parked at the curb. Jerome Monroe.

She opened the door and let him in, delighted to see him.

"It's so good to see you," she said. "Can you come in and stay for a cup of coffee?"

"No thank you, dear," said Mr. Monroe. "I've already had two cups on the drive up here. Let's just talk."

"Is everything okay?" Abby asked, suddenly worried. Mr. Monroe would have had to have left Minneapolis around six to be here this early.

As if reading her mind he said, "I'm an early riser and thought I'd get on the road and beat the traffic. I'm just checking in to see how you're doing, that's all." He stopped and looked around the shop. "And from what I can see you're doing very well. You've done an amazing job here, Abby," he said. "This is spectacular. My client is really pleased with all the work you've done and has enjoyed watching this shop take shape and blend in so well with the other businesses. Very pleased, indeed."

"Wait, what?" Abby asked, stunned. "Your client has been in the shop? They've seen it? I've met them? I have to sit down."

She made her way to the office and sat breathlessly in her desk chair while Mr. Monroe sat opposite her. "Are you alright dear? What's wrong?"

"It's just you took me by surprise," Abby said, her face feeling hot. "You've never said anything about your client. Nothing. I was surprised when you said they've been in the shop."

"Oh, dear," Mr. Monroe said. "I just assumed you understood."

"Understood what?"

"That your benefactor is local," he said, as if it was the most obvious thing in the world. "But of course they won't reveal themselves to you."

Following a few moments of small talk, Mr. Monroe made his departure. Abby was grateful that the shop was very busy for the rest of the day and that she and Sam stayed occupied. That got her mind off Mr. Monroe's visit. Before she knew it, it was six o'clock and Sam was locking the shop door and shrugging into her parka.

"If you don't need me for anything I'm going to take off," Sam said, and Abby waved her off.

Abby turned out the store lights, leaving the paperwork for the next day. Right then all she wanted—needed—was a glass of wine or a pint of ice cream. Or maybe both. Once in her apartment, she kicked off her shoes and went looking for comfort sustenance. No ice cream. She'd have to settle for a glass of wine.

Abby opened a music app on her phone and scrolled to a big band station with beautiful, jazzy instrumentals from the 1940s. After flicking on the switch to bring the gas logs to flame, she laid back on the couch and let out an audible sigh. Ah, peace and quiet at last. In the stillness of her apartment, with soothing music in the background, she could think.

Her mind whirred back to the first day she arrived in Wander Creek and fast-forwarded through all the days since. It would be impossible to remember all of the people she'd met, but she'd certainly try. She would make a spreadsheet with the names of everyone she could remember being in the shop, limiting the list to local people and ignoring the out-of-towners. And then she could methodically gather information about each person, sort of like a dossier. With that done, she could weigh the odds of one person over another and come up with an answer. Though of course, that was crazy.

Crazy.

There was only one person who did crazy better than anyone else she knew. And that was Carmen. Abby slid her phone out of her jeans pocket and texted her friend. *Something crazy just happened.* The return text was immediate. *Tell me. You know I love crazy.* Abby tapped her phone furiously. *Not now. Can you come? You can see the shop and I'll tell you all about it.* Carmen responded right away again. *Sunday. Have brunch ready and I'll spend the night. Don't forget the mimosas.*

Sunday was two days away, and Abby felt like she might burst between now and then.

CHAPTER 18

*A*s promised, Carmen's bright yellow Mini Cooper pulled up in front of the shop at eleven on Sunday morning. Before Carmen had the opportunity to open the door, Abby ran out to the car and flung the door open for her.

"You have no idea how glad I am to see you," she gushed.

"I think I have an idea," Carmen laughed. "No one's been this glad to see me since, well, since I don't know when." Carmen stepped out of the car, looking trim in a hunter green velour track suit and matching suede ankle boots with little fluffy pom-poms. "Let's have a look at you."

Before Carmen could do her visual inspection, Abby threw her arms around her friend and mentor. "Thank you for coming," she whispered. "I needed a familiar face and sympathetic shoulder to cry on." Suddenly embarrassed at her outburst, Abby pulled away and grabbed Carmen's overnight case from the back seat and invited her to come inside.

"It can't be all that bad," Carmen said.

"It's worse," Abby said, and then remembered Carmen had never been in the shop before. She had only seen texted pictures.

"But I'll give you a tour first. It will give me a chance to pull myself together."

Abby gave a little shudder. She held her breath as Carmen walked around the retail space, taking everything in, fingering the tablecloths, inspecting the variety of greeting cards and pausing to inspect the prices on items in the kitchen display. More than anyone else in the world, what Carmen thought of the Paper Box was important to her.

"You did good, kid," Carmen praised.

"I learned from the best," Abby quipped, relieved and grateful for Carmen's approval.

"That you did," Carmen agreed. "Although I don't see a sale section," she added.

Abby gazed around the store, her eyes lingering on the expensive wrapping paper, cloth-covered desk accessories and high-end greeting cards. "I don't have one yet. Sort of breaks my heart to have to discount merchandise."

"Take my word for it," Carmen assured her, "set up a sale table, put up a nice sign and people will flock to it. Price things so you make at least a ten percent profit. At least that way you're not losing money. And the merchandise will move, I promise. You want to keep your displays clean and neat. If you have too much merchandise out because you're not selling it, people will be overwhelmed."

"Point taken," Abby said. She remembered the simple, sleek lines of the Paperie displays, as well as the fashionable boutiques she used to patronize. Carmen knew her stuff. Then Abby's mind jumped to Mona's Wander Inn and its simple, classic elegance. Less was more.

"I hope you didn't forget about those Mimosas," Carmen was saying "I'm parched from the long drive."

"Are you kidding? I've had to restrain myself and not gulp one down before you arrived!" Abby led Carmen to the back of the store and up the narrow staircase.

"I'm afraid I don't have a guest room, but the couch pulls out," Abby said, as Carmen walked around admiring the apartment. "It should be okay since you're just staying one night."

"Abby, this is so lovely," Carmen said, turning to face her. "You've really landed on your feet. But what on earth has happened to get you so discombobulated?"

Abby motioned for Carmen to join her at the kitchen island where she had laid out a cold meal of lunch meats, cheeses, fruits and crackers, and the promised Mimosas. "Let me get one of these first," Abby said, pouring champagne and orange juice into the flutes and passing one to Carmen before taking a gulp of her own.

"Steady there," Carmen said, and the two women sat on the stools.

After Abby completed her story, revealing the conversation with Mr. Monroe, Carmen said, "Well this helps you narrow down the list pretty significantly. I guess that's a good thing." She studied Abby's face. "Or is it?"

"It might be, except now every time I look at anyone in town I will wonder if they are the benefactor," Abby said. "I've already been giving people sideways glances and double takes and I'm pretty sure Grace Jacobson at the library is convinced I'm trying to throw the evil eye on her."

"Have you gone through the process of elimination?" Carmen asked. "Did Mr. Monroe say whether or not you have met the person?"

"Not in so many words," Abby said. "But it's a safe bet I have. I'm in the store almost all the time, even when Sam's working. I hope you can meet her, by the way. She's a dream. I couldn't ask for a better employee."

"If she's anything like you were for me, I can't wait to meet her," Carmen assured her.

Returning to the topic of her benefactor, Abby said, "I've

made a list," and pulled a piece of folded paper from her jeans pocket and handed it to Carmen.

Carmen read aloud, "Sam, Ken, Dennis, Telly, Elise Winters, Mona, Jessica, Chief Carter, Dennis Grey. So do any of these people have the means to be your benefactor?"

"That's the crazy thing," Abby said, trying not to whine. "The only person is Mona, the woman I told you about, who owns the Wander Inn and is filthy rich. She sold her husband's family castle to a Russian billionaire, if that gives you any idea of her financial situation." Abby paused, about to say something, but then didn't, which did not escape Carmen's notice.

"And?" Carmen prompted, arching her eyebrows, her brown eyes boring into Abby's. "What aren't you telling me?"

"And," Abby said quietly, "she knows who I am. She was in Minneapolis during one of Jake's appeals and my photo was on the news."

"How did she take it? Do you think she'll expose you?"

Abby shuddered and Carmen added, "Sorry, poor choice of words. That makes you sound like a criminal. What I meant to say was do you think she'll respect your privacy?"

"My sense is that she won't tell. She has her own secrets, and she's pretty tight-lipped about a lot of things about her own past," Abby surmised.

"What are you going to do?" Carmen asked, spreading a cracker with creamy brie cheese and popping it into her mouth.

Abby shrugged. "I haven't decided yet." She topped a cracker with prosciutto and a sliced gherkin. She had splurged for Carmen's visit and made a gourmet spread. "I'm still exploring my options. Not that I have many."

"Why do you think not knowing who it is bothers you so much?" Carmen asked.

"That's a tough one," Abby answered. "On the one hand, what if I found out who it was and then things turned permanently awkward? But on the other hand, I can't spend the rest of my year here looking at everyone as a suspect."

"That is a difficult choice, "Carmen agreed. "But it doesn't seem likely that you will learn anything from the one person who knows the benefactor."

"Jerome Monroe," Abby said. "That's an understatement. He's as close-lipped as a steel trap."

"And," Abby continued, "now that I know they're local, I feel like I'm being—not exactly spied on—but . . ." Abby paused, searching for the right word. "Maybe, assessed. I feel like I'm being judged all the time. And, if you think about it, in a way I am."

The conversation stalled as both of their brains were processing the situation and trying to come up with what to say next.

Carmen finally got the conversation going again. "Have you thought any more about whether you are going to stay here after the year is up?" Carmen asked, and Abby knew very well what Carmen would say if she asked for her opinion.

"It's too soon to tell," she said, only half-lying. She was having mixed emotions, especially about Ken, but that didn't stop her from checking out condos in downtown Minneapolis all the time and saving as much of the seed money and store profits as she could.

Carmen spent the afternoon in the shop with Abby and Sam. Sam and Carmen hit it off immediately and talked shop most of the afternoon. Abby loved seeing Carmen's enthusiasm rub off on Sam. And for herself, just having Carmen visit so she could unburden herself of the things that were really troubling her had worked wonders, even though nothing about her situation had changed. She still didn't have answers or solutions, but she felt better.

Carmen and Abby enjoyed a pasta dinner at Abby's dining

room table, then moved to the living room to sit next to the gas fireplace with cups of decaf coffee.

"Thank you for coming," Abby said for the umpteenth time.

"You don't have to keep thanking me," Carmen said gently, but firmly.

"I know, but I owe you so much. You're always saving me," Abby said, tears in her eyes.

"That would be true only if you needed saving," Carmen said. "You don't need saving—didn't need saving. All you needed was a gentle push in the right direction. So let's get you going in the right direction again. Sometimes, we already know what we want, deep down, but we're too obtuse and over-thinking everything to really get to the heart of, well, your own heart. I'm going to ask you a question and whatever flashes into your mind first, just blurt it out. Don't give yourself any time to think. Just say the first thing that comes to mind. Okay? Something will jump into your mind."

"You're making me nervous," Abby said. "Is this a test? I don't want to fail."

"You spent way too much time in school," Carmen said. "This is real life. Are you ready?"

Abby nodded.

"If you could wave a magic wand and have everything you wanted right now, what would it be?"

Abby hadn't expected that question. She wasn't sure what she expected, but it wasn't that. She was no good at these kind of things. Spontaneous things. She liked to weigh the pros and cons, see the problem, find the solution. She liked things to be in their place, liked to know what to do, liked to have the answers. Maybe that's why she had liked school so much. It was predictable, and at the end, there were always answers. Lots of answers.

Carmen had been right. Something had popped into Abby's mind, and she laughed until she cried.

"What?" Carmen asked. "Did you see something?"

"I saw school," Abby said. "I saw my elementary school from my childhood."

"Well that doesn't help anything, does it?" Carmen said, and laughed, too.

Sometimes the answers that pop into your mind are to a different question. One that hasn't even been asked yet.

AT BREAKFAST at the Bistro the next morning, after considerable cajoling, Carmen convinced Abby to introduce her to Ken.

Abby hedged. "He's probably really busy and won't have time to talk to us."

"Then we'll just go in so I can have a look. I'd like to see for myself the man that is helping to draw you out of your shell." Carmen held up her hand. "Don't argue. I came all this way and slept on that uncomfortable pull-out couch. It's the least you can do."

"Okay, you're right," Abby said. "Way to lay it on thick. Let's just keep it very casual. We'll go in and you'll buy something."

"Like what?" Carmen asked. "A fishing pole? Bait?"

"He sells souvenirs and Wander Creek t-shirts," Abby said. "The t-shirts are actually quite cute. I'd wear one. Anyway. We'll say that you need a souvenir for your nephew in Minneapolis."

"I don't have a nephew in Minneapolis," Carmen observed.

"And that matters because?" Abby retorted. "He doesn't have to know that."

After paying the check and bundling back up into their coats, hats and scarves, they got into Carmen's mini cooper and drove the two blocks to the end of Main Street.

"I'm really glad you've found someone," Carmen said on the short drive over. "And before you say anything, I don't mean you're going to marry him and live happily ever after. I'm just glad there is someone in your life to have fun with."

"Me, too," Abby said, not suppressing a wide smile. "Mostly because I feel like my life is getting back to normal. Well, as normal as things can get under the circumstances."

Abby was right about the store being very busy and that Ken didn't have time to talk to them. She and Carmen blew into the store on a gust of wind and stomped snow from their boots. Abby shivered with the cold and lamented that it would be weeks until she could wear her beloved white designer sneakers outside again without ruining them. "I don't think I'll ever get used to the cold," Abby said, shivering. "I thought it was cold in Minneapolis. But this. This is bone-chilling cold."

They moved into the store and glided over to the t-shirt display to the right.

"Do you see him?" Carmen whispered. Because she was so short and not wearing heels, she was able to hide quite sneakily behind a rack of puffy snow suits.

Abby moved to stand beside Carmen where she could scan the store but still bend at the knees enough to be hidden from view. She looked to the front where a short line of customers waited to be served, but it wasn't Ken at the counter ringing up the sales. She glanced to the left corner where the fishing gear was displayed, and then to the right at the small shoe and boot display. "There he is," she said excitedly, and they both giggled. "Over to the right by the boots."

They both turned to get a better look. "You're right, he is a man's man," Carmen gushed. "I don't think you could have chosen anyone more different than Jake."

"I think that's the point," Abby whispered as she watched a beautiful blonde woman, decked out in snug snow gear that revealed her every curve, make her way over to Ken, who was still stacking shoe boxes. "Let's wait for him to wait on this customer then we'll go over." Abby turned back so she faced Carmen and pulled out her phone. "Do you have time to wait a few minutes?"

When Carmen didn't answer, Abby looked up at her friend.

"You know what, I don't think I'll wait. I can meet him next time."

She tugged at Abby to get up, but Abby sensed that something was not right. Why the sudden change of heart? Just ten minutes earlier, Carmen had guilt tripped her to the moon and back about meeting Ken. She felt her heart quicken and her hands grew clammy. She looked back at Ken, just in time to see him lean his head to the right, and the beautiful woman instinctively move her head to the left, then move into what became a kiss. An actual on-the-lips kiss.

Abby felt like a motorist unable to take her eyes off a horrible car accident. She wanted to look away, but at the same time, she couldn't.

Her mouth went dry. "You're right. Let's go," she whispered hoarsely.

They both quickly straightened up, but Carmen's purse strap was caught on one of the racks and as she stood up the display rack tumbled over, making a loud "thwack" as it thudded to the floor. Abby was still looking at Ken and at the very instant he looked up to see where the ruckus was coming from, she and Ken locked eyes. The young blonde woman still had her hands around his waist, and she turned at the torso, looking every much the perky ski bunny in her tight black pants and short white parka that was more stylish than functional. Abby saw Ken try to move forward and out of the embrace, but the young woman's arms remained firmly around his waist, giving Abby and Carmen enough time to hurry out of the store without any confrontation.

They rushed to the car. "Drive around to the alley behind the Paper Box," Abby said. "I don't want him to see us parked out front if he happens to come out. Though based on what we just saw I think that is highly unlikely."

Carmen cranked the car into gear, and they lurched away from the curb.

"Keep straight," Abby instructed. "Now turn left here onto Hickory Street and take the first right into the alley. That will take you behind the store. It's a loading zone but we can sit a minute."

Carmen pulled up behind the store and geared the car into park.

"I'm guessing that was the last thing you were expecting to see," Carmen said, unnecessarily.

"I think I'm more surprised than hurt," Abby said, "though I'll admit it stung a little. But we've only had a few dates, nothing serious, and we never talked about exclusivity. He's free to date other people." She laughed and added, "And of course so am I. I might check out the nightlife in Two Harbors and see if I can find someone for a revenge date."

"Oh Abby, I'm sorry," Carmen said, patting her arm. "I feel terrible leaving you now."

"You know what," Abby said, nodding her head and smiling, "I'm going to be fine. This is one time I don't need saving. I got this. When it comes right down to brass tacks, this might even be a good thing." Abby didn't quite believe that, but she kept talking to reassure herself. "This puts our relationship—if you can call it that—into perspective for me. And with things being so uncertain about whether I'm going to stay or go . . ." her voice trailed off.

"Okay then, if you're sure," Carmen said, giving her a quick hug.

It had begun to snow heavily, and Abby tried to convince her friend to stay until the snow stopped. "I got this," Carmen parroted back at her. "Didn't you see the industrial strength tire chains in the back seat? If it gets too bad I'll just stop and strap them on. Don't worry."

Abby waved as Carmen rolled down the alley. Maybe that's what Abby needed now—industrial strength chains around her heart to keep all the bad things away.

Back in the store, Abby took off her coat, which suddenly looked bland and unfashionable, and grabbed a cup of coffee from the store's complimentary beverage service. Sam greeted her from the storeroom, turning around to say hello, but frowned instead.

"Wow," Sam said. "Are you okay?"

"Yes, why?" asked Abby.

"You look really pale, like you've just seen a ghost," Sam explained. Two seconds ticked by as Sam's brain searched for a possible reason for Abby's countenance, then she quickly added, "Ah, you've not seen a ghost. You went to introduce Carmen to Ken. And you saw a Misty."

"What's a Misty?" a distracted Abby asked.

"How do I put this delicately?" Sam wondered aloud, half to herself. "It's not a what, it's a who. Misty Summerville is a musher from South Dakota. She comes almost every year for the big annual race up at Gunmetal Lodge, and she and Ken sort of enjoy each other's company for a few days, then they go their separate ways until the next year."

Abby was pretty sure she didn't want to know what 'enjoy each other's company' meant, so instead she asked, "Musher, like in dog sledding?"

"Hey, now you're talking like a native Minnesotan."

"That's because I *am* a native Minnesotan," Abby confirmed.

"Oh yeah, I forgot. Anyway, it's one of the biggest races in the country and a qualifier for the Iditarod. Misty's a dental hygienist, but her parents have a big farm and she keeps her dogs and trains with them there."

"She still lives with her parents?" Abby asked, shocked. "Just how old is she?"

"No, she keeps the dogs there. She has a condo in Bismarck, the big city. She was first runner up for Miss North Dakota a few years back. And just as an FYI, don't expect much cross-over business at the Paper Box from the mushers. Those are hard-core outdoorsy folks and I doubt any of them are looking for greeting cards."

With each word Sam spoke, Abby liked Misty less and less. And Ken, even *more* less. Scraping the bottom of the barrel less.

"You seem to know a lot about Misty," Abby said. "You could have mentioned it to me, so I didn't make a fool of myself walking in on them like I did. I could have just stayed away from his store while the race was happening."

"I guess I didn't know that the two of you had gotten so serious," Sam responded.

"We haven't," Abby said, but to herself she wondered if perhaps she had been a little more serious than Ken. It had been comforting to have someone in her life after that year in isolation in the dingy Minneapolis apartment where the only long-term relationship she had with a man was with the driver of the bus she took to and from work.

"I'm sorry I didn't think of it. I've been studying so hard for my winter exams that I guess my head has been elsewhere," Sam said contritely.

Abby looked at the young woman, whose hair now had light pink streaks in it, and framed her elfin face like delicate ribbons. She always forgot how young Sam was because she often likened their relationship to the one she had with Carmen. But it was not fair to even suggest that Sam was somehow responsible for what happened. "I'm the one who should be sorry, Sam. You have nothing to be sorry about," Abby assured Sam. "Keeping an eye on the ins and outs of my love life is not your responsibility and I never should have implied that it is. You shouldn't feel as if you have to look out for me, except, for example, if the store is on fire or my fly is open."

They shared a laugh and Sam's grim face softened. "I promise I will tell you if your fly is open or you have spinach on your teeth, and we'll just leave it at that."

"Ditto," Abby replied. "Now let's get back to work. I want your opinion about the Valentine's display." She followed Sam to the front of the store and couldn't help but look out the windows to see if Ken had come to see her. To offer some semblance of an explanation. To apologize. He was nowhere in sight.

But that night he called her cell phone and on the third ring she answered saying brightly, "Hi, Ken!"

"Hey," he said, his voice contrite. "I've been wanting to call or text you all day, but the store was slammed and one of my employees called in sick this morning."

Abby didn't respond, politely side-stepping the point that he had had time to play kissy face with Ski Barbie. After an awkward silence he continued. "About what you saw in the store. It's not what you think, I promise you."

"Oh, it's okay Ken, please don't worry about it one bit." Abby smiled so that her voice would be light and cheery. "You and I haven't talked about exclusivity and there are no expectations."

Well, maybe a teeny one that crept into my brain when I wasn't looking.

Ken ignored her comment about exclusivity and continued with his explanation, which Abby did not want to hear. "Misty and I see each other once a year. I had heard through the grapevine that she wasn't racing this year, so I didn't give it another thought. She just showed up before I got the chance to tell her we needed to call things off. She totally surprised me at Northwoods and took me off guard. We just fell into our old patterns, I guess. You didn't stay long enough to see what happened next."

"Really, Ken, it's not necessary. You don't owe me any explanation at all."

"Does that mean you don't want to see me anymore?" he asked.

"Not at all," Abby assured him, and she meant it. She liked him, and there was no reason they couldn't be friends. She had enjoyed their date to Duluth, and the ride on the ATV. It had been a while since she had done anything so daring.

"I'd like to talk about things. About our relationship," Ken said quietly, and Abby imagined him in his store, leaning up against the counter surrounded by fishing poles and snow tubes. "I enjoy spending time with you," he was saying, "and I'd like a chance to explain. Are you free for dinner tonight? Or we could grab a cup of coffee."

Abby hesitated. Jake was unfaithful during their marriage, and while she and Ken in no way had any commitment to each other, it still hurt to see him in the arms of another woman. Instead of revving up into defining expectations, they needed to reverse back to the parking lot and shift the car into park.

"I have a lot to do to this week to get ready for Valentine's Day," she said. "I'm guessing that's not a holiday you have to prepare for?" They shared a laugh, which to some extent broke the ice. "I'll call you next week and we can plan something," Abby said.

While Sam straightened and dusted the items on the sales floor that afternoon, Abby did some stealth Googling and discovered that the dog sled race ended on Sunday morning and everyone, and supposedly Misty, too, would probably leave Sunday night, or at least Monday morning. She'd call Ken on Monday. Or Tuesday. Maybe Wednesday. He had talked as if there wasn't anything more between him and Misty. But it sure hadn't looked that way a few hours earlier.

CHAPTER 19

By the end of January Abby and Jessica had started to meet at the Bistro every other Friday when her ex-husband had her son.

"We haven't ever talked about Ken," Jessica said one Friday after they had settled at a table and ordered drinks and appetizers. "I've been dying to ask you, but I didn't want to intrude."

"It's alright," Abby said. "I don't mind talking about it because it's really no big deal."

"Well it is to Ken," Jessica said matter-of-factly.

"What do you mean?" Abby asked, moving the condiment holder out of the way so the waitress could serve their food and drinks.

"Apparently Naomi heard about the dust-up with you and Ken and made her move," Jessica explained.

"I wouldn't call it a dust up," Abby argued. "And does everyone know what happened?"

"Of course," Jessica said without missing a beat. "It's a small town. And everyone loves Ken and looks out for him. He is the town's most eligible bachelor."

"He's the town's only bachelor," Abby pointed out.

"There's Pete, too," Jessica countered. "Anyway. A few days after you caught Ken and Misty together Naomi showed up at Ken's house and he told her in no uncertain terms that he would never be interested in her and that at the moment he was wanting to develop his relationship with you. Then she told him that you were a lying so-and-so, and it would be his smartest move to dump you."

"Lying about what?" Abby asked, unable to move, her fork hanging in the air, halfway to her mouth. She gulped and put down the fork.

"Who knows," Jessica said. "Something about you didn't really buy your building. She has a friend in the county registrar's office."

"But the deed's in my name," Abby said. "That's ridiculous."

"Apparently there was some real estate transfer between when the newspaper sold the building and when you bought it. It's all public information. She thinks you're involved in some Mafia crime family and you used a shell corporation to launder money before putting the deed in your name. Naomi is just looking for anything that will make you look bad in front of Ken, no matter how ridiculous she sounds."

"That is the craziest thing I've ever heard," Abby said. On one hand she was relieved that Naomi was so off track when it came to the truth about Abby's circumstances. But on the other hand, it sounded like Naomi wasn't going to stop looking into her background. Had she already discovered the truth and was she waiting for the right time to spring it? All these months Abby hadn't thought of Naomi Day as a real threat. She considered her more of a nuisance.

After the happy hour with Jessica, Abby was surprised to see Mona standing in front of the Paper Box, hand raised to knock. "There you are," Mona said with a tinkle. "I've been trying to get ahold of you, but you didn't answer your phone."

"I've been at the Bistro with Jessica. I guess I didn't hear it ring."

"Never mind," Mona said with her typically dismissive hand gesture. "You're here now so let's go inside. I haven't seen your apartment yet and find myself with an unexpected quiet evening." She held up a bottle of wine. "I come bearing house-warming gifts."

Abby loved the fact that Mona always assumed that wherever and whenever she showed up she would be welcomed. And of course, Mona was right about that. Had Abby been entertaining friends, or on a date with Ken—fat chance for that now—she still would have asked Mona to join them. Mona had that infectious vibe that could liven up any circumstances.

Abby pulled her keys from her coat pocket and unlocked the door, stepping aside to let Mona enter first. Abby led her through the store to the narrow stairway in the back. "My apartment's up there," Abby said, pointing up the stairs and smiling proudly.

Upstairs, Mona slipped out of her suede coat and hung it and her Luis Vuitton purse over one of the living room chairs. "Charming," she said, and Abby knew she meant it. "This is just charming, Abby. I knew that you would have excellent taste."

Abby did not correct her. After all, she did have excellent taste as a point of fact, even if she hadn't decorated this particular apartment herself.

Mona put the bottle of wine on the kitchen island. "Glasses and bottle opener?" she asked, and Abby retrieved them. While Abby opened the wine and poured them each a glass, Mona walked into the living room and sat on the couch. "I love this ottoman. Very chic to use it as a coffee table."

"Thank you," Abby answered, passing a glass to Mona, then sitting down in one of the armchairs on the other side of the ottoman.

Mona raised her glass and Abby did the same. "Shall we toast to friendship, The Paper Box and the Wander Inn?" Mona said, and the two women raised their glasses toward each other.

"That's a wonderful toast," Abby said after the first sip. "But something tells me that you didn't come here for that."

"You are the perceptive one," Mona said, laughing. "You have very good people skills, too. And you're right. I'm here to ask a favor."

"Wow, what on earth do I have that I can help you with? You have just about everything you need or want at your fingertips."

"Not quite," Mona said, smiling. "For example, I don't have a charming stationery store that's thriving. What I do have is an injured young woman who had a procedure done on her knee and is temporarily unable to stand on her feet for very long. She's been doing some light cleaning at the Inn and helping Telly with some sous chef activities, but in light of her minor surgery, she needs to take it easy for the next few weeks."

"You're talking about Billie, of course," Abby said. "But if she worked here she'd be on her feet all the time, too. She wouldn't be any better off here than at the Inn."

"Don't be absurd," Mona quipped. "I don't want her to work for you. She's an excellent artist and I want you to sell her greeting cards in your store."

"Done," Abby said. "I'm happy to help. In fact, Sam and I have even talked about stocking relevant inventory made by local artisans." She paused. "What's her story anyway? Seems like she just appeared out of nowhere."

"She did," Mona said. "I think I told you the right person would come along to help me soon, and she did."

"How much help can she be until her leg heals up? I guess I'm just wondering what your plan is?"

"Once she's healthy, which should be just a few weeks, she can take on the job full-time. She'll be a combination Girl Friday, personal assistant and Jack of All Trades. And before you ask, she's living in one of the tiny houses on the far edge of the property next to Telly."

"Where was she living before?" Abby asked.

Mona didn't say anything, and just stared into her wine glass.

Abby immediately understood Mona's reluctance to say.

"She was homeless, wasn't she?" Abby guessed.

"Yes, poor thing. She hitchhiked all the way from Duluth, and this was as far as she got, although I am not quite sure why she would come north. Anyway, she thought she could stay a few nights at the Inn and figure out what to do next. She had the money for a room."

"What's her story?" Abby asked, genuinely interested and concerned.

"It's simple," Mona explained. "And something you yourself can understand. Like you used to be, she's a lost waif who needs help and I'm in a position to help her. I need the extra pair of hands and she needs work and a place to stay."

"When did you get tiny houses?" Abby asked, not remembering seeing them before. "Are you talking about the metal container looking things behind the big hedgerow?"

"I am indeed. Those also came to me in a roundabout, serendipitous way a few weeks after the Inn opened," Mona explained, as if it was the most natural thing in the world to just stumble upon two tiny houses unexpectedly. "The person who built them was a nice man from Minneapolis on his way to the Canadian border to deliver them to their new owner. He'd been to the Inn before and really liked it, so he stopped here for the night. But that night he learned that the buyer had died. Without paying anything beyond a small deposit, I might add. To make matters worse, his widow refused to take possession. I took a look inside, and they were fully furnished and just charming. You never know when you might need a tiny house, so I bought them on the spot. The tiny house man stayed a few more days, you know, to consult about how to get them livable, and we found a contractor who hooked up all the utilities and water, and voila."

"You are a marvel," Abby conceded. "So is that where Telly lives?"

Mona nodded. "Now both houses are fully occupied, which is how it should be. The energy that comes off an empty abode is not good, and there is an aura of neglect and sadness that goes away only when someone moves in."

Mona stood up, the conversation apparently over. As she grabbed her purse she brought out a signed blank check and handed it to Abby. "Would you please order Billie a supply of blank cards and envelopes? Standard sizes are good, but make sure they're made from good watercolor paper. She'll also need those plastic sleeves to cover them in. Maybe get a set of colored pencils and graphite pencils, too. Erasers. Whatever she needs to get started on her cards. She already has a full set of watercolors and brushes. You can have them delivered to me at the Inn. Toodleoo."

And then she was gone, as if she was a guardian angel who had dropped down from the sky to do some good in the world before returning to heaven.

After Mona's visit, Abby sat on the couch going over their conversation. Mona was doing for Billie what Abby's benefactor had done for her. Mona was lifting Billie up from a bad situation and setting her up for success. She had given her the promise of a future and reassurance that everything would be alright.

Something Mona had said was particularly striking. In describing Billie, Mona said, *Like you, she's a lost waif who needs help and I'm in a position to help her.* Had Mona let slip that she was Abby's benefactor? It certainly seemed that way. Unless someone in Wander Creek was a secret millionaire-next-door type the only other explanation was that it was Mona. And Abby wasn't quite sure how she felt about that.

～

FEBRUARY WAS ANOTHER SUCCESSFUL MONTH. While Abby's clientele were mostly women, many of them came in asking for gifts for the special men in their lives. Just in time for Valentine's Day she purchased notepads, notebooks and stationery embellished with classy and attractive hunting and fishing motifs, as well as Valentine's Day and birthday cards appropriate for a man. She found handsome leather travel journals which could be used to record hunting and fishing triumphs. She even found password keepers with masculine covers, and beautiful stone paperweights carved into the shape of fish. Adventure sports enthusiasts, tourists looking for the quaint cozy town experience, and of course a steady stream of guests from the Wander Inn flocked to the Paper Box, all enamored with her new stock. After only a few days she had to re-order her masculine-themed stock and pay to rush delivery. The idea that she was responsible for the success of the Paper Box thrilled Abby. She couldn't remember the last time she had been good at anything—besides volunteering, shopping, and living an indulgent lifestyle. *I was sure good at that. That's kind of sad.*

She and Ken saw each other a few times, very casually and impromptu, but Abby continued to enjoy his company and agreed to go with him for dinner at the Bistro on Valentine's Day. He met her at the restaurant, sharply dressed in khakis, a pressed light blue dress shirt and a navy blazer. After the hostess seated them he produced a single red rose and a box of chocolates he had obviously gone to Duluth to get. They were the coconut creams she had gushed over during their date to Duluth in what seemed like eons before.

After four months in Wander Creek Abby was no closer to making a decision about her future. On some days she felt as if she had lived in this community for years. She had friends in Jessica, Mona and Sam, experienced friendly exchanges with the other merchants, and felt the camaraderie and simplicity of small town living. And then there was Ken. On other days, the pull of the city was strong, and she longed for fancy restaurants, the theatre, museums and luxury vacations.

Of course, she had agreed to stay for a year, so whatever she decided couldn't be executed for another eight months. But somehow it seemed important to settle things in her mind right now once and for all. The trouble was that the answer that had been so clear to her a few months earlier was losing its clarity. And once again, she didn't trust her gut. It had failed her so atrociously with Jake. And now all it had to offer was indecision.

AT THE END OF FEBRUARY, following the flurry of Valentine's Day shoppers, Abby finally did what Carmen had suggested and created a sales table. She had a variety of holiday items left over, from Christmas napkins and coasters to Valentine's Day cards and heart-shaped notebooks. Just as she and Sam were putting the finishing touches on the display both of their cell phones buzzed at the same time.

"That's interesting," Abby remarked. "First time that's happened." They thumbed their phones awake.

"Hot dog!" Sam exclaimed. "Looks like we're going to see how we did on the shoplifting exercise."

That evening, Sam and Abby walked briskly to the community center, and into the main meeting room, stunned at what they saw. The conference table was full of what Abby supposed were purloined items from their shops. Jessica, Emily, Dennis and a few other merchants were already seated around the table, looking like schoolchildren outside the principal's office.

Police Chief Carter, looking very pleased with himself, presided over the scene from the head of the table. "As you can see, the recruits hit a few of our stores. Not all, just the ones all of you own. I'd like to introduce one of the recruits who participated in the exercise. Cadet Barnes, would you like to take over?"

A handsome young man in his twenties, dressed in the black uniform of a police officer, stepped forward. "As you can see," he said, gesturing at the table, "our mystery shoplifters got away with a lot."

"I just can't believe it," Emily of Second to None complained. "I recognize tons of stuff from my store. The red high heels for one, plus those jeans and all those earrings."

Abby, too, recognized things from her shop, though not many. Someone had only gotten away with stealing two greetings cards and a stack of coasters. She was quite pleased with herself and Sam, and the two exchanged knowing glances and smiles.

Cadet Barnes was addressing Emily's comments. "You have a lot of small things in your shop," he remarked. "I was the one who took your items. And you have so much inventory on your floor that it's easy to stuff something under a coat or slip into a pocket. Plus, you only have one employee working at a time." He looked around. "Where is the owner of the Paper Box?" he asked.

Abby raised her hand tentatively, feeling as if she had been singled out by the school principal. "My fellow cadet hit your store noticed that two people working most of the time, which cuts down on opportunity for thieves. They're much more comfortable in stores where only one person is working at a time."

Cadet Barnes went through the rest of the items, dolling out praise, reprimands, and suggestions to the rest of the group. When he came to the industrial size bags and cans of food, Abby realized that she hadn't seen Naomi until Dennis Grey shifted and revealed that Naomi was sitting at the front of the table.

"I have to say," Barnes said, somewhat amused, "the most interesting items we took came from the Beanery's kitchen. Our mystery shoplifter noticed that the restaurant door on the alley was open, so she just drove up, walked into the kitchen from the alley and made three trips to and from her car before she heard someone coming."

"That's impossible," Naomi said haughtily. "I keep an eagle eye on my inventory."

Sam squeezed Abby's hand, barely able to contain her delight at Naomi's misfortune.

Oh boy, Abby thought, *I've created a monster.* But she ducked her head and allowed herself a small smile of satisfaction.

CHAPTER 20

As the calendar turned from February to March, Abby decided that there were two Springs in the world. There was Spring, then there was Minnesota Spring. Although a lot of the snow had melted, the wind was still wicked. But she resumed her morning walks and swore she saw a few blades of bright green grass as she passed the gazebo on the walking path that ran along the creek.

In the shop, it was time to decorate and stock for Easter. She closed the store one Sunday and she and Sam spent the afternoon in Duluth shopping for decorations. They stopped at a craft and fabric store first where they bought silk flowers and an over-sized fuzzy bunny rabbit as tall as Sam, which they had to wrangle into the back of Abby's car. At the dollar store they stocked up on baskets, Easter grass of all colors, and plastic eggs in bright pastels. They also purchased Easter-themed pencils and stickers, erasers in the shape of rabbits and carrots, and mini fuzzy chicks in all different colors. Abby would combine these with some Easter notebooks she had in the store and make cellophane goody bags that would be a great addition to any Easter basket.

Abby treated them to lunch at a very nice restaurant that resembled something she might go to in Minneapolis.

"These prices are crazy," Sam whispered after they had been seated and provided with menus. "Twenty-five dollars for a hamburger? I could buy five dinners for that at McDonalds."

Abby studied her young assistant and realized Sam was doing what she had spent an entire year doing: calculating what things she needed cost and agonizing over whether to spend the money or just go without.

"That's true," Abby agreed. "But you won't have this amazing view of Lake Superior at McDonald's." She gestured out the window to the immense lake in front of them. "And at McDonald's you wouldn't have the ambiance that you have here, the low lights, the soft music, the pretty décor. Sometimes it's worth the splurge. And this is one of those times."

Sam raised her glass of soda. "To splurges," she said.

Abby clinked her coffee cup to Sam's glass. "And to good friends."

Back at the store Abby was grateful that Sam agreed to stay late to complete the window. They kept the fairy lights where they were, strung in loops from the ceiling, and added strands of paper bunnies, strung together like a parade of paper dolls. After hauling out the writing desk and chair, they unrolled a remnant of artificial turf so it looked like a patch of green spring grass. Then Abby delightedly produced a vintage bicycle she had painted a soft pale yellow and placed it in the center of the window as the display's centerpiece. She had found it at a garage sale and painted it one evening in the back alley, then stored it in the storeroom. She was pleased Sam never discovered it behind some boxes where she had hidden it. She wanted it to be a surprise.

Sam clapped her hands and bounced up and down. "I love it! Here, let me help you with the basket." Sam filled the basket on the front of the bike with the Easter grass and silk daffodils.

Together they positioned the bunny on the seat, tying his feet to the pedals with the clear fishing line. To keep the stuffed toy upright, Abby sewed fishing line into the top of his head with just a few stitches, then standing on a ladder pulled the line up to the ceiling and tied it to a small ceiling hook she had placed there for that purpose. Abby had decked the handsome bunny out with spectacles, a decorated Easter hat she adjusted to fit over its ears, and hot glued an artificial carrot to one of his hands. In one corner of the window she placed a tall Easter tree of painted white twigs and she and Sam hung plastic eggs and the paper decorations Abby had ordered from one of her vendors. In the other corner Abby draped pink, yellow and white striped upholstery fabric over the stack of old apple crates and artistically arranged huge vases of artificial daffodils, tulips and lilies. She grouped the dollar store baskets throughout the display, stuffing them with the Easter grass and plastic eggs.

In a recent text exchange with Carmen she got the idea to put a tall, long table behind the display. For starters, it would keep curious children from crawling into the window display seeking any goodies that might have caught their fancy. In addition, many of the things she put in the window were also for sale and would be displayed on the table. To the table she added Easter cocktail napkins, notebooks and pocket-size copies of Beatrix Potter's book, *Peter Cottontail*.

"I think we're done," Abby said with satisfaction as she and Sam put out the last items on the table. "Nice work. Thanks for staying late, Sam."

"Are you kidding?" the young woman asked. Today Sam had dyed her hair in spring pastel colors so that it almost looked like a plaid design. Somehow, all these crazy hair colors and styles suited Sam. "This is really a lot of fun and I love watching you tie everything together. What's your secret? None of the other shops in town have nearly as elaborate or creative windows."

Abby smiled wistfully. Where did she get the knack for her

window displays? Probably from years of shopping at fine boutiques and the top department stores on Madison Avenue in New York City. And of course she decorated her homes, and it seemed like she was always changing or updating something in the house. It was so big that by the time she finished one redecorating project she was ready for a renovation or different color scheme all together.

"Years of experience," she finally said. "Stick with me, kid, and you'll pick it up in no time."

Abby loved the idea of passing on her knowledge to Sam, the way Carmen had done with her. And she knew she was giving Sam a gift, just as Carmen had given her one.

THE NEXT EVENING as Abby was locking up the store a woman appeared at the door and flashed what looked like a press credential through the window.

"Ms. Barrett? I'm Hillary Fine from KTCO radio in Duluth. Can I talk to you for a minute?"

While Abby was taken off guard by the woman's appearance, it didn't really surprise her. Deep down she had just assumed someone would find her eventually.

"What do you want?" Abby asked through the door.

"Can I come in please?" the woman asked. "I promise I'll only take a few minutes. And if you don't like what I have to say I'll go away and won't bother you again."

Feeling like she didn't have much choice, Abby unlocked and opened the door. Hillary was a tall, willowy woman in her thirties.

Abby held her tongue while she stared expectantly at the woman. Hillary had sought her out. She could start the conversation.

"Thanks for letting me in," Hillary said, shifting her over-sized handbag to her other shoulder and unbuttoning her rain-coat. Abby looked from her face to her fingers moving over the buttons and then up at Hillary again, who instantly stopped.

"How did you find me?" Abby asked, crossing her arms across her chest. She felt chilled.

Hillary looked at her kindly. "I went to college with Nora Talbot and she mentioned your name recently when she was telling me about her recent decorating clients. I remembered that Barrett was Abby Trent's maiden name. I took a chance and drove up to verify that you were Jake Trent's wife. I promise you I am not here to do an expose or try and cast you in any negative light."

Abby sighed. "You might as well come back to the office and we can talk, but just for a minute."

Once they were settled, Hillary leaned in across Abby's desk. "I do a weekly podcast that follows-up on major news stories, sort of a 'where are they now?' approach. I want you to come on my show and tell your side of the story. To set the record straight. I've done a lot of research and I know without a doubt that you had nothing to do with your husband's crimes and didn't have any knowledge of them, for that matter."

For a minute, Abby basked in the glory of hearing another person tell her she was innocent. That hadn't happened much in the previous year. And although the FBI never filed any charges, Abby always felt that the agents she dealt with did not believe she was entirely innocent.

"You've never had a chance to tell your side of the story, am I right? My show goes across many networks and specifically into Minneapolis and environs. I'm guessing you would love to set the record straight there."

Abby considered this and nodded. She hadn't thought of the situation this way before. She was so used to being vilified that it never occurred to her that someone would be interested in her side of things. And maybe doing this interview would help clear the way for her return to Minneapolis. She could stop hiding out here in Wander Creek.

"What all would this entail?" Abby asked cautiously.

"It's very straightforward," Hillary explained. "I've got some light equipment that I have with me that's easy to set up."

"You mean we're going to do this now?" Abby said, her voice rising an octave.

"We could, but we don't have to. I want you to be comfortable with this. We could schedule something for next week and before then go over the questions so there will be no surprises. It will be a recorded interview as opposed to live so we can cut out anything that makes you uncomfortable."

"How do I know I can trust you?" Abby asked.

Hillary's expression grew serious. "I guess you really can't know," she said. "All I can do is give you my word. But I wouldn't have gone to the trouble of tracking you down if I just wanted to do another smear piece. I could do that anytime without you."

Abby considered this and realized Hillary was right.

That evening over glasses of wine at the Bistro, Mona gave her no holds barred response when Abby told her about the reporter's offer to help her set the record straight.

"After you've done this crazy thing and it blows up in your face, I will try very hard not to gloat when I tell you 'I told you so.'" Mona said emphatically. "This is not a good idea. And you shouldn't do it."

"I'm going to be revealed eventually anyway," Abby countered. "Now that I've been tracked down the truth will come out sooner or later and everyone will know who I am. I might as well take the opportunity to clear my name. It was you who told me when we first met that a name is a powerful thing. And I'm going to take back my name. And my power."

Just then, she spotted Pete White, the mail carrier, standing near the bar. He waved and she beckoned him over. He picked up his to-go order from the bartender and took the few steps over to their table.

"Hi Pete," Abby said. "How's it going? I'm guessing you're glad the busy holiday season is behind you."

"It can be a bit hectic," he agreed. "But I'm used to it. Glad to hear you're doing well at the Paper Box." He moved his to-go box from one hand to the other and turned to Mona. "Hi Mona," he said, as he waved his goodbye and departed.

"He's such a sweet man," Abby said when he was gone. "He always comes into the shop to hand me my mail, even if Sam's closer."

"He is," Mona agreed. "He's a fixture around here, too, and there's nothing he won't do to help. He does a lot of work for military families around the holidays, sending care packages and such overseas. He also organizes the Fourth of July parade. It runs like a well-oiled machine, let me tell you. The only time that he has not delivered the mail in the ten years I've been here was a two-week vacation he took about six months ago. But don't think for a minute you're going to distract me. I still need to talk you out of doing the radio interview."

Abby asked, "Why do you think it's such a bad idea?"

"Sweetie, I just have a terrible feeling in my gut about this. I can't explain it. I hope I'm wrong, but I don't think I am."

Despite Mona's fervent admonishments, Abby agreed to the interview with Hillary and drove to the studio in Duluth the following week for the recording session. Although she was nervous, she had come to like the idea of telling her side of the story. Hillary had emailed a list of questions she would ask and they even roll played a few questions on the phone. True to her word, Hillary asked softball questions and steered the conversation so that Abby could tell her story. Abby had rehearsed her answers to the point where she could recite them by memory.

She parked in a visitor spot outside the radio station and entered confidently, telling the receptionist who she was.

"Oh, they're expecting you," the young woman said, smiling. "Go on in." She motioned behind her. "It's the second door on the left."

Abby did as instructed and tapped lightly on the door. The man inside, wearing earphones and a scowl, motioned her inside. The room was a small studio with two chairs opposite each other and an elaborate microphone set-up between them. Abby looked to the right through a glass window where another man sat at what looked like a sound board, speaking into the microphone and gesturing wildly.

Abby turned back to the scowling man. "Where's Hillary?" she asked.

"She's out sick today," the man said. "She sends her apologies and asked me to do the interview." He smiled then, and Abby felt better.

"Go ahead and take a seat." He gestured toward the empty chair and she sat, but kept her purse in her lap, as if it were a safety blanket.

All of a sudden, she had a very bad feeling about this.

The man raised his hand in the air, pointed at the man in the other booth, then said in a very officious and deep radio voice, "We're live here in the studio with Abby Barrett Trent, wife of the Ponzi scheme king Jake Trent, who stole hundreds of millions of dollars from his clients and is now serving a fifty-year term in federal prison." The man turned his eyes on Abby, and she saw the anger flash in them. "Mrs. Trent, how does it feel to know that you spent millions of dollars on your exorbitant lifestyle while your husband's clients lost everything, including their houses, life savings, and many even having to declare bankruptcy?"

This was definitely not the kind of interview Hillary had promised. Mona's warnings came back in a rush. *Why didn't I listen to Mona?*

"That's not how it happened," Abby said, trying to recover from this sneak attack. "You've totally misrepresented me."

"Oh, is that, so?" the man snarled, his face growing red and sweaty. He poked his finger at her. "Isn't it true that while your husband's swindled clients have nothing, you have a very successful stationery store and own property on Main Street in the tourist town of Wander Creek? Isn't it true that while your husband's clients suffer extreme financial loss and heartache, you hired a decorator for your store and your luxury apartment?"

Abby had to get out of that room. She rose quickly and made a bee-line for the door as the interviewer was saying, "And there she goes folks. Abby Barrett Trent is refusing to answer this reporter's questions and is on her way out the door. I can't think of a bigger admission of guilt than running away. Now let's take some calls."

Hugging her purse to her chest Abby ran out of the station. It took her a minute to find her car keys and unlock the car, her hands were shaking so badly. At last she was in the safety of the SUV. She frantically locked the doors, as if the interviewer might come after her with his microphone, started her vehicle, and peeled out of the parking lot. Hot tears stung her eyes. She was not naïve enough to think that no one in Wander Creek heard the interview. Only one person had to hear it and her shame would be all over town. Instead of driving north to Two Harbors and up to Wander Creek, she hopped on the Interstate heading south. At the exit for the Lake Superior Zoo, she veered off and pulled into the parking lot, taking a spot as far away from the entrance as possible. She needed to sit a while and plan what to do next. Her cell phone on the passenger seat rang and Abby hesitated, but decided to answer.

"What the heck, Hillary?" she barked. "You said I could trust you. You promised this wasn't going to be a smear campaign!"

"Abby, I'm so sorry. You have no idea. When I told my producer you were coming in he sent me out on another assignment and said he would do your interview. I protested, of course, but he said he would fire me on the spot if I didn't go. I tried to call and text you over and over again to tell you not to go, but I couldn't get a signal. I am so sorry. What can I do to make this right?"

"Make this right?" Abby asked, incredulously. "You tell me, Hillary. What do you think you, or anyone else can do to make this right? Because if you have an idea I'd like to know." After a few beats of silence Abby continued. "I didn't think so," and ended the call. Hillary called back but Abby ignored it. Then her phone started to blow up. First Mona, then Ken, and then a bunch of numbers she didn't recognize.

Then a text came in from Mona. *It's all over the television and internet, too. Come to the Inn. It's only a matter of time until the Minneapolis stations send news crews up.* This time, Mona skipped the pleasantries and old-fashioned etiquette typical of her texts. This was bad. Really bad.

CHAPTER 21

*A*bby texted back thanking Mona for the invitation, then declined it. The only thing she wanted at that moment was the safety and comfort of her own apartment. She turned off her phone and made the hour trip back to Wander Creek with only the noise of her tires on the road and the wind whooshing by to keep her company. She parked on Hickory Street two blocks away from the Paper Box and was grateful she didn't see anyone as she ran down the alley and let herself in the back door. By that time, it was after six and Sam had already locked everything up and gone home. After checking to make sure that the doors were locked, the shades drawn, and the alarm system set, Abby ran upstairs. Breathless and distraught, she sank onto the couch. She had made it home. She was safe from the outside world for now. Despite her better judgement she turned her phone back on and heard the pings as a dozen voicemails came in all at once. She deleted all of them without listening to a single one. Then she tapped over to the browser and Googled herself. Sure enough, the radio station had put the story on its website. She scrolled to the Minneapolis television stations and watched a brief news cast about herself, which gave a detailed account of her location.

And although the words spoken and written about her were untrue and unkind, in the midst of it all, she realized to her surprise that the only thing she felt was relief. The big hairy monster of shame and embarrassment that followed her to Wander Creek from Minneapolis was of her own making. If she didn't allow what other people thought to impact her, she would be free from all of the judgement and hatred. And isn't that what she wanted all along? To be free? It had just taken her a year-and-a-half to realize that the freedom she craved was inside her all along. She just had to let it out. And she'd have to face her friends and neighbors in Wander Creek.

THE NEXT MORNING, Abby went down to the store bright and early and chose a medley of upbeat eighties songs to play on the sound system. As she straightened the shelves and restocked, she hummed along to the music at first, then burst into song, belting out the lyrics of a favorite track from her youth.

At nine-thirty, Sam rushed in the back door and quickly locked it behind her, as if a strong wind had blown her inside.

"What?" Abby asked, concerned. "Are you okay?"

"There's a film crew outside filming you through the display window," Sam announced, and the two women turned to look. "Should I call Chief Carter?"

"Don't worry about it," Abby said. "I've decided not to let it bother me. But I do need to explain a few things to you. Let's go into the office."

The women sat in their customary places—Abby at the desk and Sam in the chair across from her. Taking a deep breath, Abby launched into her story, trying to make it as brief as possible.

When she was done Sam just stared at her for a few beats, and then said, "Oh, that. Lots of us know all about that. Except Naomi. She's so wrapped up in her stupid idea that you're a Mafia wife on the run that she didn't see this coming."

"You knew?" Abby asked, stunned, thinking back to all the people she'd met and all the friends she'd made, wondering how many of them had known from the beginning who she was. "Other people knew? Did Ken know?"

"That I don't know," Sam said. "He's too much of a gentleman to gossip. If he did know, he kept it to himself."

"But why didn't you say anything to me?" Abby asked, genuinely confused. Her so-called friends in Minneapolis had not wasted any opportunity to throw it all in her face and were relentless in their endless judgement and reprimands.

"I figured if you wanted us to know you'd tell us," Sam said. "It's not like any of us were going to ask you for financial advice or anything like that." Sam grinned and Abby responded with a groan.

"Everyone has their secrets and they usually deserve to keep them," Sam continued, and Abby appreciated the young woman's attempt to make her feel better.

"Oh, yeah?" Abby asked playfully. "So what's your secret?"

To Abby's great surprise, Sam immediately burst into tears.

"What's the matter?" Abby asked. "Are you okay? Did something happen to you? Your family? Is it Naomi?"

Sam shook her head miserably. "I can't bear it," she said, and wiped her nose on her pretty pink sweater, making Abby cringe. "It's just so terrible."

Abby reached into her desk drawer and pulled out a box of tissues. "Here, this will help. Now just take a breath and tell me what's up. Are you hurt? Did someone hurt you? Is it school? It can't be so bad that we can't work it out together."

"No, it's just the opposite," Sam said, drying her eyes with a balled-up tissue. "I'm the one at fault. I did something really bad and I'm afraid if I tell the person they won't forgive me and I'll have to go back and work for Naomi at the Beanery and wear that stupid Burger King uniform."

"But why would you have to leave your job here?" Abby asked, suddenly realizing what Sam was saying, without actually having said it. "Oh. I'm the one you hurt. I'm the person you think won't forgive you."

Sam nodded miserably and Abby studied her. How many times had she sat in the back office with Carmen, long after they had closed the Paperie, and cried about Jake, her miserable apartment, her utter loss as to how she could possibly lift herself out of her circumstances? But she had never hurt Carmen. Never done anything that would break the trust between them.

"Whatever it is Sam, just tell me, straight out. Once it's all on the table we can figure it out."

Sam took a deep breath and closed her eyes. "I'm the one who cut up the box of greeting cards during the grand opening party."

Abby gasped. Whatever she thought Sam was going to say, this certainly wasn't it.

"But why would you do something like that?" she asked. "I don't understand."

"It was Naomi," Sam explained quietly. "She offered to give me a thousand dollars if I vandalized some of your stock. And I needed the money. The school raised tuition again. I was supposed to wreck a whole bunch of stuff over the course of a few weeks, but I felt so sick after the first time that I gave the money back and told her I wouldn't be involved in her stupid vendetta against you. Are you going to fire me? Never mind. Of course you're going to fire me. I deserve it. And I will pay you back for the stock I ruined even if it means I have to leave school for a semester."

Abby stared at her trusted employee, the lovely young woman who had been with her since she opened the Paper Box. She wished she could text Carmen right then and ask her what to do. They had never covered personnel issues during her crash course in starting a business. Never mind. She'd trust her gut. After all these months her intuition was finally getting stronger and she felt she could listen to what it was telling her. She leaned back in the chair and let out a breath. Sam was looking at her expectantly under her light pink bangs. It also appeared as if she was shivering a little, too. The poor girl was suffering. The person Abby should really be mad at was Naomi, who put Sam up to it in the first place. Abby had seen Naomi's nastiness firsthand. Being anywhere near her was like waiting for the other shoe to drop. Or rather, to bang down on your head.

"You aren't saying anything," Sam said. "Why aren't you saying anything? Should I just leave now? I should leave. I'll leave."

"No one is going anywhere or dropping out of school," Abby said, flashing Sam a wan smile. "I like you Sam, you know that, very much, and you're an important part of this business. What you did was terrible, yes. But I understand why you did it and I know what a bully Naomi can be. I'm just sorry you didn't come to me first about the tuition money. We could have worked something out."

Abby remembered the day she broke an expensive porcelain desk set at the Paperie. It was a beautiful blue and white trellis pattern desk blotter, lamp, letter opener, pencil holder and a little stamp dispenser. That evening as she was straightening the store she tripped and crashed right into the display so hard everything went flying and broke into so many pieces that the set was ruined. The retail price was three hundred dollars. The wholesale price was probably half that amount. But still. A hundred and fifty dollars was a month's worth of groceries. In her previous life it was what she tipped the cute valet who retrieved her car after the Christmas party at the country club. She had picked up the pieces and put them all in a paper bag, cleaned up the display table and spent a miserable night stewing about it and worrying what Carmen would do. When she arrived at work the next morning she recounted the story and put the paper bag on Carmen's desk. Carmen peeked inside.

"Yep. It's a goner. Just trash it and put out another one." Then she reached into the bag and brought out the gold letter opener with the blue and white porcelain handle. "Aha!" she exclaimed, as if she had just found a treasure. "This is still pristine." She handed it to Abby who took it, puzzled.

"I understand if you need to take the money out of my paycheck," Abby said, using the words she had rehearsed the night before. She had only worked at the Paperie for a few weeks. "But if you could spread it out over a month or two that would really help me. I need . . ."

Carmen put up her hand, then flicked her wrist as if to wave the whole thing away. "Cost of doing business," she said. "Stuff like this happens. It was an accident. Besides, you got yourself a new letter opener out of the deal."

Abby had forgotten she was still holding the sole survivor of the accident. She looked at it, then back up to Carmen.

"A little reminder," Carmen explained, "that when something breaks, there's usually some small part that is salvageable."

Abby knew Sam was looking at her expectantly. She glanced at the large glass jar of pens on her desk, her eyes resting on the blue and white handle of the letter opener. She made her decision.

"I know this was a one-time thing and that you would never do it again," Abby said. "I'm not going to fire you and I'm not going to garnish your wages."

"What are you going to do?" Sam asked, sniffling.

"I'm going to give you a second chance," Abby said, smiling. "And a raise to help you with your tuition."

"Oh, thank you! I'll make it up to you. I swear!" Sam assured her. "But what about Naomi?" Sam asked, tentatively. "What are you going to do about her?"

"Naomi is a bully, there's no doubt about that," Abby said.

"But I'm sure she's also really insecure, though I have no idea why. She's a successful businesswoman, and reasonably attractive. If she wasn't so mean, she could actually be a good person. She craves attention. She wants me to react to what she had you do to the stock. But If I just ignore her, she's lost her power."

"I can see that," Sam said hesitantly. "I just hope she doesn't try anything else."

Abby shrugged. "If she does, she does. I'm going to stop being afraid of her." To herself she thought, *I'm going to stop being afraid —period.*

CURIOUS AS TO why she hadn't heard from Ken lately, Abby snatched up the phone as soon as his number appeared in the caller ID two days after the news story broke. She said a tentative, "Hi," and was so relieved to hear his cheerful reply.

"Hi babe, sorry I've been out of touch. I was up in the Boundary Waters with the tour group I told you about and the signal was worse than usual. I've never seen it so bad. None of us could use our phones. I'm guessing a cell tower was offline or something. I'm just grateful we didn't have an emergency."

Abby didn't know what to say. Should she pretend as if nothing happened? Should she take the bull by the horns and jump into an explanation. As it turned out, she didn't have to decide.

"I heard what happened while I was gone," Ken said gently. "Are you okay?"

"Did you know all this time?" Abby whispered.

"I did," Ken said, "but it didn't bother me. Still doesn't. You are you. You're not your ex-husbands mistakes. And getting to know you all of these months, well, you've proven that over and over again. Besides, I would never fall for a fallen woman," he joked, and they both laughed. "Listen," he continued, "Can I come over tonight so we can talk?" he asked.

"I'd like that," Abby replied. And she meant it. To be so accepted for herself rather than berated for something she had nothing to do with was an invigorating feeling.

She let Ken into the shop at six o'clock and he gave her a reassuring hug and passionate kiss, as if he was proving to her that he didn't think less of her. Hand in hand they went upstairs to the apartment and sat on the couch. Ken still held firmly to her hand.

"I should apologize to you for not letting you talk more about what happened with Misty," she said. "I was jealous and hurt but I didn't want you to know that. I was afraid to make myself vulnerable."

"Do you believe me?" he asked. "As soon as you and I started dating I decided I wasn't going to see her anymore. Like I said, I just hadn't gotten around to telling her. I guess I was avoiding it," he admitted. "Do you forgive me?"

"If you can forgive me from keeping my big secret from you," Abby said, squeezing his hand.

"There's nothing to forgive," he said, and squeezed back. "Are you going to be okay?"

"I'm embarrassed, of course," she answered, "and surprised that so many people already knew. And I guess shocked that no one confronted me or treated me like an outcast. I never would have known that people in Wander Creek knew all along."

"That's a small town for you," Ken explained. "People band together and look out for one another. You're one of us, now," he said. "Especially since you've been out on the ice and survived. That impressed a lot of people."

Abby laughed. "Is that all it took? If I had known that I would have gone out as soon as the lakes froze over in December."

"Can we talk about exclusivity?" Ken asked, turning serious. "We've not gone there, yet, but I want to. I only want to date you and see where this takes us. I'm crazy about you, and I think you feel the same way, but I sense a hesitation that I'm hoping isn't related to how you feel about me."

"That's very perceptive," Abby said, shifting uncomfortably on the couch. "I'm crazy about you, too. But you're right, the whole time I've been here I've been torn between whether to stay or try to salvage part of my old life in Minneapolis. But I have to tell you, knowing that the people of Wander Creek knew the truth about me and welcomed me so generously anyway—well, that's pretty amazing. This place has helped me heal and to get to know myself again. For the first time in a long time, I like what I see when I look in the mirror."

Ken took her face in his hands. "Me, too," he said, as he kissed her again.

CHAPTER 22

*T*he next day when Pete brought in the mail he asked Abby if he could speak to her after closing time, and Abby readily agreed, assuming he wanted to ask her to help with some civic activity or something similar. And maybe that wouldn't be such a bad idea. Maybe Pete was offering her an olive branch from the town.

Pete showed up precisely at six and after locking the door Abby led them back to the office. Pete was still in his postal uniform and he seemed very nervous, looking everywhere but at her.

"I don't know how to do this, or how to handle it," he said, looking at his hands resting in his lap. "So I'm just going to come out and say it. I'm your benefactor. I'm the one who set all of this up for you."

Abby was dumbfounded and she was certain her mouth was hanging open in surprise. She heard the words Pete was speaking but they didn't quite register. Pete was her benefactor. Quiet Pete who lived in a modest cottage on the outskirts of town? Unassuming Pete who lived on a mailman's salary?

"You?" she asked, sputtering.

"I hope you're not disappointed," Pete said, finally making eye contact with her.

"No, it's not that. Of course it's not that. It's just, I expected my benefactor to be, well, rich. It's just that, I never considered you . . ." She was struggling with how to tell Pete she could hardly believe he had the means to be her benefactor.

Finally, Abby decided to take a different tac, and to just say thank you. "Oh, Pete. I don't know what to say. But why? I don't understand. This was just so generous of you. It's so much money."

"Generosity comes from the heart, not just the checkbook," he said. "And there's more. This is going to shock you, but there's no other way than to just tell you."

"You're scaring me," Abby said.

"I knew your mother almost forty years ago," he said. "She came through Wander Creek one summer and we fell in love. But of course, it didn't last. It turned out to be just a summer fling. We were so young. So carefree. It wasn't long after she went back home that she married your father. She called and told me she was pregnant and I was the baby's father. She made me promise that I would never tell our secret to anyone, especially not to you. She felt the best thing was for you to have parents who were actually married, and a loving solid home. So I kept that promise for almost forty years. I kept it even after the man you knew as your father died, and after your mother died."

"So you're saying that my father isn't my father. Not my true father?" Abby asked. "You're telling me that you are my biological father?"

Pete nodded. "I'm sorry to shock you in this way."

"I don't know what to say, or even how to feel about this," Abby said, resting her head in her hands, feeling drained and confused. Suddenly everything she knew to be true about her life was up-ended.

"I've kept up with you since you were born," Pete said. "I've been to all of your graduations." He ticked them off on his fingers. "High school, college, the first master's degree, the second master's degree. I would just sit in the back. No one noticed. And no one knew I was there, especially not your parents. In fact, besides me and Jerome Monroe, you are the only person who knows I am your true father."

Pete continued with his revelation. "You were in the news a lot after you married Jake. I had to subscribe to the Minneapolis magazines and news sites so I could keep up with your charity work. The Children's Hospital annual fundraiser auction and the Golden Ridge Humane Society fundraising pet walk. And of course, your photo was all over the society pages. You did a lot of good work. I know you have beat yourself up over and over again about your husband and everything that he did. I saw you at the trial. I know how devastated you were. When everyone else was watching the lawyers and the jury and the witnesses, I was watching you. I saw you cringe. I saw you shake your head and wipe away tears."

"You were at the trial?" Abby hiccuped, now crying.

"Every day," he said. "I had to take two weeks of vacation to be there. But I wouldn't have missed it. You needed me, even if you didn't know I was there. Well. All I could do was be there."

Abby cocked her head and sat very still. "I always kept an eye on who attended the trial," she remembered. "I think it was my way of trying to determine who was against Jake and who was for him. I guess for and against me for that matter. But in the end it didn't matter. Everyone either ignored me or gave me hateful glances. I can't believe I didn't recognize you after all these months. I mean, I see you practically every day."

"I'm glad you didn't. That was never my intent. I didn't plan to reveal myself. Ever."

"So why now?" Abby asked. "Why come forward now?"

"I suppose it was inevitable that as soon as you stepped into my life, my own flesh and blood, that I would want to know you. I guess I thought I would be strong enough to just be close to you, to make sure you were okay, without revealing myself. But, obviously, I wasn't that strong. Nobody could be that strong. You look so much like my mother, your grandmother. Sometime, if you want to, I can show you some pictures. But please know that I don't have any expectations."

"But why this dramatic ruse?" Abby asked.

Pete shrugged. "You needed me. And this was the only way I could think of to help you and get to know you, without breaking my promise to your mother. I had a brother, your Uncle Nathan. He died twenty years ago and left me an inheritance that I wasn't expecting. I let the money sit in my account until I finally decided what to do with it. I decided to give it to you, for a fresh start."

"But that's so much money just to give away like that." Abby hiccuped again. "Couldn't it have made your life easier or helped you in some way?"

Pete held up a hand. "Now don't you worry about me. That was extra money. Unexpected money. I had no idea that my brother even had that kind of money. It was a shock, let me tell you. I still have my job and my salary and when I retire I will have a nice pension and Social Security. I like my life here in Wander Creek. I have everything I need. I didn't need that money. But you did."

"How did you come up with the idea of giving me the building and opening a shop?"

"After the trial, I asked Jerome's firm to keep an eye on you and report back. There wasn't much that they could tell me, and I didn't know anything about your interests besides you going to the library every few days and working in a stationery store. Jerome reported that you seemed to enjoy your work and that you and the store manager seemed close. I don't have much imagination, I guess. So I decided to give you what you already had and enjoyed, I suppose."

"And why are you telling me all this now? I still don't understand," Abby said.

"Things have taken a turn for the worse for you now that your secret is out," Pete said. "I understand that, though believe me, people here don't hold anything against you. People here love you—they really do. And you've brought another successful business to Wander Creek, and that helps everyone. But I know you probably feel differently now about everything. I'm here to tell you that you can leave anytime you want. You don't have to stay for the entire year, and you can keep the building, sell it if you want. Start over someplace else if that's what you need to do. I don't want you to leave, of course. But if you want to, I won't hold you back."

AFTER PETE LEFT, with promises that he wouldn't tell anyone about their connection, Abby washed her face in the small bathroom off her office and stared at herself in the mirror for a long time. She always thought that she looked like her father, Frank Barrett. They had the same startling blue eyes and when they went to the Twins baseball games, they always sat the same way, right leg crossed over the left and hands clasped in their laps. Knowing what she knew now she supposed that was just a learned gesture, not an inherited trait. Had her father known that she was not his biological child? If he had, he never showed it. He was a man of few words and often distant, but she had no doubt that Frank Barrett loved her dearly. She took great comfort in that. So what did this new information change? Would knowing that Frank was not her father change her somehow? And how about the fact that her mother had taken her secret to her grave? Had Betty Barrett ever considered telling her? Abby thought back to the weekly visits she made to her mother after her father died and she was married to Jake. As she got older, had her mother ever considered telling Abby the truth? Abby would never know.

CHAPTER 23

That evening Abby called Sam and asked her to open and close the store the next day. Abby wasn't sure where she was going, but she knew she had to get out of Wander Creek to clear her head. All of a sudden Wander Creek was suffocating her. Next, she texted Ken and told him she'd been called out of town unexpectedly and she didn't know when she's be back. She couldn't tell him about Pete—not yet anyway. Ken didn't know the truth about how she found herself in Wander Creek either. That would be a discussion for another time. Or not.

She left Wander Creek the next day before dawn. Despite spring's efforts, snow was still piled up high on either side of the roadway, and the trees were dusted by an overnight flurry as if someone had scattered powdered sugar on them. Even though she had not planned her destination, she knew subconsciously where she was going. She drove through the quiet streets of Two Harbors, then southwest along the bluffs overlooking a Lake Superior, through Duluth, and then south on the Interstate.

As she approached Minneapolis, she took the familiar exit for the University of Minnesota and then drove the few blocks to the neighborhood of her childhood. It was almost ten when she pulled up and stopped in front of the buttery yellow stucco house where she had grown up. It was a modest house, with an interesting and pleasing roofline and cement steps painted a light grey leading up to a dark red front door. The small lawn and low scrub bushes were covered with snow, and Abby remembered the many times she and her mother had made snowmen and snow angels in that yard.

Someone had kept the house in great shape, and not much about it had changed in the five years since Abby had last been there. How was that possible? So much else had changed in her life. It was somehow reassuring that something had remained the same. Maybe if she could just see the inside, just one more time, it would help her come to terms with her mother's deception.

She turned off the engine and got out of the car. Looking up at the house she thought she saw a curtain flutter in the large picture window, like someone had been watching her from inside.

Abby walked up to the front porch, an eerie sense of Deja vu accompanying her every step. She knocked on the red door.

"Yes?" a faint voice answered from inside.

"Hi," Abby said loudly. "I grew up in this house and I was wondering if I could come inside and look around, just for a few minutes."

"Who did you say you were?" the voice asked.

Abby hadn't said, not wanting to admit who she was, but then the door opened slightly, and a white-haired head peaked through the crack.

"Hello," Abby said. "I grew up in this house and I just wondered if I could take a look around. I'm feeling sort of nostalgic. It's amazing, but the outside looks just like I remember it."

"That's right," the woman said. "I bought it after Mrs. Barrett died. She kept it real nice, and I love the red door."

The old lady opened the door a little wider and beckoned for Abby to come inside. Abby was immediately greeted by the rush of warm air that enveloped her as soon as she stepped into the foyer.

"Thank you," Abby said. "I really appreciate this."

"Not a problem," the woman said. She was short and compact and wore a faded floral dress and a pink cardigan sweater, lumpy and out of shape. "I don't get many visitors. I'm seventy-five years old and don't get out much these days. Go ahead and look around. I'll be in the living room."

Abby walked slowly through the first-floor rooms, then headed upstairs. There were two bedrooms and one full bath. She peeked inside what used to be her small bedroom. It was now a sewing room with a machine and large table filled with bolts of fabrics and a large thread spool holder. Now that she was standing in the place where she had grown up, she wondered what she had expected to feel. What was this visit supposed to accomplish for her? Was she looking for clarity or insight into what she should do with the rest of her life?

She went back downstairs to the living room where the woman had laid out a tea set and was pouring two cups. She handed one to Abby and invited her to sit down.

"I'm Cora Michaels," she said, adding casually, "and I know who you are."

"Oh?" Abby asked, surprised. "How so?"

"You're Abby Barrett. I never forget a face. When the realtor showed me around the house your picture was plastered everywhere."

"It's me, in the flesh," Abby said. "Sorry I didn't introduce myself, but I have sort of gotten in the habit of shielding my identity."

"I can understand why," Cora said, "after what your husband did. I was a teacher in the Minneapolis schools for forty years, and unfortunately our union representative put a lot of our retirement funds into your husband's fund. Or his *scheme*, I should say. A lot of teachers—working people like me, not rich people like you—lost everything overnight."

Stunned at the revelation, Abby put down the cup and saucer, afraid she would drop it, her hand was shaking so badly. She felt as if she was having a panic attack. She clutched at her neck, gasping for air. "Do you mean you are one of the people he swindled?"

"I'm afraid so," Cora said. "Not directly, but he swindled my retirement fund, so yes—he swindled me. But I've forgiven him for it," she explained. "I've come to terms with what he did to me. I lost my entire retirement savings, and now I live on just my Social Security and a small inheritance from my sister. Thank goodness the house is paid for—otherwise, I don't know where I'd be now."

Abby's heart was racing, and she felt as if she might pass out. Cora could see Abby struggling, and she sat down on the couch close to Abby's side.

"There, there, dear. It's okay," Cora soothed, genuinely concerned.

Cora reached over and began to softly rub Abby's back, as a mother would comfort a suffering child. "Put your head between your knees and take deep breaths for a minute, otherwise you're going to pass out."

Abby already knew many of Jake's victims, but had never met one outside her social circle. She had never met a victim like Cora, who had lost her life's savings, and at this point in her life, hardly had the means to recoup them.

"I don't know what to say," Abby said.

"There really isn't anything to say," Cora responded, patting her hand. "This isn't your fault."

Abby looked up to the hallway that led from the front door to the living room, remembering the photos of the Eiffel Tour,

Great Pyramids, Venice Canal, Acropolis in Greece and Mt. Rushmore she had passed when she walked into the house.

"After I retired I planned to travel the world," Cora said wistfully as she followed Abby's gaze. "Now I have to make do with my imagination. I cut those photos out from *National Geographic* magazine. Aren't they pretty? But I have a roof over my head. Sort of." She looked up and Abby followed her gaze to the water stain on the living room ceiling.

"How can you forgive Jake after all he took from you?" Abby asked.

"I didn't have much of a choice," Cora explained. "It was either that or hold a grudge against him for whatever time I have left on this earth. That's not how I want to spend my golden years."

Abby wiped a few tears from her cheeks, as Cora continued speaking. "I'm guessing he took a lot from you, too, and I don't mean just money."

Abby nodded. "I landed on my feet, though, but I had some help. I don't think I could have done it on my own," she said.

"In a way I did, too," Cora said. "I may not have everything I want, but I have everything I need. I'm very happy here. That's what's important."

The two women sat silently for a few moments, then the kind, grandmotherly Cora said, "You need to forgive yourself. And until you do that, you won't have any peace. Whatever it is you're running from—your guilt, your fear, whatever—it's time to face it. It's time to let go."

CORA HAD BEEN RIGHT that it was time to let go. Whether Abby stayed in Wander Creek or not, she would never resume any semblance of her old life. And she didn't want to. It was time to say good-bye to the old Abby. A week after returning from her odyssey to her childhood home, Abby decided just exactly how Abby Barrett would say goodbye to Abby Trent for good.

Abby stood in her closet and lovingly felt the fabrics of the designer clothes that for so long were the one physical connection to her former life. She knew the only reason she had kept them was that when she did return to Minneapolis, she could look the part. One by one, she slipped the gowns, shirts, pants and skirts off the hangers, folded each item carefully into tissue paper, and packed them into a suitcase. Next, she turned to the shoes, jewelry, purses, and other accessories, and repeated the process. In the end, she wrapped up about ninety percent of her designer wardrobe, keeping only a few favorite pieces and accessories that were more appropriate for the life she now led.

When she was done, she texted Ken who came over and helped her load what turned out to be several suitcases into the SUV. "I just have to go to Minneapolis one more time," she told him, kissing him lightly, "and I should be back before dark."

She made the trip south to Minneapolis with a light heart. As she drove slowly past her old haunts, she noticed nothing had changed. Everything looked exactly like it did when her life had suddenly collapsed. It seemed strange to Abby that everything from her old life had stayed the same when she herself had changed so much. She drove past the Paperie, disappointed that Carmen was on vacation and she couldn't see her old friend. But she knew they would get together again.

Abby parked in front of the upscale second-hand store that sold only very high-end designer items. Even at second-hand prices, items in this store sold for thousands of dollars. Abby wheeled in the four Louis Vuitton suitcases and the saleswoman came out to help her. Abby had made an appointment in advance and the saleswoman led her into the back room where she laid out each piece, inspected it carefully for flaws, then made notes on a tablet. Finally, after almost an hour, she looked up, smiling.

"You've got an amazing collection. I bet I can move most of

this in a matter of a few days. I'm so grateful that you brought these to me."

Abby nodded. "That's great," she said, sensing that even though everything was slightly used she would still get a substantial sum. And she was right.

The saleswoman tapped on a calculator on her phone with long red fingernails, then wrote a figure on a piece of paper and turned it around for Abby to see. "Does this figure sound about right?" she asked.

Abby was stunned. She hadn't expected nearly that amount. "That would be awesome," she said.

The woman sensed Abby's surprise. "You have several pieces here that are clearly one-of-a-kind. And some of these gowns are no longer available new but are still in very high demand. They'll be gone like that." She snapped her fingers for emphasis. "If you have anything else you'd like to sell, I hope you'll bring them to me first."

The saleswoman reached into a drawer and pulled out a large, elegant checkbook. "Who should I make the check out to?"

"Cora Michaels," Abby replied. "Please make it out to Cora Michaels."

Afterward, sitting in her car looking at the check, Abby thought of the many things Cora could do with the money. For starters, she could certainly do some traveling. There was also enough to get the roof fixed.

Abby grabbed a pen and envelope from her purse. On the memo portion of the check she wrote, "Bon Voyage, from A.B." On the way out of town, she stopped at a mailing store and sent the check by overnight express. By this time tomorrow, she hoped Cora would be planning her first trip abroad.

At the end of the day, Abby had done what she could to help one of Jake's victims. It was just a drop in the bucket, but it was something.

Abby returned to Wander Creek that afternoon and arrived

exhausted from all the driving. Back at the shop, Sam was getting ready to close up, and an incredible smell of Italian herbs wafted from the back of the store. "Ken's here," Sam grinned, and slipped out the front door.

"You're back," Ken said, emerging from the office carrying a pizza box from the Pizza Den and a bottle of red wine. He kissed her tenderly. "I figured you'd be beat from all that driving and in need of sustenance." He held the pizza box up high.

"Perfect," Abby said. "It's just what I need. Dinner, drink, and a handsome dude."

Then they both turned to look toward the front of the store when the bell on the front tinkled.

"Oh, shoot," Abby said. "Sam forgot to lock the door. Let me just get rid of them and then we can eat. I have a lot more that I want to tell you." And she thought to herself that she also had a lot more that she needed to do. She needed to talk to Pete again. And she needed to walk around Wander Creek with her head held high. She'd help the Post Office with the Santa Claus letters next year, and get a letter writing workshop put together in time to make it into Mona's brochure.

Abby and Ken watched as an older woman walked through the front door. "Oh, I'm sorry," she said, in a surprised voice. "Are you closed?" She looked around the store. "I just wanted to get a birthday card for my grandson. If I don't get it in the mail tomorrow it will never arrive on time." She stood hesitantly by the door.

"By all means, please come in," Abby said, gesturing toward the greeting cards on the wall. "There are many to choose from. My boyfriend and I were just closing up but please take your time."

The woman chose a card quickly, and once she was gone, Abby and Ken took the narrow staircase up to Abby's second floor apartment.

Ken diverted to the spotless kitchen with its white cupboards, granite countertops, and generous island. He zapped the pizza in the microwave and poured the wine. Meanwhile, Abby sat on the couch, laying her head back on the cushions. It had been a long day.

When they settled in with their plates in their laps and glasses balanced carefully on the ottoman, Ken said with a shy smile, "You called me your boyfriend."

"I did," Abby said. "Hope that's okay."

"Only if you meant it," Ken said, grinning broadly now.

"Of course I do," she said. "I mean, we've been seeing each other for five months now. I figured that's where we were in our relationship."

"You were saying just before the card grandmother arrived that you had something you wanted to tell me," Ken prompted.

Abby took a fortifying sip of wine. "I do, and you need to hold on to your hat because it's a doozy." She took a deep breath. "Before I moved here I was living in a dumpy apartment working a dead-end job, which, by the way, I was grateful to have. After Jake's crimes came to light and people watched their savings and investments go up in smoke, I became the social pariah of the season. I even got kicked out of the country club. Escorted off the property like a common criminal. Anyway, last October, an anonymous benefactor gifted me this building, with a few caveats. I had to move to Wander Creek, open a business, employ at least one person and stay for a year. After that I was free to do with the building what I wanted, including selling it and moving away."

Ken's eyes widened with each word she spoke. "That's unbelievable," he said. "Like something that happens in a fairy tale."

"Yep. A Minneapolis lawyer named Jerome Monroe showed up on my doorstep one evening and laid it all out for me. It was unbelievable, literally. But it was all legit, all there in black and white. The more I thought about it, the more I figured, why not? I had pretty much lost everything already. There was nothing left to lose. Literally. So I accepted the gift and here I am."

"Do you know who your benefactor is?" Ken asked.

Abby nodded. "I do now, but I didn't when I first moved here. And now that I've told you, you're one of only five people who know anything about this."

"And you're not going to tell me who the benefactor is," Ken guessed. "No worries. I don't need to know. But there is one thing I do want to know."

"Oh?" Abby asked, hoping she would have the answer he was looking for.

"Will you stay in Wander Creek after the year's up, or move back to Minneapolis?"

Abby hesitated a beat longer than she meant to. For months she had asked herself that very question almost every day. And each day the answer seemed to change. But she loved her life in Wander Creek and everything she had built.

Ken held up his hand, smiling. "It's okay, you don't have to answer," he said. "I know it's a big decision. And besides, you'll be here another seven months at least. I'll take that."

Abby knew that Ken would stay in Wander Creek for the rest of his life. He built his business from nothing over the course of a decade, and people came to his shop even if they had to drive miles out of their way. He was a good and generous man, and the polar opposite of Jake. And while Abby was quickly putting down roots, she still felt the pull of the city. She knew she could never return to her once glamorous high-flying life where money was no object. And that's not what she wanted. Not anymore at least.

After dinner and a second glass of wine, Abby walked Ken down the stairs and out the front door of the shop. Ken kissed her again, and as he got into his truck he said over his shoulder, "By the way, I love that my girlfriend is a woman of mystery and intrigue."

The End

IF YOU ENJOYED *A Place to Start*, please leave a rating/review. Thank you.

ALSO BY AMY RUTH ALLEN

FINCH'S CROSSING SERIES

Finch's Crossing is a heartwarming series following the lives of the four Hamilton sisters as they search for love, personal fulfillment, and a renewed connection to the place they call home. Each Finch's Crossing book evokes the special joys of the seasons and the charms of small town life. Fans of Debbie Macomber's Cedar Cove series will be happily drawn into the life of this beloved community. To read excerpts and reviews, and learn more about the real town that inspired the Finch's Crossing series, visit amyruthallen.com.

Autumn (Book One)

How could she let this happen?

Autumn's life used to be idyllic. Now she may have to leave her happy life and lovely home in Finch's Crossing to save her career.

And here she is, with her own life in turmoil, standing in a pumpkin patch trying to save a little girl. The orphan is supposed to be moving with her new guardian to New York City.

Autumn may escalate things by trashing his car. He may call her a pumpkin bumpkin.

And she tells him in no-uncertain terms that he is obviously out of his league.

Autumn can't stand by and do nothing. It's in her nature to fix things. *She won't give up, and she's soon to find out, he will never back down.*

While she schemes to make things right, she's also battling a secret shame. Is it the reason why it's been so long since she's let a man into her life?

Gradually, he shows Autumn that he isn't a bad guy after all, and they can no longer deny the mutual attraction that has been building for months.

But a cruel revelation on Christmas Day changes everything.

Now what? Are they friends or enemies? Feelings don't just disappear overnight . . .

Spring (Book Two)

Is this a second chance, or a second mistake?

Spring expects to see beautiful yellow and pink tulips blooming when she arrives in Finch's Crossing.

But she does not expect to see him. The man who broke her heart twenty years earlier.

And has he named his little bookshop after her? *Really?*

How dare he even try to talk to her!

She has only come for a quick visit with her sister. After all, she has an exciting future in New York City where she will be feted as one of the country's top models.

But the heart wants what the heart wants and they cannot resist the pull of the past.

Until his explosive secret past catches up with him. And catches her by surprise.

Is it time to pack her suitcases, *or should she give him another chance?*

Summer (Book Three)

His timing couldn't be worse . . .

Summer has returned to Finch's Crossing to put down roots for the first time in a decade. She has a vibrant new business. A lovely childhood home full of happy memories. Good friends.

And *now* he comes into her life? This wonderful, wandering man.

Picnics. A shared interest in nature and well-being. Surprise gifts. *He loves her. She has found her soulmate.*

So his abrupt departure is as unexpected as it is painful.

What happened to the kind, genuine and nurturing man she has fallen in love with?

And why does she hear another woman in the background when they speak on the phone?

Is it time to let go, or time to make a grand gesture?

When the truth finally comes out, will she give him the chance to explain, or wonder forever what happened to their love?

∼

Winter (Book Four)

When the mean girl meets her match . . .

Winter blows into Finch's Crossing with a broken leg. Taking over her lovely childhood home. Imposing on her sister. Alienating everyone around her.

Watching her perfect life in the city slip away one unanswered email at a time.

She knows she is bossy, selfish, ruthless and cold-hearted. It's how she climbed the corporate ladder and became a millionaire.

So it's hard to fathom that he sees beyond her icy demeanor to what's really in her heart. Pain. Regrets. Sadness.

As they grow closer, profound and dangerous circumstances lead Winter to do the unexpected.

Is it enough to make people like her? *When all is said and done, will the kindest man she's ever known become her champion?*

Then his kind nature leads him far, far away from her.

There is no ways she can go with him. Her leg has healed, but is her heart big enough now to make a sacrifice so they can be together? *She's not the only one who doesn't think so . . .*

∼

WANDER CREEK SERIES

If you love wholesome women's fiction that celebrates friendship, second chances and the joys of a life well-lived, all against the backdrop of small-town living, you will fall in love with the Wander Creek series.

~

A Place to Start (Book One)

What does she have to lose? She's already lost everything . . . literally.

Abby is still reeling from her husband's bombshell. Overnight, she went from rich and carefree socialite to social pariah.

She needs to lay low and out of the spotlight. A small town she's never heard of is as good a place as any. *But should she take the outrageous opportunity offered by an anonymous benefactor?*

Why not? She can't sink any lower.

He is her first friend in Wander Creek, but another woman has her hooks in him and many more want to paddle his canoe.

But he's taken a shy shining to her. He helps her set up her business and literally takes her on her first walk across a frozen lake. *And that sunrise ATV ride along Wander Creek . . .*

But then there's that snow bunny and Abby's public humiliation. *How could he do that to her?*

So what's the point in staying in Wander Creek? According to her crazy arrangement, she can leave after a year with the money. A lot of money.

She'll have to muster all the sass and moxie she can to decide whether to stay or go. Or is it possible that she can she do both?

When Abby's humiliating past is revealed another secret comes to the surface and shocks Abby to the core.

All of a sudden, his betrayal is the least of her worries . . .

~

A Place to Stay (Book Two)

What happened to all the reasons she had to stay?

Abby runs a successful business in Wander Creek and has wonderful friends, including the irrepressible owner of the Wander Inn on the shores of the creek. *Abby could stay here forever.*

And the man in her life is kind, loving, and adventurous. A real man's man.

But then he sees something he wasn't supposed to see. She tries to explain, but his taillights are the last thing she sees of him for some time.

And the mean girl is back and determined to chase Abby out of Wander Creek. *The trouble is the law is not on Abby's side.*

But Abby isn't about to back down from a challenge. Especially since the mean girl has her sights set on Abby's beau. *Or is it ex-beau?*

Meanwhile, Abby finds herself in the middle of a magical mystery. But a dangerous situation makes Abby re-evaluate her life. Life is too precious to waste in arguments with people you love. But can Abby persuade her beau to give her a second chance?

Probably. Hopefully.

But then Abby sees something she wasn't supposed to see . . .

A Place for Christmas (Book Three)

What's a little spying and breaking and entering between frenemies?

Abby has gone from disgraced socialite and social pariah to successful entrepreneur and civic leader with a steady and comfortable love interest.

Christmas would be a romantic time to propose. If only Abby was certain she wanted him to.

Wait. Was there an engagement ring in the small velvet box she wasn't supposed to see? How did things get so muddled?

Christmastime in Wander Creek is magical, with the small hamlet decorated to the nines under a snowy blanket. Abby plans to enjoy every cozy moment at her stationery store, the Paper Box, and her new venture, the Book Box. Her nemesis has left town in disgrace and all seems peaceful in the quaint town. Until. . .

But old ghosts appear, Abby's own version of the Ghost of Christmas

Past, and things get out of control. What's a little spying and breaking and entering between frenemies?

Will the Ghost of Christmas Past ruin the new life she built for herself?

Readers **LOVE** Wander Creek!

"**I absolutely loved this book.** I enjoyed all the characters, the good ones, bad ones, and crazy ones. The descriptive environment is wonderful, from her shabby apartment to her adventurous walks and rides around Wander Creek. **The story pulled me in** and I joined Abby on her decisions, friendships, goals and new love...maybe. What will Abby's future hold? Will her decisions help her for the better? Will all end up during spring time at Wander Creek or will she fall through the creek ice? You'll have to read this amazing book to find out. I'd highly recommend this book by the very talented author Amy Ruth Allen. **I look forward to the next book and all her books to come.**" – Reader

"**Another great read by Amy Ruth Allen. I thoroughly enjoyed reading this book and am looking forward to the next one in the series**. The main character, Abby is likable and all of her friends (and foes) are fun to get to know. The aura of mystery on who the benefactor is and who sabotaged her inventory keep you guessing until the very end.
– Reader

PRAISE FOR AMY RUTH ALLEN

"I found the book Autumn on my kindle. The characters and the story were wonderfully written. It was a joy to read. I immediately purchased the book Spring and have read it in one evening. It also was wonderfully written. I have purchased the entire series with pre-order for Winter as it wasn't unavailable yet. With all that we are facing at this time in our country, these books take me away to another place for awhile. It was also fun to see that Amy Ruth Allen lives in my town Minneapolis, Minnesota."

— READER

"Felt like a good Hallmark movie. This was a sweet little book that felt like a good Hallmark movie. I liked the characters and the plot (except the sister). I was looking for an autumn themed book and this was a perfect choice. I can almost feel the autumn leaves rustling at Finch's Crossing."

— READER

"I have read Autumn and Spring back to back and have pre-ordered the next one due 1st August. I loved reading these books. Easy reading and feel good - especially good during the pandemic. I love that this series in set in a small village and everyone knows each other. Would recommend if you like easy reading and stories that wrap up eventually in each book."

— GOODREADS READER

"This was such a good book. I fell in love with the characters. Amy hit a homer with this!" –

— GOODREADS READER

"Oh I'd love to go on a vacation to Wander Creek. The great thing is I did while reading this book. This story is full of beautiful descriptions and wonderful, loving and caring characters. Including, a not so right in the head character that I love to hate. Through out this book you'll experience hard work, friendships, despair, worry, mystery, hardship, doubt, new beginnings and love. I absolutely enjoyed the wonderful writing from this very gifted author Amy Ruth Allen, and want everyone to experience this adventure throughout this marvelous book. I'm eager to know what's ahead for Abby, and can't wait for the next book!" –

— READER

"I thoroughly enjoyed reading this book and am looking forward to the next one in the series. The main character, Abby is likable and all of her friends (and foes) are fun to get to know. The aura of mystery on who the benefactor is and who sabotaged her inventory keep you guessing until the very end."

— READER

ABOUT THE AUTHOR

Amy Ruth Allen writes wholesome, uplifting women's fiction that celebrates the power of friendship, love and self-discovery, the charms of small town life, and the joy of a life well-lived. Lose yourself in her two feel-good series, Wander Creek and Finch's Crossing. Stay in touch by joining her newsletter at amyruthallen.com/newsletter. Amy lives in Minneapolis, Minnesota with her husband and their rescue pup Jessica Fletcher.

For Leigh, always.

Made in the USA
Las Vegas, NV
10 August 2024